C.T. Sullivan lives in Surrey with his wife, Deborah, and golden Labrador, Woof. A twenty-five-year career as a foreign exchange broker in the City was followed by spells as a lorry driver, landscape gardener, pub singer, film extra and musical comedy entertainer whilst learning his craft as an author.

He began writing poems and short stories from the age of ten, shortly after the death of his mother. His love of the written word is equal only to his passion for music, sport and humour.

REASONABLE FORCE

To Tom
Best Wishes
C Bullen

C.T. Sullivan

REASONABLE FORCE

Vanguard Press

VANGUARD PAPERBACK

© Copyright 2015
C.T. Sullivan

The right of C.T. Sullivan to be identified as author of
this work has been asserted by him in accordance with the
Copyright, Designs and Patents Act 1988.

A CIP catalogue record for this title is
available from the British Library.

ISBN 978 178465 037 7

Vanguard Press is an imprint of
Pegasus Elliot Mackenzie Publishers Ltd.
www.pegasuspublishers.com

First Published in 2015

Vanguard Press
Sheraton House Castle Park
Cambridge England

Printed & Bound in Great Britain

To Deborah, for her love, support and inexhaustible faith.

Acknowledgements

My thanks go to Eve Seymour for her advice, guidance, availability and enthusiasm.

To Sandy Eddy for her enjoyable company, time and invaluable input on technical matters.

Cheers, James. Enigmatic. Inspirational. Too young. You will be missed.

CHAPTER 1

His mother was seriously ill in hospital. A bout of viral pneumonia had developed into a bacterial version of the disease. His worried father worked long hours in the City – arrangements would have to be made.

It was mid-June – hot. Nicholas Summers thought people only caught pneumonia when it was cold. He was twelve.

He sat on the corner of his bed, door open, listening intently to the conversation in the downstairs hall. 'I really appreciate this, Barry. It's just until Lindre gets back on her feet,' said his father.

'He can stay as long as it takes. We always love to have him. You know that,' came the reply.

Nicholas turned and launched himself upwards, his smiling face ploughing into his royal blue pillow as he crash-landed down onto his single bed.

So, it was arranged. His aunt and uncle, who lived just under a mile away and were childless, would look after him until his mother was well again.

Uncle Barry and Auntie Rena were more than just relatives. His aunt, a softly spoken woman, fussed over Nicholas as if he were her own. He revelled in the attention. His Uncle Barry, who had a wicked sense of humour, was his favourite adult.

The first week of his stay flew by. On the Friday afternoon, when school had finished Nicholas set off for home. The journey had not been a pleasant one. A group of boys had followed him and his friends, shouting insults and hurling stones at them along the route. To escape their loutish behaviour, he had run the last half mile back to his temporary abode.

Uncle Barry, who taught science at Ashford Technical College, arrived back at the house an hour later. 'Right, Nicholas. Want to help me clean the car?'

In the comforting presence of his uncle, the incident with the group of boys was soon forgotten. 'Yes, of course,' said Nicholas.

The silver Vauxhall Vectra was parked in the road outside the three bedroom bungalow. Buckets were filled; sleeves were rolled; sponges were dipped. 'Let cleaning commence,' announced Uncle Barry. 'And, if you do a good job, you get two pounds. One now, and the other when you reach twenty-one,' he said, with a straight face.

The first stone hit the windscreen, leaving a small v-shaped scar in the glass. The second hit his uncle on the back of the neck, drawing blood. He spun around to see where the missiles were coming from. There were at least seven of them. Nicholas recognized the boys immediately. He guessed they were about three years older than him.

'Oi! You old paedophile,' shouted the tallest boy. He wore an orange hooded top and a white, reversed baseball cap.

'Paedo, paedo,' the others chorused, as they swaggered nearer to the car.

Nicholas' uncle moved towards the gang. At six foot and fourteen stone he was an imposing figure. He dabbed his injured neck and noticed the blood. 'Who threw that?' he demanded.

'Me,' said the leader in the orange hood. 'What you gonna do about it, old man?'

'You cheeky little sod,' replied his uncle. 'If you *were* a man I'd punch you on the nose. But you're a silly little boy trying to be big. Now bugger off, all of you, before I call the police.'

Nicholas, standing at the far side of the car, grasped his wet sponge close to his chest with both hands, paralysed with fear. He wanted his uncle to back down. He wanted this gang to go away. The group of cocky lads moved closer. His Uncle Barry took two more steps towards the leader. He stood, defiant, a mere few paces from the mob.

'Come on then, old man,' said the leader, as he pulled a small knife from his orange top and waved it in front of him.

'So you need a knife to be big, do you?' his uncle replied, standing his ground. Unfortunately, the knife had been a distraction. Nicholas noticed that his uncle was now surrounded by the menacing gang. Suddenly, two of the boys lunged at him from behind, aiming kicks at the back of his legs. Nicholas' mouth dropped open as he saw his uncle, off-balance, fall to his knees. A powerful urge to run forward to help him seared through his nervous system. But he could not move. Fear had turned his muscles to rock.

Seizing on his chance, the well-built leader raced forward and swung a fist. The blow landed flush on the left side of the man's lower jaw causing the bone to fracture in two places.

Nicholas watched in horror as his uncle's unconscious body collapsed sideways. The sickening crack of his skull, as it hit the concrete kerbstone, jolted his own head backwards as if he had felt the impact himself. On seeing the rapidly expanding ruby red stain emerge from the head of the figure on the ground, the gang scattered like a flock of spooked sheep.

In a matter of seconds, the street was empty apart from Nicholas and his injured uncle. Nicholas remained motionless, dazed, mouth open, as a mass of gloomy clouds overhead opened their sluice gates. The rain fell heavily – he didn't notice. He was too scared to move. Slowly, he turned his head towards the bungalow. His chest filled with air – a desperate scream exploded from his lungs.

Nicholas stood shivering as his Auntie Rena ran from her home and knelt at her husband's side. Her high-pitched wail speared through Nicholas' brain as she stroked her husband's limp hand and wept over the man she loved.

As the rain soaked their clothes, Nicholas' attention was gripped by a river of diluted blood as it swept over the pavement and down through the iron grid of a drain.

Shortly after the ambulance arrived, his uncle was rushed to the same hospital that housed his mother. After a series of X-rays, his unconscious body was moved to the intensive care unit.

The following day, the police took separate statements from the gang of boys. They admitted to harassing the man, but said their leader had struck out in defence after he swore and then lunged at him. These versions of accounts would tell a totally different story to that of Nicholas.

When Nicholas was required to give a statement, he was still consumed with guilt and fear as the stern-faced police officer began to question him.

'And where were you standing when this assault took place?' the officer asked.

'Outside, with my uncle,' he replied, surprised at the obvious question.

The officer pulled a glass ashtray to the middle of the table, by way of re-enacting the scene. 'If the boys and your uncle were here,' he said, putting his fist one side of the ashtray, 'where were you standing?'

After a slight pause, Nicholas pointed to the opposite side of the glass object. 'Around the other side of the car,' he replied.

'So, you didn't have a clear view of the incident then?' quizzed the policeman.

Nicholas hesitated. He hadn't expected to be put under pressure. He didn't like this man's approach at all. 'I saw it through the windows of the car and over the bonnet. They kicked my uncle and a boy punched him in the face,' said Nicholas defiantly.

Nicholas saw the policeman writing on his pad as he spoke. But, by the look on his face, he thought the officer hadn't believed a word he had said. He began to resent this person's presence in his house. After a few more questions the interview was terminated. The policeman said a few whispered words to Nicholas' father and departed.

His uncle remained in a coma for three days. On the morning of the fourth day, his eyelids flickered and opened for a short period. His heartbroken wife was greatly encouraged by this brief step forward as she sat in hope by his bedside.

Just over three hours later that hope was crushed as the only man she had ever loved lost his fight for life.

After some deliberation, the DPS decided that there was insufficient evidence for a realistic prospect of conviction. They declined to proceed with a prosecution and dropped the case against the fifteen-year-old boy. The local community was astounded.

In the ensuing years, Nicholas watched his Auntie Rena deteriorate from a contented wife to an empty, broken woman. In his eyes, the loss of his uncle and the demise of his auntie was all his fault. He had not tried to help his uncle; he had just stood and watched them attack him – helpless, useless. He was smaller than the pack of yobs but he could at least have been a diversion had he entered the fray. Many sleepless nights followed.

Nicholas experienced three things on that unforgettable afternoon. He saw a woman lose her loving husband. He lost his best friend. A seed was planted.

CHAPTER 2

Nineteen years later

Saturday 30th October 2009. It was a date that should have been carved deep into Nick Summers' brain. This was to be the last Saturday he would wake without having to share his bed with resounding whispers of regrets – with incurable pain.

He lay in bed looking at the beautiful face of his wife, Mel. Her hair, a jumble of honey and ivory curls, fanned across the white pillow. As she slept, the swell of her breasts rose and fell above her satin nightgown with each shallow, rhythmic breath.

Nick propped himself up on his elbow and wondered why this gorgeous creature had fallen in love with him.

Quietly, he slipped from under the heavy duvet and left the bedroom. Fifteen minutes later he was gone.

Nick passed beneath the row of mature oak trees lining the gravel path that wound its way around the perimeter of the local park. Every Saturday he rose at seven thirty, pulled on his tracksuit and trainers and ran the half-mile to the park at the top of a rise.

The sun had begun to pull away from the bruised skyline, firing needles of light through the branches that arched over Nick's route. The late season pigments: golds, russets, blood reds suddenly lost their splendour. His thoughts darkened.

Mel had arranged for them to go out that evening with two neighbours and their female guest for a few drinks in the local. He was not looking forward to the gathering. The woman was pleasant enough but her husband, a police officer, was not someone he would have chosen as a friend. His general demeanour and the way he looked at Mel made him feel uncomfortable. He'd never met their guest, either. Two hours of forced conversation was not his idea of fun.

The cold air stung his lungs and cleared his negative thoughts as he jogged along the path that dipped and curved between two rows of hydrangeas. Nick wiped the sweat from his forehead with the back of his hand. His arms, piston-like, drove him up a gradual incline that continued through a brick archway opening on to a lake.

A swan, floating motionless near the centre, had assumed ownership of this flawless aquatic canvas. Unhurriedly, she turned her regal head and watched Nick's progress along the margins of her estate.

Nick absorbed the magical environment and held one main thought in his head – *Life doesn't get much better than this.*

CHAPTER 3

The dimly lit bar was filled with ruddy faces and bright conversation. In one corner a black Labrador lay slumped across his owner's feet, eyes closed, mouth twitching into an occasional smile.

Nick Summers finished his beer. 'Right, same again? That's two pints of Fiddler's, one house white and two Diet Cokes.' The circle nodded their approval as he moved to the bar.

Nick pushed back his chocolate brown hair carelessly with his fingers and dipped into his back pocket for his wallet. The attractive teenage barmaid acknowledged that he was waiting to be served. She lowered her head and offered him a shy smile. Nick recognised the type of look – he was flattered. He smiled back at the young girl and ordered his drinks.

The thought flitted across his mind that ten years ago he may have followed up on the barmaid's flirtatious body language. Not any more.

It was shortly after his twenty-fifth birthday that he'd met Mel at a friend's party. He'd asked her to dance. She had said no. 'Do you mind if I dance on my own then?' he replied. It made her laugh. It broke the ice. They were married two years later and moved into a house in the quiet village of Bourne in Kent.

Tonight he and Mel were out with Nathan and his wife Cathy, who was six months pregnant. Detective Sergeant Nathan Ballack had thinning, biscuit-coloured hair, sharp features and was in his late thirties. He was in charge of a pod of three officers in the SCD unit attached to the station in the nearby town of Ashford.

Jo Major, whom Cathy had invited along, made up the group of five. Jo had recently been transferred to Ballack's small team. Cathy had become more friendly with Jo since her mother's death, aware that her social life had not been good of late. She was pleased that Jo had accepted her invitation to tonight's get-together.

'That's sixteen pounds thirty,' said the barmaid. Nick gave her a twenty, got his change and began to ferry the drinks over to his crowd. As he passed a drink to Jo, she hung on to Nick's wrist. He saw her admiring the gold wedding ring on the finger of his tanned, rugged hand. It had an impressive oval cut diamond set in the top.

'Mmm! That's an unusual wedding band for a man. It's lovely,' said Jo, hanging on to his ring finger whilst she switched her drink to her other hand.

'Yeah, thanks. Mel chose it for me – didn't pay for it – just chose it,' he replied mischievously. Jo smiled and released his finger. Nick thought he saw a touch of envy within the smile.

Nathan, as usual, was performing for the women – relating a story of his early days in the force. His hand was resting on

Mel's shoulder as he spoke. Nick registered that Nathan was making a habit of touching Mel at every opportunity he got.

'... the muscles went into some kind of spasm. I don't know what was worse for the bloke, the pain or the embarrassment. Anyway, it took the doctors three hours to get the bottle out. And d'ya know what? As it finally emerged, the vacuum sucked the cork clean out with a bloody great pop!' The three women giggled, slightly embarrassed at the lewd tale. 'Well, we couldn't let a nice chardonnay, albeit a bit warm, go to waste could we?' said Nathan.

'Oh, that's disgusting!' said Mel. 'You didn't really drink it?'

Nick realised that this was one of Nathan's crude attempts to impress the ladies. 'Goodness, Mel, you're so gullible. Anyway, cheers!'

Everyone but Nathan lifted their glasses and returned the toast. The detective's attention was elsewhere.

CHAPTER 4

Nathan had his eyes fixed on a man across the bar. The figure was raw-boned; short, black hair brushed forward; his eyes uneasy. The man looked back at the policeman over the top of his pint glass and sucked down a large amount of lager.

Nathan dipped into his leather jacket pocket and pulled out a pack of cigarettes. 'Right, I'm off for a fag.' Aware that Jo had recently given up the weed yet again, he knew he was the only smoker in the group. As he walked outside, the thin man finished his pint and followed.

The policeman stood a few yards from the white stuccoed walls of the country pub, placed a cigarette between his lips and lit it with a cheap plastic lighter. The furtive individual that fidgeted beside him pulled out the stub of an unfinished roll-up from his grey hooded top and did the same. Without saying a word, both men moved around to the car park at the rear of the premises. They stood together in the shadows.

Nathan looked down at the thin man's baggy tracksuit bottoms that corrugated over a pair of off-white trainers. In a slow, deliberate movement, his eyes travelled back up to his face. Suddenly, he lurched forwards, grabbed the thin man by the throat and slammed his back against the craggy red-brick wall at the rear of the pub. He slapped him – once, hard, across the face. The stinging blow knocked the short roll-up from his string-like lips. Nathan's mouth hardly moved as he spat out in a whisper, 'What the fuck you doin' here, Scrivens? This is my fucking local.'

The thin man looked scared. 'Sorry, Mr Ballack. You said you needed the stuff as soon as I got it.'

'Yeah, but not here, you scrawny little prick. Not when I'm out with friends.'

'Well, I been trying to get you on your fucking mobile for days now and I knows you drink here sometimes. I already owe me supplier from the last lot I got you. He's all over me at the moment.'

'You'll get your money when I get mine. I'm like you: I move the gear on and wait for the payout. So far I've had jack shit.'

'I'm dead if I don't pay this back by next Tuesday. I'm fucked. And then you'll be fucked 'cause then they'll come for you,' said Scrivens.

Nathan's hand went down and grabbed Scrivens' testicles. He squealed. Nathan put his mouth close to Scrivens' ear. 'Don't you dare threaten me, you little piece of shit. I'll have it by Thursday.'

'If you don't, Mr Ballack, I'll have no balls left to squeeze,' he whined.

The DS released his grip on the thin man's privates. 'Where's the gear?'

'In me motor,' Scrivens replied, clutching his groin area.

Nathan reached into the pocket of his jeans. 'Here are my keys. It's the red BMW. Go and put it in the boot.' The detective took a long drag on his cigarette. Then he grabbed Scrivens' arm as he was about to head off towards his car. 'And for fuck's sake, don't forget to lock it after.'

When he returned, Nathan handed him a few folded notes. 'There's a ton there. That's all I got on me at the moment. I'll get the rest next week.'

'But, Mr Ballack...'

'How was I supposed to know you'd turn up tonight with the gear, you doughnut? Next week, I said! And don't ring me on the mob – it's knackered. I'm getting a new one. I'll ring *you*. Now fuck off!'

As Scrivens sloped away, Nathan pulled deeply on his cigarette. The detective looked up at the clear, star-studded sky. He blew the smoke out into the cool night with a loud sigh, flicked the butt into the darkness and left the car park.

Back in the bar, Mel and Jo were discussing clothes. 'I'm quite annoyed, actually. I'm going to have to get another winter coat,' said Mel. 'I bought a new one only last month and I've worn it perhaps three or four times. But it has a fur collar that brings my neck out in a rash. Maybe I'll advertise it in the local paper.'

'Actually, Mel, I might be interested. I could do with a new coat. We're about the same size; maybe I could come over and try it on some time?'

'Yes, of course. Well, if you've got a spare moment tomorrow, pop over and have a look at it. Do you know where we live?' asked Mel.

'No. Can you put it on my mobile?'

As Mel was punching in her address and number on Jo's mobile, Nathan appeared at the door of the pub. As he neared the group, he noticed Jo was watching him. She took a few steps towards her boss. 'Why don't you give it up, Nathan?' she said quietly.

Nathan was caught unaware. 'What d'you mean?'

'You know exactly what I mean.' Jo's gaze sharpened to a point, piercing the detective's dark, wary eyes.

Nathan felt his temples constrict. He went on the defensive. 'What you talking about?'

'Look what smoking did to John Webster at work. He was forty-eight and he could hardly breathe for the last six months of his life. You're bloody mad, if you ask me'

Nathan sucked in air through his nose, blew it out through puffed cheeks and breathed a sigh of relief. 'I will, Jo. In the New Year, I will.'

CHAPTER 5

Scrivens sat bent over the steering wheel of his car. He was in serious trouble. He already owed his cocaine supplier £700, and now he was another four hundred short from this evening's deal. He needed to get some more money from somewhere. He would have to fall back on his other occupation.

'Fuckin' arsehole coppers,' he breathed. The words hit the driver's window in a ball of mist that slowly evaporated. He turned the key in the ignition. His next task was to cruise the immediate area looking for some likely hits.

On an ideal night he'd spot an open downstairs window in a darkened house. But this was not to be a lucky evening. After five minutes of driving around residential backstreets he had not seen one obvious target. He needed to get out of his car and continue his search on foot.

He parked his unwashed, green Ford Fiesta at the end of an affluent-looking road, killed his engine and switched off the lights. He picked up the crumpled Black Sabbath tee-shirt lying on the passenger seat and stuffed it in the front pocket of his cotton top. A pencil-shaped torch from the driver's door went in with it. Then he opened the glove compartment and pulled out a pair of black leather gloves. A broken-toothed smirk climbed the left side of his face at the thought of where he kept them. He pulled them on and got out.

Scrivens' heart began to race, his sweat glands working overtime as he tugged his hood up over his head. He had gone through this routine countless times before, breaking into houses from his early teens. But still, on each occasion such as this, his every move was ruled by overpowering tension.

He walked along the length of the dimly lit road as nonchalantly as his nerve ends allowed. At the end, he crossed over and started back up the other side. There wasn't a soul to be seen in the vicinity and most of the houses had their curtains drawn.

If you had asked him precisely what he was looking for, he couldn't have told you. The initial and most obvious answer was the absence of an external alarm box. After that, he relied on his instinct – he had to have a feel for a place. He was like an animal sniffing out its prey – its next victim.

One of the possibilities along the road was a bungalow that sat behind a white gated entrance. But it had little in the way of trees and bushes as cover. But the property seemed to ring a bell. Then he remembered. He had cased this and the one two houses further on months before. He deemed the second one a worthy hit. It was a two-storey cottage partly screened by tall fir trees. But on the night he returned hoping to carry out his mission the owners had been in. And, this evening, so was his luck.

The man and woman, who he had seen through the open curtains of the brightly lit sitting room, he was sure were the same two people drinking with Ballack in the pub. Now, the property was shrouded in darkness and no car was parked in the drive. So, the only residents that lived here, he assumed, were the two he'd just seen. A possibility of an elderly parent upstairs asleep, he thought, but it was a risk he was prepared to take. This would be his first target.

He moved unhurriedly to the shadowy, ivy-covered cottage, walked up the garden path to the heavily-grained, oak front door and rang the bell. If a light went on upstairs he was out of there. He waited for over thirty seconds – the house stayed dark, silent.

It would take him ten minutes, at most, to complete the job. He was confident that he had ample time to get in and out before the owners returned. He walked casually around to the side of the house. Given his relaxed gait, he could easily have been the owner.

He was a professional burglar. He employed a blasé demeanour: moved in an unhurried fashion. The calmer he appeared, the less likely he was to alert suspicion; less likely to get caught.

The side door was solid mahogany and locked as expected. Next to it and just three feet off the ground was the original single-glazed, six-panelled leaded light window – just as he had hoped. This would be his point of entry.

He pulled out the tee-shirt and folded it into quarters. Then he held it against a square of glass and punched through it. Scrivens put his gloved hand through the gap, lifted the latch, opened the window, pulled his lightweight frame up and climbed in. The whole process took less than twenty seconds.

Once inside, the torch led him through the kitchen, up the carpeted staircase and on to a narrow landing. There he found a bathroom and three bedrooms all with their doors open. Each room was unoccupied.

The first bedroom was large, square and looked out onto the rear garden. The faint smell of lavender met Scrivens' nostrils as he stepped into the room. It housed an enormous bed, two cane bedside tables and a double wardrobe. Inside the drawer of one of the tables was a box in which Scrivens found some folded notes – perhaps a couple hundred pounds. A good start. He took the money out, replaced the box and closed the drawer. He may be a common thief but he saw no need to leave the place in a mess after he'd burgled it. He regarded himself as a professional and took pride in his neat approach. It was his calling card.

The next thing he wanted to find was lying on top of the wardrobe. He pulled the light-brown canvas holdall down and threw the money inside. A jagged smile lifted the left side of his mouth once more. He was always grateful when the residents of the house provided a decent getaway bag for him. When he had accrued half a dozen holdalls, he would move them on to a receiver in exchange for decent beer money. His receiver would then sell them at out-of-town car boot sales.

The wardrobe itself held nothing of interest so he moved on to the second room, which was a lot smaller. It housed a single bed, a pine table, a china doll and not much else. He knew from experience that these fancy, glazed porcelain dolls could be worth quite a lot of money. He used both gloved hands to pick up the item and placed it carefully in the bag. He proceeded swiftly on to the third bedroom.

This appeared to be more of a changing room. Racks of clothes lined both sides of the room. In front of him was a large bay window. He lowered his torch quickly, fearful that someone may spot it from a neighbouring house. The beam of light then fell upon the object that was to be his next target. Beneath the window sat a cream coloured dressing table with a large mirror. On top of the table was a jewellery box.

Scrivens watched the shadowy image of himself in the mirror as he approached the table. He picked up the pink, satin-covered jewellery box and emptied the contents into the holdall. The box was placed neatly back on the dresser. He checked the drawers and found two credit cards. He left them alone. Credit cards were traceable – too risky.

He turned away from the dressing table and stopped. He thought he heard a noise. He waited – listening. There it was again. It was close. The slamming of a car door? Someone putting rubbish in a bin? Every one of his senses was put on alert as he stood, frozen, tense.

CHAPTER 6

The Saturday evening get-together was brought to an early close at nine forty-five. Nick was aware that Nathan and Jo had both been on duty that day and were ready to leave. That afternoon, he had finished off landscaping the garden of an investment banker in a neighbouring village so was glad of the early night. There were no complaints from Cathy, who was heavily pregnant.

Jo, who had drunk Coke all night, was the first to depart in her sleek black Ford Cougar. She lived three miles away in the village of Ludbury. Nathan and Cathy were next to go and headed off to the car park and their red BMW 3 Series. Although they lived two streets away from Nick and Mel, Nathan never walked anywhere that was further than the end of his garden.

Nick watched them leave the pub then turned to Mel. 'Right! Ready, Freddy?' he asked. He went to retrieve their coats from the stand that stood like a sentry by the gents' toilet door. On his return he held up his wife's coat for her to slip into. 'Looks like it's just you and me, sweetheart,' he added in a passable Sean Connery impression.

As they left the pub, Mel took Nick's arm. 'Jo's a nice girl, isn't she? I'm surprised she hasn't got herself a man.'

Nick flipped up the collar of his coat with his free hand, the middle of his mouth and eyebrows arched upwards. 'Nathan told me tonight that she's married to the job. Sad – she's a very good looking woman.'

'Oh, is she now?' Mel said, digging him in the ribs.

'Boy, is she. Unlike you...' – he paused as long as he dared – '...who's absolutely gorgeous.' Nick pulled away from her arm and started to tickle her. 'Anyway, I didn't see you complain when playboy Nathan took every opportunity to slip his arm around you tonight.'

'He does that with all the women. You must be joking; I couldn't fancy any man whose dearest love is himself.'

'Mmm.' Nick smiled and let the conversation die as they set out on the walk home.

CHAPTER 7

Cathy pulled the seatbelt over her extended belly as her husband shot out of the pub car park. 'Nathan, slow down. What's wrong with you? You'll get caught drink driving one night, lose your job, and then where will we be?'

'If you hadn't been so bloody stupid and got pregnant again you could've driven.'

'That's rubbish and you know it. Even if I could, you wouldn't let me drive. You never let me drive. And don't blame me for falling again; there are two of us in this relationship.'

'Don't remind me,' said Nathan.

'You wanted children when we married and now suddenly it's a disaster.'

'I didn't want a fucking child before we married, though, did I? But you had to go and get pregnant,' he replied.

'So, you only married me because I was pregnant?' Cathy asked, close to tears.

Nathan ignored the question. 'I wanted us to enjoy life first without bloody kids. All I've ended up with is a load of hassle and debts up to my sodding earholes.'

The rest of the short journey continued in strained silence. Nathan pulled into the drive of their three bedroom semi and switched off the ignition. He got out, slammed the door and let his wife struggle out of the passenger seat. He entered the house and Cathy followed him. She started to climb slowly up the stairs. 'Are you coming to bed or staying down until all hours again?'

'What's the point in coming to bed? Look at the state of you.'

'You bastard! You complete bastard.' Cathy wept silently as she continued her laboured journey up to her bedroom.

Nathan headed over to the drinks cabinet in the corner of the living room. He pulled out a bottle of Johnny Walker and poured himself a large scotch. Staring vacantly across the room, he brought the cut glass tumbler to his lips and threw his head back to down the contents in one. The spirit made him wheeze. 'Fuck it!' The words came out in a low rasp. 'How am I gonna get out of this God awful mess. Shit!'

He reached for the bottle once more and poured himself another drink, then grabbed a silver cocktail shaker. He twisted off the lid and pulled out a small plastic bag of white powder. The detective put it carefully between his teeth and replaced the shaker in its original position in the drinks cabinet.

He took glass and bottle through to the small study at the end of the living room and closed the stripped pine door behind him with his foot. He took two steps forwards, leant over and let the bag drop from his mouth onto his desk. He then placed the drink next to the bag and sank into a black leather swivel chair.

The detective emptied some of the contents of the bag onto the back of his hand and sniffed the powder deep into his nostrils. His eyes watered. He wiped his face with his sleeve, leaned over and pressed play on his CD player. The haunting tones of Radiohead's 'High and Dry' flooded the room. The irony of the song registered immediately as he closed his eyes.

He put his head back against the shiny headrest where his thoughts turned to Mel Summers. *Why didn't I meet you first, Mel,* he mused. *That middle-class wanker Nick doesn't deserve you, darling. Landscape fucking gardener – what kind of profession is that for a bloke?*

He had lusted after Mel from the first moment Cathy had introduced him to her. He felt his wife didn't have the class or the looks of Mel. He decided that he deserved better. He deserved Mel.

He hadn't admitted it to himself, but he was envious of the college nerd Nick – of his comfortable background and his middle-class, easy-on-the-ear accent. Nick had received a privileged upbringing and had benefitted from a good education. He was also earning a great deal more than him. The last bit hurt the most.

Sitting at his desk with his eyes still closed, Nathan started to fantasise about Mel. It was becoming a regular habit. There had been no sex between him and his wife for over three months and this was his outlet. In fact, it was becoming a fixation. His drug misted fantasies were so real to him that part of his mind believed he was already having an affair with Nick's beautiful wife.

'It's only a matter of time, Mel, my little darlin',' he whispered as his fingers slowly undid the zip on his denims and moved along the length of his growing penis. He released himself from his boxers. At that moment Mel was straddling him, sliding up and down on his erect member. He visualised her facing towards him, her weighty breasts swaying to and fro in front of his eyes.

'Fuck me, Nathan – fuck me.' His lips mouthed the words as his imagination accelerated through the gears. His clenched fist now sped up over the end of his swollen member as he imagined his warm hand to be Mel's tight vagina. She swayed forward, rubbing her erect nipples across his outstretched tongue, releasing a low, animal moan as he bore deep inside her. He echoed that moan as he brought himself to orgasm.

Nathan breathed deeply and let out a long, satisfied sigh. 'One day, Mel, my little darlin'. One day.'

CHAPTER 8

The noises outside had stopped. Scrivens' heart slowed a few beats as he moved on. He was pleased so far with his haul from the unoccupied cottage. He left the changing room and headed for the bathroom at the far end of the corridor. Occasionally, extra odd pieces of jewellery were to be found in bathrooms. *This is going to be a very nice start to the night's mission,* he thought. Another few houses should get him the money needed to sort out his immediate financial problems.

Suppliers had two simple rules for their dealers: don't squeal if caught, and all debts are to be paid on time. Failure to adhere to either rule was met with pitiless retribution.

Nick and Mel reached the weathered oak front door of their house and paused to embrace. 'Ooh, I love you, Nick Summers.' She pressed her lips firmly against his. 'And when we have our little Summers, I will love you even more – if that's possible.'

'And I love you, darling,' Nick said, avoiding Mel's reference to a family. They had been trying for a child for four years without success. Mel was approaching her thirtieth birthday and was getting fidgety.

Throughout Nick's early adulthood, getting one of his casual girlfriends pregnant had been a constant worry. He now recognised the irony of his position; the nightmare had turned full circle. The longer this situation went on the more he tried to avoid discussion on the subject. He believed that it just put more pressure on them both.

Mel was the love of his life but he felt that this state of affairs was nudging its way between them like an unwelcome mother-in-law. It was confusing. What really worried him was that it was beginning to irritate him.

As Scrivens walked back out onto the upstairs landing the sound of voices coming from outside the front door alerted his ears. The thief froze. Off went the torch. A key went into the lock. 'Fuck – oh, fuck!' The words squeezed from his tight mouth as he edged backwards and into the small bedroom.

Nick opened the front door, patted Mel's bottom and ushered her into the house with a sweeping wave of his arm. As they entered the hall, he thought he heard a noise upstairs. He stood still and listened for a few seconds – all was quiet. He dismissed it from his mind.

Nick closed the heavy front door, drew across the top and bottom bolts, and secured the mortise lock. He then lobbed the bunch of keys towards the wooden fruit bowl that sat on the small antique table in the hall a few paces from the door. The keys hit their target, landing softly in between three shiny oranges, nestling quickly into their spongy, aromatic home.

Mel watched her husband's performance. 'Boys!' she said, rolling her eyes.

Scrivens slid the torch into the holdall and sank down into a foetal position behind the single bed. This was not part of the plan at all, he thought. He replayed in his head his movements from the moment he had entered the house. Then he remembered – the kitchen. He prayed they wouldn't go into that room and see the broken glass on the floor from the window.

The downstairs lights sprang to life, illuminating the upstairs hallway. Scrivens, his heart now thumping against his oesophagus, shrank closer to the floor. From beneath him the muffled conversation between a man and a woman ebbed and flowed as the owners moved from the hall into the sitting room.

Mel crossed the sitting room floor and headed towards the stairs. Nick followed her and then took three steps further to the arched kitchen entrance. He hooked his arm around the wall and put his forefinger on the light switch. 'Fancy a quick nightcap or coffee before bed?' he asked.

He flicked the switch down and the kitchen lit up behind him. His feet were now inches from the pieces of broken glass that had been punched out from the shattered kitchen window. The light sent champagne spangles dancing across the slivers of glass that now bejewelled the kitchen floor.

'No. I want you upstairs immediately to the baby factory with me. It's day twenty-one and my temperature is still point four degrees higher than normal.'

'I love it when you talk dirty,' Nick replied, deadpan.

'Come on. Turn that light off,' Mel insisted.

Nick flicked the switch back up and reflected on how wonderfully erotic his sex life had now become. 'Wow! Point four degrees. It doesn't get more provocative than that,' he mumbled.

'What's that?' Mel called over her shoulder as she climbed the stairs.

'Coming, darling!'

A cool breeze blew through the jagged edges of the broken window and across the glass-littered floor that hid in the darkness once more.

The voices got nearer and nearer as the owners reached the landing outside the main bedroom door. Scrivens could now feel the blood in his veins pulsing through his temples. He was aware of the acrid smell of fear seeping from his scrawny body. The voices moved even closer, just a few feet away from his hiding place. The man and woman were now standing directly outside the door of the small bedroom having a conversation. Scrivens hardly breathed for fear of them hearing him.

After a short time, the footsteps passed by his bedroom hideaway. Their voices faded behind the bathroom door as it swung shut. He filled his lungs with air for the first time in over a minute and immediately felt light-headed.

He waited for a few minutes, uncertain of his next move. He knelt upright from his hiding place, his mind racing. Should he make a break for it now or wait for the occupants to go to bed? He didn't know the ground floor layout very well. If the front door was locked, his exit would not be easy.

But the urge to get out of the house was overpowering. Just as he climbed to his feet, the bathroom door opened and the voices emerged once again. Scrivens recoiled behind the single bed, his sweat-soaked forehead buried in a sheepskin rug.

This time, much to his relief, the soft footsteps passed by the door to his hideaway and entered the main bedroom. There was another brief conversation before the door closed.

Scrivens, still lying face down on the rug, decided to wait ten minutes or so until they were asleep. He would then get the hell out of there. He pulled the torch from the holdall and shone it onto his wristwatch. It read *10.05 p.m.*

In bed, they went through the same monthly ritual. The middle ten days of Mel's cycle had become more important in their house than the invention of television. Although Nick was tired, he knew he had to perform.

This isn't how sex should be, Nick thought. This certainly wasn't how sex used to be. He was becoming aware of a growing tension between them on their 'lovemaking' nights. He sensed that Mel felt the same.

After he had finished, he lay on his back, exhausted. Nick stared at the insides of his eyelids. He hoped that the alcohol wouldn't affect the stamina of his semen. *Swim, you buggers, swim,* he urged silently as he drifted off to sleep.

Mel turned over on to her side, contracted her abdominal muscles, crossed her fingers, crossed her legs, bit her bottom lip and prayed that tonight was the night she would get pregnant.

Unfortunately, sleep did not come easily to Mel. She lay in bed looking through the darkness. She hadn't been sleeping well for months and tonight was no different. Her mind was too busy. The thoughts and concerns that she shunned during the day returned, uninvited, at night. Would her marriage survive if they were to be denied children? Had she married purely for love or for the overwhelming need to have a family? It was impossible to separate the two emotions.

She loved Nick, but this overriding problem was beginning to make her question the whole concept of love, of marriage, of family. A long-term relationship was never easy at the best of times. But the prospect of two people living together on their own for maybe forty, fifty years until one or the other died – well, was it feasible? It worried her.

Children were the binding agent in a marriage. How many couples would stay married if they remained childless? Not many, Mel surmised. All these questions scrambled her senses. The future used to be so clear, the direction so obvious. She was beginning to feel lost and a little bit scared. She was starting to panic.

Her restless brain now wandered back to previous relationships. She'd had only one serious boyfriend before she met Nick: an advertising executive called Martin. He was six feet tall, privately educated and gorgeous, and she'd been hopelessly in love with him.

Sadly, the relationship had lasted only three years and then finished, rather spectacularly, in tears at her twenty-second birthday party. During the evening's celebrations, when Mel took a trip upstairs to her bedroom to reapply her make-up, her dreams of a long and happy future with her man vanished in a flash.

There, kneeling on top of her bed, was the gorgeous Martin with his trousers around his ankles. That wouldn't have been so bad if her best friend Susan had not been kneeling in the same direction in front of him with less clothes on than

Martin. Susan's pert chest was jiggling rhythmically in time to Status Quo's hit, 'Whatever You Want'.

Unfortunately, what the cheating couple *didn't want* was to be caught doing it doggy fashion by the hostess of the party. Following a monumental outbreak of blue language and red faces, the party finished abruptly, as did Mel's friendship with Martin and Susan.

Unsettled by the memory, her mind hurried back to the present as she turned to look at the slumbering body of her husband. His broad, naked shoulders rose and fell with each breath as he travelled a private, subconscious world.

Mel realised that she wanted to be part of that world. She was suddenly reminded of how lucky she was to have a loving husband. An honest husband. She pushed all previous thoughts from her mind. Apart from one. She needed a pee.

CHAPTER 9

All was now quiet in the house. Scrivens turned on his torch and checked his watch once more. Ten thirty-five. He had been waiting longer than he had anticipated. The muffled noises from the bedroom had ceased well over ten minutes ago. They must be asleep by now, he reasoned. It was time to make his exit.

He hadn't moved a muscle whilst in his hiding place and his knees and lower back had stiffened up badly. He rose slowly to his feet, stretching his aching joints as quietly as he could. He then gathered up the holdall and crept forwards to the bedroom door. After a quick check to see the landing was clear, he turned left towards the stairs.

As he drew level with the main bedroom, the door swung open and the naked figure of Mel walked straight into him. He let out an involuntary squeal as their heads bumped together in the darkness.

In an automatic reaction the intruder threw his skinny arms out in front of him, knocking Mel over onto her back. She lay sprawled across the hall carpet, her eyes fixed on the shadowy figure above her. Her initial shock rapidly turned to terror. An involuntary scream exploded from her lungs – a scream that pierced the silence of the dark house.

Scrivens knew he had to move fast. He vaulted over the body of the woman in front of him and raced down the stairs.

In a blind panic, he turned at the bottom, entered the sitting room and ran straight into the chrome leg of a glass-topped coffee table. The protruding corner of the glass dug deep into his shin, felling him sideways. He slammed into the back of a sofa. He shrieked in pain, his leg badly damaged.

Nick was immersed within a troubled dream. He was remonstrating with Nathan. 'How can that be fair? It's all right for you, you've got kids.'

'Yes, Nick, but we reached the full offspring complement for this area of Kent three years ago. That's why we treat the domestic water supply with the oestrogen hormone. You're too late, mate.'

'This is ridiculous. It's not fair! We've only been married for four years,' Nick pleaded.

'If you'd been in the force, I may have been able to help you. But you're just a bloody gardener. You've got no chance. Anyway, why do you want kids? You'll ruin Mel's fantastic figure; her lovely breasts will sag and sex will never be the same, mate.'

Something inside Nick suddenly erupted, and as Nathan went to turn away he leapt at the policeman, raining blows down on his head. Surprised at the onslaught, Nathan let out a cry of anguish. The cry got louder and louder until the screaming in his head was not coming from within any more.

It was surrounding him. But the tone had changed from pain to alarm.

Nick's body shook violently as he awoke from his ridiculous yet disturbing nightmare. It took a few seconds for him to realise that it was his wife who was screaming.

'Mel! Where are you? What's wrong?' he shouted into the blackness.

'Nick, oh God, Nick!' Mel's voice was coming from outside the bedroom door. Nick leapt from his bed and rushed out onto the landing. Mel had curled up in a ball on the floor, afraid to move. 'Someone's in the house, Nick. He ran straight into me and knocked me over.'

'What? Are you sure?' Nick replied, still groggy from sleep.

'Of course I'm sure. He ran downstairs.'

'Are you okay?'

'Yes, but please be careful,' Mel replied as she uncurled and propped herself up against the wall, still in shock.

Nick ran back into the bedroom and pulled on a pair of boxers. He stooped down and pulled a baseball bat from beneath the bed. He had put it there a few years ago after a spate of burglaries in the area.

Gripping the heavy wooden bat, Nick ran out onto the landing. He swerved past the trembling figure of his wife and reached the top of the stairs. Then he stopped dead. It was as though an invisible force was holding him back. In one pounding heartbeat his demeanour changed from one of anger to uncertainty. Fear now controlled his every movement.

His mind was racing, firing questions at him at a demanding rate. *How do I handle this? Do I shout to scare him off the property? Should I confront him and get involved in a possible fight? What if he has a knife? A gun? There may be more than one intruder!*

All these thoughts clamoured for attention in his overworked brain. Steeling himself, he edged down the stairs with the bat held aloft. With each downward step the muscles in his arms and legs began to tighten. His semi-naked body felt alien to him as he broke out in a cold, clammy sweat.

Still clutching the holdall, Scrivens picked himself up, wincing at the pain coming from his injured shinbone. He leaned forwards to rub his leg only to feel a sticky wetness seeping through his tracksuit bottoms. He was bleeding heavily.

In twenty years of burgling houses this was the first time he had ever been caught on the premises. And leaving blood on the floor wasn't very clever either. There had been a few close calls but never like this. He had to get out, and quick.

He limped across the sitting room floor through the hall and reached the front door. He pulled back the bolts and turned the handle. The door didn't move. 'Shit, it's locked,' he whispered. 'Where's the fucking key?'

He quickly scoured the windowsill for the small piece of metal that would secure his freedom. He looked behind the curtain. He bent down and lifted the coconut-fibre doormat. Nothing! It was no good; he'd have to get out the same way he got in. He turned quickly, brushing past the wooden fruit bowl that contained the means to his salvation. He thought he heard a noise on the stairs. As fast as his injured leg could carry him, Scrivens headed for the kitchen, picking his way around the furniture in the darkness.

Nick reached the bottom of the stairs. He stood as if frozen – listening. He heard a shuffling noise coming from the sitting room. Should he turn on the light? At least then he'd be able to see who he was dealing with. But then that would make him an easy target. 'Christ!' The whisper came out in a breathless wheeze. What was he supposed to do?

The polished ash handle of the bat rotated a few degrees in Nick's moist hands as he tightened his grip on the weapon. He took a few tentative steps forwards, turned, and entered the sitting room. Through the gloom he thought he saw a shape move. Then, another sound.

Just at that moment a figure emerged at speed from the shadows straight towards him. There wasn't even time for his response to register in his brain. It was a reflex reaction that came from deep within him, born out of abject fear, of raw survival.

He swung the bat chest high at the threatening shape closing in on him. At that height he was sure of hitting something whilst not doing too much damage.

CHAPTER 10

As Scrivens hurried towards the kitchen, he looked up just in time to see a dark object heading at speed towards him. He ducked to avoid the blow. Sadly, his quick reaction proved to be his nemesis. He lowered his head straight into the path of the weighty missile. The sound at impact was sickening – like a sledgehammer driving a wet fence post into the ground.

The blow lifted Scrivens clean off his feet and propelled his light frame back into the room. This was followed by a nauseating groan mixed with the shattering of glass that shredded Nick's senses. The holdall had continued forwards and landed just behind him.

Nick stood in the dark, frozen to the spot, the bat still held high in his trembling hands. He stood as if turned to stone. He waited for what seemed like minutes for any other sounds coming from within the house. There was only silence.

'Nick?' The call came from behind him. It made him jump so violently he felt as though his heart had climbed up into his throat and was fighting to get out. He looked over his shoulder. He could just make out the dim figure of Mel. She was sitting halfway up the stairs, wrapped in an oversized dressing gown. She was hugging her knees tightly.

He turned back towards the sitting room, still not sure whether any more dangers lurked in his house. He started to speak but it was as if the voice was coming from someone else: 'I hit him. I hit him hard, but I'm not sure if...'

Before Nick could finish the sentence a light sprang on. It made him jump once again. Mel had reached the foot of the stairs. She had flicked the switch.

The sight that met his eyes was horrific. The carnage before him made his stomach feel as if it had folded over on itself. His arms sank to his sides and as his clenched grip loosened, the blood-spattered bat fell to the floor. The weapon that, a few moments ago, was his means of security, his ally, was now alien to him. It repulsed him. He took two steps forwards trying to absorb the horror that lay before him.

'Oh! Jesus.' Nick's mouth swung open as the enormity of his actions tore into every emotion he possessed. He turned to prevent Mel seeing the same picture. It was too late. Her despairing scream echoed throughout the house.

'Oh my God! Nick, what have you done? Oh my *God*!' Her emotional reaction quickly swung from shock to distress as she began to sob uncontrollably. Nick pulled her close and turned her away from the ghastly scene. As he held Mel, he surveyed the room that now housed a dramatic picture of surreal proportions. He began to take in every grisly detail.

A bowl of coloured glass balls and broken glass from the coffee table had been scattered over the rich ivory rug and across the polished wood floor. When Scrivens' unconscious body had fallen it had twisted through one hundred and eighty degrees. This had caused his face to whiplash downwards and straight through the plate glass surface of the coffee table.

His body lay awkwardly over the chrome frame. One arm had fractured so badly in the fall that a large piece of white snapped bone had pierced through the skin, jutting out from his wrist at right angles. His bloodied hand had been snapped back and lay flush, squashed against his forearm. His right leg from the knee downwards was a bloody mess.

When his head had struck the table, the impact had caused his neck to twist back on itself. His face was now pointing straight at Nick. One eye was looking directly at him, penetrating his soul – it was wide, staring, questioning. Where his other eye should have been there was now a six-inch shard of glass embedded deep in the socket. Glutinous blood poured from the grotesque wound. It ran down his colourless cheek, over his gaping mouth and onto the rug, forming a large, slowly expanding, dark crimson stain.

His attention then focused on a blood-matted cleft in the side of his skull. This was the spot where the perfectly weighted baseball bat had struck him. It had split his cranium from the crown to just above his right ear. Splinters of bloodied bone clung to his black-and-red-streaked matted hair, dappling the ugly crevice like some macabre mural.

Nick suddenly pushed his wife aside as bile flooded his oesophagus. 'Don't look round,' he managed to choke as the contents of his stomach poured out over his bare legs and feet and onto what used to be their beautiful, deep-pile Persian rug.

At the same time, the strength drained from his body. He sank slowly to his knees, leaning forwards on to his hands in an effort to clear his spinning head. As he did so, he looked up again at the fast-cooling body of Scrivens that was now directly in front of him. He retched and threw up again over the thin man's tracksuited legs.

Keeping her gaze away from the dead body, Mel swung around and helped Nick to his feet. She pulled him away from the horror that lay in front of them. Her first instinct was to wash the streaks of blood and vomit from her traumatised husband. She gripped his arm and turned him around. Using all her strength, she pulled a disorientated Nick towards the downstairs bathroom. It was like leading a blind man across a hazardous road.

Nick sank down onto the side of the bath. Mel lifted her husband's head and looked deep into his face. It was not a face she recognised. His skin appeared thinner than usual; the colour of dough. His eyes, usually soft, blue, thoughtful, were now lifeless. It was like looking into the eyes of a sheep – vacant, unresponsive. Nick appeared to have aged ten years in the last ten minutes.

Mel stripped off his shorts and cleaned his naked, trembling body with a wet flannel, then towelled him dry. She worked swiftly and in complete silence. She then went upstairs with her dazed husband and they dressed together. Neither was sure why they had decided to dress again in their day clothes – it was an unspoken, natural reaction. Perhaps if they were fully dressed they would not feel so vulnerable.

Still nothing was said as they went back downstairs. They edged past the mutilated body of the intruder, trying to avoid looking at the horrific scene, and entered the kitchen in a daze.

Avoiding the broken glass on the floor, Mel pulled out two of the arrowback chairs from the gnarled oak farmhouse table.

Together, they slumped down into the wooden seats. They had been a wedding present from his grandmother. At that moment neither of them appreciated the attractive period furniture.

Mel leaned towards her husband and took his hand. It was cold, quivering. She spoke softly, 'We have to phone the police, Nick.' She stood and moved towards the pine Welsh dresser and picked up Nick's mobile phone.

'No!' Nick barked, snapping out of his inertia.

'What do you mean, no?' Mel sat down once more opposite her husband.

'I need time to think. For God's sake, I've just killed a man. In fact, I haven't killed him. I've slaughtered the poor bastard.'

'A burglar, Nick. A low-life who broke into our home and attacked me outside my own bedroom door. How do we know he just came to rob us? He could have killed us. Who are the poor bastards here?'

'That's not how the police will see it. Don't you see? I've read about these cases. He wasn't brandishing a knife or a gun. He was just a common thief. Reasonable force. That's what they say you can use. Reasonable fucking force. Look at him. I've destroyed the bloke.'

'You didn't mean to kill him. It was an accident.'

The word 'accident' registered a change in Nick's demeanour. 'He breaks into our house, invades our privacy and scares the life out of us. How did I know he didn't have a weapon? All I do is try to protect my home, my family – and bingo, he dies. And I get ten years inside.'

'Oh God. Nick, that can't be right.' Mel's stoicism suddenly evaporated. She started to cry again.

'It's not right. But that's what will happen.' Nick leant forward onto his elbows and dropped his head in his hands.

'We must call the police. We have to put our trust in the law. We've never done anything wrong in our lives, they must see that.' Mel was now pleading with her husband.

'Yes! Like that farmer. What's his name? Martin someone. He'd never done anything wrong and look what happened to him. He shot that intruder – one of those boys who kept breaking into his farmhouse. He trusted the law and where did it get him? Ten years for murder.'

'I don't think he did ten years, though,' said Mel.

'No, it was reduced to five and manslaughter. And this was a man who was burgled on a regular basis. A man who was at the end of his tether. This is our first break-in. What understanding or leniency are we going to get?'

Nick sat back in his chair and stared at the ceiling. His mind rewound back to when he was twelve. He had stood, helpless, and watched as his uncle was attacked and killed. He had been unable to do anything about it then. He had also lost faith in the police, who had failed to get justice for his family.

This time he had done something to protect himself and the person he loved. But he was still confused, still scared – because he was now the killer. After a pause, he said, 'What's the time?'

Mel looked at her watch. 'It's five to eleven. Why?'

'I'll phone Nathan. I realise I will have to call the police, but, I don't know, maybe he will tell me how to handle this – give me some assurance that I won't have to go to prison. But it doesn't look good at the moment does it?'

'But he is the police?' said Mel.

'Yes. But he's sort of a friend. I need all the help I can get, Mel.'

Nick reached forwards, unfurled the reluctant fingers of Mel's hand and scooped up his mobile phone – it was wet with perspiration. He wiped it on his shirt front. 'I think I've got his mobile number in my phone. I just hope he's still up.' Nick located the detective's entry, but, as he went to ring the number, his trembling forefinger hovered over the call button, unable to move.

He looked up at Mel, whose eyes were locked onto his uncertain hand. The tension in the room was suffocating. He had to make a decision.

He pressed the button.

CHAPTER 11

Nathan sat slumped at his desk, eyes closed, still clutching the empty whisky glass. He was almost asleep when his mobile phone, which he had switched from ring to vibrate, began to pulsate in front of him. The irritating buzz snapped him out of his drowsy state. He glanced at his watch. 'Who the…?' He picked up the phone and saw the caller's name – Nick S. He pressed the answer key.

'Hello, Nathan?' Nick's voice was barely above a whisper.

'Nick. Do you know what bloody time it is?'

'Nathan, there's been a terrible accident.'

It took a few moments for the words to register. Then Nathan's senses were jolted back to life. 'Is it Mel?'

'No. We're both okay but it's serious. Could you come over?'

'Yes, of course, but can't you tell me…'

'I'll tell you when you get here. Is Cathy there?'

'No. She's upstairs in bed. She'll be fast asleep by now.'

'Good. Keep it that way. I'd rather she knew nothing about this at the moment.'

'Of course. I'll be over in five.' Nathan turned off his mobile and went into the kitchen. He ran the cold tap for a few seconds, threw a few handfuls of water on his face to freshen himself up, picked up his car keys from the table and left the house as quietly as he could.

On the short journey to Nick house, his imagination was galloping around inside his head. He had no idea of what he was about to see but a part of him was excited to be going into Mel Summers' home for the first time. When he arrived, Nick was waiting for him at the front door. The sight of Nick's ashen face told him that something very serious had happened in this house.

Nick kept Nathan in the hallway while he related the incredible sequence of events of the past half hour. The detective could not believe what he was hearing. Having prepared him for what he was about to see, Nick showed Nathan into the sitting room.

'Jesus! Fucking hell!' Nathan spat out the words as his mouth dropped open. He then repeated the blasphemous curse in a whisper.

Nathan Ballack had been a copper for almost twenty years. He'd heard plenty of gruesome tales, had some frightening scrapes and dealt with the lowest of the low. But he'd never attended a scene such as this. Yes, he had seen a few dead bodies at close quarters, but they were mainly heart attack or drowning victims. This guy was a mess.

Nathan walked methodically around the bloodied corpse, his policeman's mind taking in every detail of the scene. When he reached the front of the body he looked into the disfigured face of the dead man.

It couldn't be. Nathan stepped towards the buckled figure and took a closer look. He checked out his clothes. He looked in amazement. Was it Scrivens? Yes it was. It was Tony Scrivens. Once more his jaw swung downwards. His initial reaction was one of incredulity. It was quickly followed with one of cautious relief. If this was handled carefully, he thought, it could get him right out of the financial mess he was in with his suppliers. He couldn't believe his possible good fortune.

Nick interrupted Nathan's scheming thoughts. 'I need you to tell me what to do, Nathan. This doesn't look like reasonable force, does it? But I only hit him once.'

Mel, who was sitting at the foot of the stairs, keeping her gaze away from the mutilated body, added her support. 'And it was dark, Nathan. He couldn't even see what he was aiming at.'

'I just swung the bat at the middle of the oncoming shape,' Nick continued. 'I know what that farmer got for killing that bloody boy thief. What chance have I got with this mess?'

'Have you searched the body for a weapon?' said Nathan.

'God, no. I haven't touched him.'

Nathan quickly checked Scrivens' clothing and found nothing. 'He's not carrying.'

'That makes it look worse, doesn't it?' said Nick, sweeping the hair back off his pallid face with his fingers.

'It's not good, Nick. If the bloke attacked you with a weapon, you may have an argument. You could put a knife in his hand but, to be honest, it's too risky. If they find your or Mel's DNA on the weapon, you're dead.' Nathan was pleased with the way he was guiding the proceedings. But he had to appear to be impartial. 'The SOCOs may corroborate your story – the sequence of events – but no weapon, the level of violence. Well?'

His mind was racing ahead. Part of him wanted to help them both, but he was beginning to enjoy the power he had over Nick – this man who had everything he wanted.

Beneath his outward demeanour of concern, he took pleasure in watching Mel as she gazed at her husband. Her usual look of loving admiration was now replaced with doubt and fear. It gave his twisted mind some hope.

'You've got two choices,' Nathan said.

'I'm not sure I want to hear this,' said Mel. She left the two men standing over the body, picked up the holdall and went into the kitchen where she filled the kettle and pulled out a bottle of whisky from a cupboard.

Nathan continued: 'Your first choice: you ring the police now. You've already wasted time reporting it and they'll want to know why. But he's a bloody mess. Anyone witnessing this scene will be surprised at the severity of the victim's injuries.'

'Victim? Christ!'

'That's how they'll see it,' said Nathan. He now had to lay it on thick to achieve his desired outcome. 'Taking into account the force you have used here, you're quite possibly looking at a murder charge, mate.'

Nick's face dropped. He felt light-headed. 'Murder?' he choked. Mel, on hearing the word, moved to the sitting room door to listen to the conversation.

'But, hopefully, you'll just go down for manslaughter. You're looking at five years minimum, I reckon – out in three probably.'

Nathan studied Nick. He displayed the body language of a cornered animal. The policeman could see that the lesser sentence for manslaughter was hardly a comfort to this frightened individual.

'Of course, there's a chance you could get off, people do. But it's a slim one. Even if you do, you will still be arrested, locked up, your fingerprints and DNA taken, which will always be on file. I've seen these cases before Nick. You and Mel would be plastered all over the front pages of every daily paper. The TV cameras and hacks will camp outside your door.' Nathan saw Nick shrink as he tried to absorb the information that was being fed to him.

Nathan continued, 'I'm afraid the papers won't stop with this incident. They will delve into every aspect of your past and Mel's. However personal, it will be in print for all to see. And if you're found guilty? Well, I haven't got to tell you what it would do to your business. Couples break up over less than this.' Nathan shook his head. He turned to see Mel at the door. He took a deep breath. 'I'm sorry to scare you two, but I have to paint the picture as it is.'

Nick raised his eyes from the floor and looked at the detective. He filled his lungs with air. 'You said I had two choices. What's the second one?'

Mel had heard enough. She returned to the kitchen.

'You get rid of the body. It's the middle of the night; no one would have seen him enter your house. That's his job. You've got no motive to kill anyone so the police won't come knocking on your door. He won't have told anyone where he was going tonight or which house he was going to do. As long as you can get him out and bury him without anyone seeing you, you should be okay.'

Nathan realised that if Scrivens was never found, it would suit his own cause perfectly. *Scrivens' suppliers won't know who owes him money; they will just think he's done a runner.*

Nathan also knew Scrivens' background from when he had first arrested him for dealing. He was one of seven children from an impoverished, fatherless family living in Wolverhampton. He had left home at the age of thirteen and made his way down south, living on the streets, stealing and begging.

He'd eventually got involved with the drug scene in his late teens, which provided enough money to rent a flat on the poorer outskirts of Bourne. He lived on his own and had no dependents and no job. If he disappeared, no one would care or even question it. The plan was coming together nicely in his calculating brain. Nathan had made up his mind: the quicker Scrivens disappeared the better for everyone.

Nathan could see Nick wrestling with the two options. 'It sounds like an easy choice when you put it like that... Jesus! I can't believe I'm talking like this,' said Nick. Nathan had to make him think logically about doing something that was foreign to his moral beliefs.

'As far as I'm concerned, that's your only sensible choice,' he urged. 'There's risks, course there's risks. But even if you get caught the circumstances of the killing won't have changed. You were in shock, you panicked and tried to dispose of the body – the body of someone who broke into your home. The length of your sentence won't differ an awful lot either way, so you might as well go for it.'

'Are you sure about that? It won't make much difference to my sentence?' Nick asked, his words wrapped in desperation.

'Yes,' Nathan replied starkly, with as much sincerity as he could muster.

Nick was stuck in panic mode. He had no time to clear his head or check out the detective's words.

Nathan could see that he still needed to convince Nick. 'Anyway, I've just realised who this is. He's a drug dealer and habitual thief. His name is Scrivens. I wasn't sure at first because of the mess he's in. But I'm certain now.' He looked down at the pathetic body of the thief. 'He lives on his own and has no family. No one will be looking for him. It's your choice, mate. It's not an easy one. But I know what I would do.'

Nick closed his eyes. He saw the ruinous newspaper headlines, the media intrusion. He imagined the prison cell door; heard it slam shut. Then there was Mel, on her own, broken, vulnerable.

He looked at Nathan, took another deep breath and nodded, 'Okay. How do we do this?'

'You've got your car in the garage, right?' said Nathan.

'I've got the van I use for work. The Jag's in for a service at the moment. We can take him through the integral door so no one will see.'

'The van's perfect. Right! I'll help you get him in the back of the van, then you're on your own. I can't get involved any more than that. I shouldn't even be doing this.'

'Sorry. No, I realise that. I really appreciate this, Nathan.'

The two men moved into the kitchen and explained the options in full to Mel. 'I heard it all, Nick. I just can't believe…' she couldn't finish the sentence.

'If you heard everything then you know what the consequences would be, whether I am found guilty or not. I've got to dispose of the body, Mel.'

Mel's reaction made it obvious to both men that it was not the option she had wanted to hear. She covered her mouth with her hand, shaking her head in disbelief. Her eyelids squeezed closed, forcing more tears down her troubled face.

Nick stepped forward and held his trembling wife in his arms. Nathan could see that Nick was still not convinced he had made the right decision. The detective looked upon the domestic scene with mixed emotions.

Over a cup of whisky-laced tea, the detective tried to convince Mel that if she did not want her husband to go to prison – didn't want their lives to be turned inside out – getting rid of the body was the only option to take. As he watched her lukewarm reaction to his suggestion, two things suddenly struck him: Scrivens must have parked his car somewhere close, and he had a hundred pounds of his money on his blood-soaked body.

Nathan needed to act fast. 'Look, you two talk it over. It's just dawned on me that your intruder might have a car parked somewhere near. You don't want the police finding it so close to your house. You two discuss what I've been saying and I'll just go and search him for car keys. I'll take care of the car. I know someone who can get rid of it.'

Nick looked over at Nathan. 'Oh! Right. Thanks.'

Nathan left them sitting at the kitchen table and moved into the sitting room. Taking care not to tread in the still-expanding pool of blood, he found Scrivens' keys in the front pouch of his top. Then, checking to see that he was still on his own in the room, he retrieved a small bundle of folded notes from a zipped pocket in his tracksuit bottoms.

A triumphant grin unfolded across his face as he slipped the money into the back pocket of his jeans. Events were going his way at last. In fact, they could not have been going any better. When he returned to the kitchen, Mel was talking to Nick. 'Is this what you really want?' she asked.

'Of course not. The last thing I want to do is drive out to some desolate place in the middle of the night and bury a body. But I don't want to go to prison either. The law, many years ago, didn't look after my bloody family when we needed them. Why should I believe the law will protect me now? If it's murder, Mel, they'll lock me up for... I don't even know! But it'll be a lot more than a few years.'

Mel looked up at Nathan. He gave her a confirming nod. She looked at both men. They seemed to have already decided on a plan of action.

'I realise that whatever I say is not going to change your mind. I'm not happy with this at all. But, if what you say is true, I'm equally unhappy with the alternative. It's not a decision I would want to make. You must do what you have to do,' Mel said reluctantly.

The horrifying strategy was to go ahead.

The plan: after the body was put into the boot of his car, Nick would drive out to Dunley Marsh that lay twelve miles east of their village of Bourne. There, he would dig a grave and bury the body.

Dunley Marsh was a twenty-five-thousand acre site of low-lying wetlands. It was a largely uninhabited location with areas of dense undergrowth and tangled forests. The surrounding roads were narrow and winding due to the hundreds of sewers and small drainage ditches that interlaced the boggy terrain. There were few villages in the vicinity and consequently few road signs. This made navigation across the marsh very confusing for the unwary. For that reason, it received few visitors.

After a brief discussion, both men agreed that the marsh would be an ideal spot to bury a body. Nick was familiar with the location as he had been there on a field trip many years before as part of his honours degree. The atmosphere was dank and hostile. The site had an overpowering smell that reminded him of when he had left his wet, muddy rugby kit in his closed sports bag only to discover it two weeks later, covered in mildew. Now he had to return to the marsh not to take from the soil but to add significantly to it.

Nick's mind was now a farrago of conflicting emotions. Could he actually go through with this macabre course of action? The concept chilled the blood in his veins. The skin over his entire body prickled – it suddenly felt one size too small.

He remembered feeling very uncomfortable during the six-hour fact-finding mission at Dunley Marsh. He recalled how the clammy conditions sat heavy on the lining of his lungs. It had impaired his breathing and made it difficult for him to concentrate on what he was doing.

Tonight he must ignore the uncomfortable conditions and control his fears. Tonight his concentration must be total.

CHAPTER 12

Nick went into his garage and switched on the internal light. The exposed brick walls were lined with wooden shelves that were covered with a miscellany of objects. He walked past the partly-filled paint pots, household tools and numerous glass jars that contained anything from screws to discarded buttons, and pulled a plastic decorator's sheet down from one of the top shelves. He unfolded it on the floor, took a pair of scissors from his tool box and cut it in half. He then dragged it back into the sitting room and laid it next to the lifeless body.

Without further discussion, Nathan took the arms and Nick took the feet as they lifted the blood-soaked creature that had been Scrivens off the table frame and onto the sheet. Nick was surprised by how light the dead man felt between the two of them. He tucked one end of the sheet over the corpse, then, together, they rolled it up into a tightly wrapped parcel. He tied up the bundle and secured both ends with garden twine.

When he had finished, he stood up and looked across at Nathan. They nodded at each other in silence, bent down and lifted the body up from the floor. The men carried it across the sitting room, through the utility room and into the garage.

Nick put his end of the grisly package down on the cold concrete floor and opened the back doors of the van. Together, they slid the body into the back of the vehicle. The seven-year-old white van was the same size as a standard car but with just two seats at the front. At the rear were two windowed doors that opened onto an area of flat storage space – just long enough to house a top-to-toe human body if placed diagonally. Nick retrieved some old compost bags from the corner of the garage and used them to cover the human parcel.

Despite being encased in plastic, Nick could still smell the sickly odour of his victim. He brought his soiled hands up to his face. Repulsed, he jerked his head backwards. They reeked of Scrivens' blood and perspiration.

As Nick closed the doors of his van, Nathan broke the silence: 'Haven't you forgotten something?'

'No, I don't think so,' Nick replied, surprised.

'What are you gonna bury him with, Nick?'

'Oh, shit!' Nick hurried away, collected a shovel from the garden shed and put it in the van.

'And you're gonna want a torch,' Nathan added.

After putting one in the glove compartment, Nick once more closed the van doors. Nathan spoke again. 'And what you gonna do with the rug?' He was talking to him now as if he were addressing a naughty child.

'I've got a huge pile of leaves and garden rubbish ready to be burnt. The rug goes up in smoke with the rest of the pile tomorrow morning,' replied Nick.

'Good! Look, I'm gonna shoot off back home. I'm done in,' said Nathan. As they moved back into the sitting room, Nathan looked across at Mel, who was busy clearing up the mess of blood and broken glass. 'Bye, Mel,' he called.

Mel, still numb with shock, joined them as they reached the front door. Nick went to open it, then paused. 'I think it would be best not to tell Cathy about this,' he said.

'No way. The fewer, the better. If she's noticed that I went out tonight, I'll tell her that I went for a drive. She'll be fine. I doubt she even woke up. She could sleep on a stiff breeze, that woman.'

The policeman leant forward and kissed Mel's cheek. 'Don't worry, Mel, he's doing the right thing. There's one less piece of trash in the world now. That's the way to look at it. G'night and good luck,' Nathan said, almost flippantly, as he turned away. He climbed into his car and was gone.

'Can we trust him, Nick?' Mel said, as Nick closed the front door.

'We haven't got any choice. Anyway, what does he gain by telling on us?'

'Oh, I don't know. There's something about him I don't like. What you see isn't what you get with Nathan. He's a shifty bugger!'

'Look, I'm just grateful he's helped us out. And anyway, after what he did tonight he's an accomplice. His prints or DNA or whatever are going to be all over the body and the sheet. So I hardly think he'll turn us in,' Nick said, in hope.

As they re-entered the sitting room he surveyed the scene. 'Where's the rug?'

Mel did not reply.

Nick looked at his wife, who was staring trance-like at the spot where Scrivens had been killed. 'Mel. Where is the rug?' he said more forcefully.

Mel tumbled out of her stupor, trying to shift the ghastly imprint of the bloody scene from her immediate vision. 'It's rolled up outside the back door waiting to be burnt,' was her barely audible reply.

'Right! Well done. You've done a great job already cleaning some of this lot up. This is bloody weird. Standing here now, it's as though it was all a terrible dream,' Nick said, wishing it were true.

'I've got a lot more to do yet. When I've cleaned up this mess I'm going to wipe down everything in the vicinity with hot water and disinfectant. There are probably tiny specks of blood everywhere. You'd better get on with it,' said Mel, looking towards the connecting door to the garage. Nick nodded at his wife and closed his eyes for a few seconds as the reality of the evening came rushing back. A veil of nausea descended upon him once again.

Nick took a deep breath though his nose and slowly exhaled through his mouth. He checked his wristwatch. The stylish Armani timepiece indicated twelve minutes past midnight. 'Okay, I'm going. Wish me luck. Oh, and don't forget to close the garage door when I've gone – quietly. The last thing we want is for some neighbour who can't sleep looking over here and wondering what the hell is going on,' said Nick.

'Oh God,' said Mel, 'please be careful.'

Nick leaned forwards and kissed his wife on the forehead. 'I will be careful. I just hope that I'll be lucky.'

He picked his bunch of keys out of the fruit bowl and opened the front door of his house. As he stepped outside, he scanned the surroundings for any signs of life. Bray Road was peaceful and deserted. A gentle breeze ruffled his hair as he looked up into the night. The sky was completely overcast. The clouds were set high – he hoped that was a good sign. He did not want it to rain tonight: it would make his job messy and infinitely more difficult.

Moving quickly to the garage door he pulled it up and over his head. Then he climbed into his van. His hands went to the wheel. He couldn't stop them shaking at the thought of being in such an enclosed space with the dead body. As he pulled out of the drive, he glanced back to see Mel close the garage door and enter their house. He knew that the next few hours would be indescribable torment for both of them.

She would be alone and scared. Which was exactly how he felt.

CHAPTER 13

Nick Summers drove slowly away from his house. Behind every curtain every eye in the neighbourhood was watching him. Or so he thought. Each time he had to stop at a red light or junction, he sat, shoulders hunched, huddled over the wheel. Twice he turned to check that the back doors of his van were locked.

As he drove down Bourne High Street and approached a set of lights, he noticed a mobile stall parked in a lay-by next to the junction. Standing around the stall were several small groups of alcohol-fuelled, young men munching kebabs and hamburgers. The last thing he wanted was people seeing his face and looking in through the van's back windows. He prayed that the lights would stay green long enough for him not to have to stop. But he dared not increase his speed for fear of being spotted by an unseen police car or getting caught on a speed camera.

The green light got nearer and nearer as his hands tightened around the steering wheel. With forty yards to go on came the amber light – maybe he could still just make it.

Thirty yards, twenty… With ten yards to go the red light suddenly filled the front windscreen like a warning hand. 'Damn!' Nick's right foot hit the brake. As the van screeched to a halt the body in the back shot forwards and slammed into the back of the driver's seat.

Nick was pushed forwards, his nose stopping just short of the windscreen. He was then sucked back into his seat. The groups of teenagers all turned to see the cause of the noise. He sat there, not daring to look sideways at the gathering of late-night snackers.

A gang of three teenagers wearing hooded tops, the closest to Nick's van, started to laugh and shout insults at Nick. 'If you can't drive it, mate, get out and fuckin' push it. You wanker!' said the tallest of the three. His mates laughed.

The youth finished his final mouthful of kebab, screwed up the paper wrapper and threw it at the van. The missile startled Nick as it hit the driver's window, making him flinch. The louts found that hilarious.

'Come on, lights. Come on,' Nick pleaded through clenched teeth as he continued to stare straight ahead of him. The youths, encouraged by the driver's timid response, moved threateningly towards the van. This was the last thing he needed right now. Suddenly, part of him was twelve once more. His heart sped up as the picture of his uncle surrounded by the gang of boys flashed across his brain. Now he had the nerve to stand up to these bullies but there was no way he could get out and remonstrate with these lads. Not tonight.

Closer they came, just a few feet from his window. He had to do something, and fast. Just as he contemplated taking a chance and jumping the traffic signals the amber light lit up.

Nick shot away from the junction, causing Scrivens' body to now slide backwards, thudding against the rear doors of the van.

He heard the louts cheer in derision as he left the mob gesticulating in the middle of the road. 'God! Did I not need that,' he said as his lungs expelled a balloon of air. The last thing he wanted to do was draw attention to himself. *Not a great start,* he thought. It was an incident he could have done without.

He glanced in his rear-view mirror at the bundle that was now wedged up against the rear of the van. He prayed the doors of his ageing vehicle would hold securely as he continued his journey.

At the next crossroads, Nick turned left on to the main road that led directly to the marshlands. The incredible events of the evening spun wildly around his brain as he drove on through the night. Every few minutes he checked his speedometer to make sure he was keeping just below the speed limit for the road. He could feel his body growing progressively tense as he drove towards his destination.

Piloting his van in a safe and efficient manner, something that was normally such an easy task, had suddenly become an uncertain operation. The pressure he put on himself to get every manoeuvre correct and not make any silly mistakes was as fierce as the day he'd taken his driving test at the tender age of eighteen.

The journey took just short of twenty-five minutes; to Nick it seemed to last a lifetime. Every so often he would look in his rear-view mirror at the crumpled body behind him, struggling to come to terms with the fact that he had ended a human being's life. Whenever he glanced back, an overwhelming infusion of guilt raced through his senses.

The repeated visual checks were also to confirm that the corpse, by some unearthly way of retribution, had not come back to life behind his back. He half-expected a grasping hand to descend upon his shoulder at any moment. He was aware that his imagination was out of control, but until the body was in front of him where he could see it, he was not going to feel comfortable. In fact, if it was at all possible for him to experience any feelings of ease, it would not be until after he had buried it beneath a huge quantity of earth.

The illuminated blue road sign he saw to his left came as a welcome relief. Dunley Marsh was indicated as the next road on the right, half a mile further on. As he neared the turning he moved across to the centre of the road, flicked down the right indicator and drove off the two lane route onto a minor road.

It came as a relief to see that his was the only vehicle in the vicinity. But not as a complete surprise. Who in their right mind would want to visit such a bleak place as this in the dead of the night? Only those, he thought, who had something to hide. Or someone to bury.

He continued at a slower pace along the deserted road, looking for an appropriate pathway into the centre of the swamp. Dark towering trees with low, overhanging skeletal branches sprang forward, then disappeared like gigantic black spiders as he moved forwards into the unknown.

Occasionally, a small dead branch or seed pod would fall, hitting the thin metal roof of his van with a crack, causing him to recoil in his seat. It was if nature was expressing her displeasure with Nick – warning him not to continue with his vile plan.

After five hundred yards or so he took a left onto a narrow and poorly lit track. Nick put his main beam on then immediately turned it off. 'Don't draw attention to yourself, you idiot,' he said out loud. He continued to berate himself as he drove slowly down the winding route.

Three hundred yards further on, the track split into two. He decided to leave the main track and take the smaller left fork, which led into denser vegetation. The pathway was now reduced to a mere car's width with only his sidelights to guide him.

Nick dared not go above a crawl as he negotiated the pitch-black, pot-holed causeway. 'Surely no one sane would venture this far down into this God forsaken place,' he whispered, trying to reassure himself.

Suddenly, visibility improved and his surroundings became a lot clearer as the moon appeared unexpectedly through the wind-tossed clouds for the first time since he'd left his house. It was only then that he realised he was almost totally surrounded by water – foul, grimy, weed-filled water.

At first he welcomed the extra light, but the moon's reflections, now bouncing off the swamp, mixed with the low trajectory of the van's lights began to confuse him. It made his progress more hazardous. He was aware that there was perhaps only a foot of track either side of his vehicle. Beyond that he was looking at guaranteed disaster.

The van was now lurching in and out of sludge-filled hollows. Nick tried desperately to keep the vehicle from disappearing into the threatening quagmire that began to lick at his mud-covered tyres. Twice he struck his head on the roof of the van as he and the body in the back were thrown around like rag dolls.

On and on he crawled into the blackness, not knowing where he was going or what pitfalls he may encounter. He was driving blind – he was convinced that he was driving into the bowels of hell.

Then he got his first piece of luck that night. He found what he was looking for: a clearing large enough in which to turn his van around and carry out his grim course of action. He swung the van around full circle. It was now facing the way it had come. Then he reversed back to a dense thicket that sat close to the edge of the swamp. Behind the thicket lay a small section of land cut off from the track that jutted out into the bog.

He turned off his lights, killed the engine, grabbed the torch and stepped out of the van. That same damp stench of rotting matter that he'd experienced all those years ago attacked his senses once again. It crept up his nostrils and slithered its way down his throat to his lungs.

Nick flicked the switch of his torch and surveyed his surroundings. Dark, dank, remote and wildly overgrown just about covered it. He hated it; it frightened him – but it was perfect.

He moved to the back of the van and turned the door handle. As he did so the doors sprung open and a pair of plastic-encased arms shot out at him as though they were still alive. He jumped back in shock. 'Fuck!' Nick shrieked. 'Fuck!' He didn't want to shriek. He didn't want to make any sound whatsoever. He placed his hands over his chest and felt his heart kicking against his ribs. He took three deep breaths. 'Come on, I've got this far. Let's get this done and get the hell out of this accursed place,' he told himself. He ducked into the van, lifted Scrivens' legs to one side and retrieved the shovel.

He picked his way carefully around the back of the compact scrub and laid the torch on the ground by his feet. Here was a track of land, perhaps ten feet square, between the trees and the edge of the swamp – just enough, he thought, for his purpose.

Apart from the thin beam of light coming from the torch, the location was in complete darkness. To complete his task Nick realised that he needed more light to work with. Turning on the powerful headlights of the van was not an option; it could attract attention.

He picked up the torch and approached the small trees and shrubs that stood between him and his van. After a few unsuccessful attempts he managed to wedge the small flashlight at a downward angle between the fork of two branches of a tree.

It was not the most powerful shaft of illumination, but the section of land that was to be the grave was now visible enough for Nick to carry out his mission.

He started to dig.

Nick was grateful that this was part of what he did for a living. At least his body was used to this particular physical exertion. Years of digging out dead tree stumps and stubborn, deep-bedded roots had equipped him with strong upper-arm, neck and back muscles along with a good technique. The earth beneath his boots was loose and moist, which made his job considerably easier. He worked fast and economically.

In just over an hour and a half he'd dug a three-foot-deep grave. By the time he had finished, despite his good level of fitness, his body was soaked in sweat due to the clinging humidity; his lungs felt raw as they sucked in the putrid air.

Nick pulled the corpse from the van and dragged it around the thicket to the side of the freshly dug hole. He then untied the garden twine and rolled the body out of the sheeting and into the grave. The body tumbled into the murky pit and landed on its back.

There it was again – the horrific sight of Scrivens' mutilated face, with one eye still snapped open. The chilling, swollen, doll-like eye was staring straight up at him. Nick's brain threw out a panic bulletin that reverberated down every nerve in his spine. His skin prickled, his muscles tensed. Drunkenly, he reeled away from the ghoulish spectacle.

Leaning forwards with his hands on his knees, Nick gagged and swallowed hard. If he had allowed himself to be sick, there would have been very little in his stomach now apart from bile.

He had to be strong. He had to do this – his and Mel's future depended on it. Averting his gaze away from the grisly spectacle, Nick folded and tied the plastic sheeting into a small bundle and threw it in next to the body. He figured that, unwrapped, the corpse would rot much faster.

He picked up the shovel and started to fill in the grave, throwing the damp earth on top of Scrivens' dead body. It took him another half an hour to replace the mound of stinking mud and sludge into the pit.

When it was completed, he walked over the surface of the grave, treading down the loose earth. Gathering a handful of brushwood from the surrounding area, he used it to comb the top of the grave to level the earth and hide his footprints. Finally, he covered the area with dead branches and bracken.

Nick lumbered to his van and threw the shovel in through the rear doors. He reached his arms over his head and stretched backwards, his overworked vertebra grateful of some respite. Then he turned and looked back onto the small copse. Most of it was hidden by the bushy scrub in front of the burial site and what little you could see of it looked quite natural and undisturbed.

He was satisfied that he had done a good job. To the untrained eye the area looked virtually untouched. All he had to do now was negotiate his way back to the main road without driving the van off the track and into the swamp. *Easier said than done,* he thought.

As he was about to get into his vehicle a glimmer of light grabbed his attention. Out the corner of his eye he saw a faint gold reflection, ripple snake-like on the stagnant water. In his tired, agitated state he had almost forgotten about it. How stupid was he? The dim torch was still wedged between the tree branches. Why not put a sign up stating, *Body buried here,* he thought as he retrieved the flashlight and returned to the van. 'Think, Summers, think,' he said, slapping himself twice on the cheek.

He closed the rear doors, put the torch into the glove compartment, took one more look at the scene and climbed into the driver's seat. As he turned the engine on he was momentarily stunned by the sound of high-pitched screeching. Shocked, he quickly turned the ignition off again. After a few seconds he realised the terrible noise was coming from a flock of low-flying geese passing overhead.

'God! What next?' Nick dropped his forehead onto the top of the steering wheel. 'Fine fucking time to decide to fly south for the fucking winter,' he said to the dashboard. He lifted his head, shook it and started to laugh. It was an ironic laugh; a hysterical laugh. He was aware that his ragged nerves could not take much more.

As Nick made painfully slow progress back along the twists and turns of one of the many strands of earth that intersected Dunley Marsh, he began to see the perversity of his position.

Were the three years spent studying plant life and soil conditions, working outdoors and keeping fit meant to prepare him for this moment? Without them, he wouldn't have been familiar with Dunley Marsh – the ideal spot to bury a body. He surely would not have had the strength and the knowledge of local biomass to have completed such an efficient job tonight. Had fate delivered these skills in the knowledge that he would one day have to use them in an emergency?

For the first time in his life, Nick started to question everything he had previously taken for granted. Having studied psychology in his last year of school, he was aware that a high percentage of people who experience a serious crisis undergo this re-evaluation process. He looked for reasons why he should be in this predicament and struggled to find any.

Does every occurrence in your life have to have a reason? he pondered. *Does destiny actually exist – or are all these things such as time, place and outcome merely random coincidences?* He could not find one convincing answer that satisfied his questions.

'That burglar could have decided to break into another house tonight and I would be fast asleep now next to my lovely Mel with a bright future to look forward to,' he said out loud.

'Instead, here am I, a murderer with a distraught wife and the possibility of a prison sentence that would screw up my life forever. Unbelievable!'

His mind was wading in and out of remorse, self-pity and abject fear as he negotiated the hazardous return journey through the labyrinth of narrow, slippery passages. More than once he lost concentration and had to slam on his brakes as his van threatened to disappear into the swamp.

Finally, Nick guided his vehicle onto the larger track that took him back to the minor road. He breathed a sigh of relief to see that he was still the only one in the location. When he got to the junction of the main road he stopped the van and put it into neutral.

He sat back into his seat for the first time since he'd left the marsh. The muscles in his neck and back were a series of clenched fists. He dropped his shoulders and began massaging the area around the base of his neck with his mud-covered fingers. It felt good.

'Right, Nicholas Summers, you've done it. Let's get home,' he said to himself. His hands returned to the steering wheel, but this time with a slightly looser grip. He put his van into gear and turned left onto the road home.

He told himself that this was not going to ruin his life. He needed strength of mind. He switched on the radio. The station was playing 'Yesterday' by The Beatles. His mouth formed a wistful smile.

CHAPTER 14

On the return journey, Nick went over his actions time and again from the moment he'd left his house. Had he made any mistakes? Years ago he had read somewhere that it was always the stupid errors, the small details missed by the perpetrator of the crime that led to their downfall.

Most murders were committed in the heat of the moment when the offender was out of control or in a period of stress when the brain was muddled and not able to think rationally. Nick now had time to think. Had his planning or movements been sloppy? He was an intelligent man but that was not enough. He had to think like an intelligent criminal. If he didn't make any careless mistakes, he should be safe.

Then it hit him: his van was a mess. It was covered in sludge from the marsh and would surely draw attention from his neighbours if they saw it in that state.

It would only take one light sleeper from his housing complex seeing him arrive home in the early hours of the morning in a mud-spattered van to set tongues wagging. He lived in a small community where not much went on without some busybody making a note of it and passing it on to any willing ear. More to the point, he didn't want to take all that incriminating evidence back into his garage.

Rational thoughts. Where? How? As Nick headed homewards he tried desperately to form a picture in his mind of his geographical position. After a few minutes of scanning the location in his head, the answer came to him.

He knew of an all-night petrol station that had an automatic carwash. It was just off the slip road of junction ten of the M20 motorway, only a small detour from the route he was taking and no more than a ten-minute drive away. He hadn't driven past the station for well over a year but he prayed that it was still there and still open twenty-four hours a day.

As he turned into the road where he remembered the petrol station to be, he saw the bright yellow and blue neon sign lit up like a welcoming beacon. He breathed a deep sigh of relief. He swung his van into the station and parked it at the entrance to the carwash, grabbed a handful of coins from a small compartment under the dashboard and walked across to the service station night window. He was the only customer there.

A Pakistani assistant sat behind the reinforced glass window reading a paper. 'Any petrol?' he said without looking up.

'No. Just a gold car wash, please.' As soon as the words left Nick's mouth he wondered whether they would strike the employee as strange. *Who bothers to get their car washed at this time of night without getting petrol? Shit!* A needless mistake: he should have filled the van up as well.

The assistant put his paper down and gave him a quizzical look.' No petrol?' he repeated, as if he disbelieved what he had heard.

Nick went to speak but the words stuck in his throat like a wad of wet blotting paper. He coughed. 'No. I, uh, forgot to bring out my wallet. I've just enough for a car wash,' he stuttered, pleased that he was holding a fistful of cash. It was a ridiculous explanation. A simple *no* would have sufficed.

Nick avoided making eye contact with the assistant and passed his money through the small gap at the bottom of the window and was handed the gold car wash token in return. As he walked towards to his car, he glanced backwards. The assistant was watching him intently, through his window. Nick forced a smile and climbed back into his van. He just hoped that the assistant would not remember his face.

As he sat inside with the soap-filled revolving strips whipping away the mud from his vehicle, he decided that tomorrow he would scrub its interior. And tonight's clothes had to go on the bonfire along with the blood-soaked rug.

When the washing part of the procedure had finished, he watched, with trepidation, the heavy metal bar as it moved up and along the bonnet towards the windscreen. Like an enormous industrial hair dryer, it blasted out hot air to dry the van. Nick had never trusted this part of the car wash process. He had always half-expected the machine to get stuck at the bonnet level, carry on and smash straight through the windscreen and decapitate him.

Tonight all his irrational fears were trebled. As he followed the machine up and over the roof, he found himself slipping down in the driver's seat. He imagined the headlines in the morning paper: 'Man slays intruder and buries body in bog – then loses head in carwash. Poetic justice!'

The journey back home was, thankfully, without incident. The whole operation had taken just over three hours. Nick drove up the short driveway to his house and stopped in front of his garage doors.

Mel was frantic. From the moment Nick had left the house, she had been convinced that he would be caught trying to dispose of the intruder's dead body. After she had cleaned and scrubbed most of the sitting room and swept the glass from the kitchen floor all she could do was wait.

She'd been sitting, thinking in the darkness by the hall window for the past two hours, waiting for her husband. A husband who had just killed and buried a man. Occasionally, she had got up and wandered aimlessly throughout the house, looking for any other evidence that there had been a thief in their home. Then she would return to sit by the hall window once more, waiting, worrying.

Mel's head was a mixture of conflicting emotions as she struggled to come to terms with the night's events. She was battling with how on earth they had arrived in such a perilous place as this. Why had it happened to them? What had they done to deserve this nightmare? Had Nick made the correct decision to bury the body?

He had been brave to protect her from a potential assailant; he had shown strength in carrying out the disposal of the intruder. That half of her brain was proud of her husband. But it was fighting the other half that condemned his reckless action. She was struggling to silence the inner whispers that wanted to blame him for putting them in this dreadful situation.

Just as she was beginning to despair of ever seeing Nick again, the distant noise of a car engine broke the silence. She stared out into the night. A rush of adrenalin, a tidal wave of relief, surged through her as she saw her husband's van approach the house. In those few seconds the negative doubts retreated to the back of her mind. The man she loved had returned home safely to her.

She walked through the utility room to the garage and pulled the door up and over, allowing Nick to drive the van in. Without delay, she closed the garage door and turned towards the spotlessly clean vehicle. Standing still, mannequin-like, a tangle of tightly entwined fingers pushed against her chest, she waited for her husband to appear. It was a good few seconds before the driver's door was pushed open when Nick climbed wearily from his van. Mel was shocked by his dishevelled appearance.

'Oh, Nick! Are you okay?' Mel asked, aware that it was a hopelessly inadequate question. Nick nodded slowly as he started to undress. 'I've got to wash this muck off. I can still smell him on me,' he said, grimacing. Mel gave an understanding nod as she watched in silence while he stripped down to his boxers. He left the muddy bundle of clothes in a heap by the vehicle, ready for tomorrow's bonfire. Then he went straight to the downstairs bathroom to shower.

Afterwards, he dressed in a bathrobe and added his boxer shorts to the pile in the garage. When he entered the sitting room, Mel was waiting for him. Their eyes met in confusion as they moved close to each other and fell into a desperate embrace.

'How did it go? Was it awful?' Mel asked as they stood holding each other.

'It was... indescribable. Horrific. But I don't think anyone saw me. Christ! I was so nervous, Mel. I don't know how I managed to drive the van.' Nick held his wife out in front him. 'But it's done. And I think I found a pretty good place to bury him. In fact, good isn't the right word. It was bleak – grim. I can't see any reason why anyone would want to go sniffing around a spot like that.'

'What if someone does, though, and finds him?' Mel asked.

'The chances are very slim, Mel. And even if they do, there's nothing to tie him to us. We were just a random hit. And Nathan recognised him. He told me he's a known burglar and peddles drugs. He lives alone and hasn't got any family. So no one's going to be looking for him.'

'Nick, I'm scared,' Mel said as her tears returned.

Nick pulled her back in, close to his chest, and put his arms around her. 'I know. At this moment so am I. But we can't let this thing ruin us, Mel. You and I have led honest lives and worked hard for what we've got. We have to get our heads around tonight's disaster. Eventually, put it out of our minds – our lives.'

His impassioned words gave Mel a small crumb of courage.

'Okay. I'll try. I know you're right,' she said.

'Come on, we need some sleep.' They turned and walked towards the stairs when Nick stopped. 'Oh! I need to do something about that broken window in the kitchen before I come to bed,' he added.

'Don't worry, I've taped some cardboard over the hole. But we must get someone in to fix that tomorrow.'

'Okay!' Nick paused. 'Actually, I might do that myself. I don't want anyone to think we might have had a break-in. The less people involved, the better, Mel,' he said as he took her hand and led her up the stairs to their bedroom.

As Nick lay in bed, he hoped his talk with Mel would convince her to put this night of horrors behind her. He had his doubts.

Now that the evening's dramas had come to an end, the adrenalin in his body had subsided. It was replaced with utter exhaustion. As his mind gave in to the demand for sleep, he had one last thought: could Mel ever live with the awful truth that he had killed another human being and buried the body? More importantly... could he?

CHAPTER 15

A detailed account of cheats, liars and murderers was being edited with great care on the small screen. When made public, this information would almost certainly make the front pages of all the nationals.

Jo Major sat at her home computer typing out the report. It was a slow process – a typist she was not. A report, especially one as detailed as this, took her over three hours to complete.

'Oh bugger! Buggery! Bugger it!' Jo said in frustration. She had just typed: *the situation was becoming impissible*. It was the third time on the same page she'd hit the *i* instead of the *o*. She'd already transformed *shot* to *shit* and *drop* to *drip*. 'Come on, Major, sharpen up. More haste, less speed – whatever that bloody means,' she added, wiggling her fingers like a classical pianist.

Despite having to write these reports she liked her job. *Detective constable after ten years – nothing to shout about*, she thought. But after her recent move, she could feel the pulse of ambition grow stronger. For the past six months she had been attached to the Specialist Crime Directorate unit, working within the middle market drug squad. Her head of department boss, Detective Superintendent Jack Jolley, who had worked and been good friends with Jo's father, was responsible for her move to his department.

It had been a long and stressful week and one that she hadn't enjoyed. Being part of a covert operation was never easy, but this one had been a bloody nightmare. Twelve-hour days, irregular meals and fear of being caught skulking around in the shadows had taken its toll on this twenty-eight-year-old.

Jo pushed her chair back and stood up from her desk. She began rolling her head from side to side, stretching the taut muscles in her neck. 'Impissible!' she uttered, with the final turn of her head. 'I ask you.'

She needed a coffee. A barefoot pad across the small downstairs room she used as an office took her into the sitting room. On the way to the kitchen her eyes fell upon her mother's favourite chair. The sight of it still made her feel uncomfortable.

It was three months ago now. Jo stood with her hands on the back of the chair and relived the scene as though it were yesterday.

It was early evening and she was working on another report in her office. Her mother, Barbara, who was in the sitting room, had been unusually quiet, so she had wandered in to check on the seventy-two-year-old. She was in her chair, which had pride of place in front of the television. 'Like a cup of tea, Mum?' she asked.

'Why would I want a cup of tea? I've just had one,' she snapped back, taking her daughter's hand away. She knew that her mum had her last drink over three hours ago but didn't want to argue this evening; she was too tired.

Her mother's progressively strange behaviour was becoming a concern. Her memory and concentration span were beginning to ebb and flow like the tide. Vocal anger would often be followed by silent melancholy. She hadn't been out of the house for months. After Jo's father died she had increasingly lost focus over the ensuing years. She was now worried that her mother was showing signs of Alzheimer's disease.

She returned to her modest place of work to finish the report. It took another three hours. When she returned to the sitting room her mother's chair was empty. She wouldn't be in bed, she thought, not without saying goodnight. She climbed the stairs and entered her mother's bedroom. Her clothes were in a neat pile on a chair. But the room was unoccupied.

She moved along the passage to the bathroom. 'Mum, you okay?' She tried the door; it was locked. 'Mum, if you've got a man in there...?' Her attempt at humour was to mask her growing anxiety. No answer came from the bathroom. She banged with her fist on the sturdy pine door. 'Mum, if you don't answer, I'm coming in.' Still no reply from the other side.

She ran into her bedroom and thrust her feet into a pair of sturdy walking boots. She hurried back, pressed her forehead against the bathroom door and shouted. 'Mum! Can you hear me?'

Silence.

She leant back against the wall of the narrow passage and, with every ounce of her strength, kicked at the door aiming just below the handle.

The heel of her boot landed to the left of her target and hit part of the door frame. The impact sent a flash of pain that travelled from her ankle to her hip. 'Shit!' she hissed through clenched teeth. The door shuddered but stayed in place. Once more she took aim and let fly, this time hitting the perfect spot. The small bolt on the inside flew off, the door snapped back and crashed into the wall behind.

She stepped forward and looked across at the bath. Her mother's head was all that was visible above the high waterline. It was tilted back. She was staring at the ceiling with expressionless eyes, her face as white as the porcelain that surrounded her immersed body.

She raced to the side of the bath. The water was a deep red colour. 'No!' she pleaded. She lifted her mother's limp arm from the lukewarm water, revealing the vicious cut across the inside of her wrist. There was no pulse.

'Oh, Mum! Why? Oh, Mum,' she sobbed.

But she knew why. Deep down in the taut muscles of her stomach, she knew why.

After the last image of her mother's lifeless body began to fade, Jo found herself sitting in her mother's chair. It surprised her. The memory of that night had been so vivid she had not been aware of moving from the rear of the chair to sitting down in the tired piece of furniture. She sprung to her feet. 'This, Jo,' she said to herself, 'is getting us nowhere.' She made herself a coffee and returned to her office.

It contained only a pine desk, a recliner, a PC and an antique brass floor lamp. A picture of her father in his police sergeant's uniform hung from the wall above her desk.

The small room suddenly felt smaller. She threw off her faded blue Champion sweatshirt and performed a few stretches in front of the full length mirror that hung from the back of the door. After a number of bends and twists, she ceased her brief workout and stared at her reflection.

The first thing she noticed were the tired lines around her eyes. 'Thank God I gave up smoking last year,' she said to the looking-glass as she stepped sideways to pick up a packet of Marlborough lights from her desk. 'Shame it only lasted three weeks,' she mumbled, frowning at herself. She pulled a cigarette from the pack and returned to her reflection.

The full image in the mirror presented a woman of medium height, pretty in a slightly boyish way, with short blonde hair cut into her neck. Her athletic figure was thanks to her years in the force – no room for soft, feminine curves in that profession.

She stepped forward a pace and studied her eyes once more. She'd never noticed the similarity before, but for the first time in her life she saw her father's eyes staring back at her. It surprised her. Then it brought a smile to her face. Reluctantly, she slid the cigarette back into the pack. Her father, George, had never liked her smoking.

Jo sat down in her faux leather chair. 'Right,' she murmured, as she resumed typing.

It took another two hours of prodding fingers to complete her report. 'Finished, you little bugger,' she said to the typed account of her ongoing investigation. She slumped back in the chair, locked her fingers behind her head and glanced at the report once more.

She was still finding it hard to believe that someone who had been so successful could be so damn stupid as to throw it all away.

CHAPTER 16

The palpitating buzz of the alarm entered Nick's nightmare for a few moments, then brought it to an end as it woke him from a short and restless sleep. He lifted his head to focus on the small piece of noisy plastic that sat on his bedside table. The illuminated figures were a red blur at first. He blinked twice and forced open his eyelids as wide as they would go. It was nine o'clock and he'd had six hours sleep. It felt like six minutes.

As he tried to move his body, it seemed as though he had trebled in weight. He and the mattress had become one. Summoning up his depleted reserves of energy, he managed to roll sideways, lean over and hit the stop button on the digital clock.

Mel was lying next to him, but he could tell by the rhythm of her breathing that she was still fast asleep. Although it was Sunday morning and he didn't have to go to work, he always had a list of tasks to do.

He would rise most Sundays at seven thirty and collect the newspapers from the local shop. He'd then have breakfast with

Mel, flick through the weekly news and sports stories, and be beavering away at some job around the house by nine.

This was not a normal Sunday. He wouldn't usually go to bed on Saturday night at three in the morning after burying someone he'd just clubbed to death in his living room. As last night's horror movie began to wind itself back in his memory, it was near impossible to take in. He had to get up and get busy to quieten his demons.

He crept out of bed and dressed quickly. There was a full day ahead of him. Starting the bonfire in the garden was the first job, then there was the interior of the van to clean. The broken window would have to wait until Monday; that was the earliest that he could buy a replacement pane of glass.

Nick descended the stairs and, trying to ignore the memory of what had taken place there last night, hurried straight through to the front door. He stepped outside into the chilly morning air and set off on the five-minute walk to the newsagent's.

On the way to buy his daily paper he berated himself for rushing through his sitting room as if it were a place of torture. He had been tentative when entering the room, anticipating that it would now possess a different aura. But of course it had nothing of the sort. The difference was inside Nick's head. Apart from the coffee table, the room was exactly as it had been before. *Locations only take on a haunted atmosphere,* he tried to reassure himself, *when the imagination starts to rule the uncertain mind.* He could not let that happen.

It was easier said than done. In every house he passed by that morning, he expected there to be a set of prying eyes watching him intently, wondering why he had been driving around in the early hours of the morning, eyes that would detect the look of guilt that must surely be on his face.

When Nick arrived at the small newsagent's two customers were waiting to be served. One was a plump girl in her early teens wearing a low-cut, thin cotton vest under a pink quilted jacket. The vest displayed endless inches of dynamically underpropped cleavage; the jacket, which hovered two inches above the waistband of her short skirt, exposed a generous tyre of dimpled flesh. She wore an expression of utter boredom.

The other customer, standing directly in front of him, made the teenage girl appear slim. He wore a white-collared shirt under a massive, maroon woolly jumper and a pair of jeans large enough to house a troop of scouts. Nick recognised him as a neighbour from a nearby street and nodded in his direction. Thankfully, the man just nodded back and didn't start up a conversation.

He knew it was illogical, but he thought that if he spoke to anyone this morning, something in his behaviour, or in the depths of his eyes, would give him away and uncover his terrible secret. Whilst he was in this frame of mind, weighed down with the unbearable feeling of remorse, everyone in that shop was a threat to him.

He picked up his usual two Sunday papers from the many piles on the floor and joined the short queue. When he reached the counter, he handed them to the female assistant to be scanned.

Mrs Hoffmann, as far as Nick and most of the other local residents were concerned, was a meddlesome gossip. She was of German origin, had worked in the shop for over ten years and boasted that she knew everyone in the area. Nick did not doubt her word.

'It's terrible, isn't it? What happened in town at the late-night burger van last night,' said Mrs Hoffmann in her Anglo-German accent, as she zapped Nick's newspaper across her machine.

Nick went cold. He couldn't believe what he was hearing. The blood drained from his face. For a moment he thought he was going to faint. He didn't speak.

The elderly assistant dipped her head and looked up over her glasses. She noticed Nick's ashen face and fixed expression. 'You feeling okay, Mr Summers?' she asked.

Nick had to recover his composure. 'Yes. Sorry. A bit too much wine last night, I'm afraid. What was that you were saying?'

'Yes, it was on the local radio news this morning. It happened sometime after midnight. A group of boys – probably drunk, I think – were standing by the burger van in the high street throwing things at passing cars.'

Nick tensed as he waited for her to continue. He guessed they had to be the same gang who'd given him a hard time last night.

'Eventually,' said Mrs Hoffmann, 'one car stopped and four lads got out. There was one hell of a fight and one poor chap got stabbed. He was taken to Ashford General Hospital. The four lads then jumped back in their car and drove off. The police are asking for any witnesses to come forward.'

Nick wondered how Mrs Hoffmann had got so much information from a radio report, but then again, she did know everyone in the area. His first reaction was one of relief and he finally managed to breathe out again.

Then it dawned on him that the police would be studying all the CCTV cameras in the immediate area in order to identify the car full of young men. His van would be seen on those cameras screeching to a halt directly in front of the burger van. The word 'witnesses' worried him.

'That's terrible, Mrs Hoffmann,' Nick replied, trying to sound concerned. But he didn't want this conversation to continue. He paid for his paper, smiled at the shop assistant and made his exit. He prayed that the police would locate the lads and not have to hunt down other cars on camera for the purpose of finding witnesses. This piece of news was not good.

On the short walk back to his house, he decided not to tell Mel the story of the stabbing and his unfortunate encounter at the same spot. She was upset enough without giving her more reason to worry.

When he arrived back home, Mel had dressed and was preparing breakfast. As they sat at the table, Nick and his wife found any attempt at conversation difficult. Whilst they ate, they were grateful for the excuse to read the Sunday papers.

Nick wanted desperately to speak to Mel, but what could he say? When he glanced over in her direction she kept her head lowered. Not once did she allow their eyes to meet. He had to make an attempt to communicate with his wife.

'Did you manage to get much sleep last night?' He knew it was a stupid question.

'Not much,' said Mel, her attention not diverting from the Sunday Mail's You magazine.

'Nor me.' Silence followed. Nick saw Mel empty her teacup. 'Another cuppa?' he asked.

'No thanks.'

A packet of cornflakes sat on the table between them. It may as well have been a brick wall. Mel was distant, uncomfortable. It was an emotion he had never before experienced from her.

Even when they had first met, Mel had seemed so relaxed in his company. They had spent the entire evening poking fun at each other's taste in music. She liked Take That and Westlife, he liked Bruce Springsteen and Guns N' Roses.

Despite their melodic mismatch they had gelled immediately. Shortly after their wedding, they had moved into their house in the quiet village of Bourne. He had never seen her so happy. The rural location sat on a hilltop with breathtaking views over the North Downs and out towards the rugged Kent coast which lay five miles away.

A primary school, two pubs, a post office-general store and a small church were just about all the amenities that Bourne had to offer. But for him and his wife it was perfect.

Nick was now struggling to come to terms with the fact that in the space of a few hours that perfection had been stolen from them.

After a tense and hurried breakfast, Nick took a bundle of old newspapers down to the end of the garden. Separating and scrumpling up the pages into fist-sized balls, he scattered them over the site where he always had his garden bonfire. Then he sprinkled them with petrol from the small can that he kept in the garden shed, covered the paper with dead twigs and leaves and threw a match into the middle of the lot. Nothing happened.

He waited for half a minute. 'Come on, you bugger, burn!' Nick urged, as he scanned the surrounding gardens to see whether anyone was watching him. He took a step towards the bundle of sticks and just as he was about to strike another match the small flame made contact with the petrol.

With a roar, the bonfire burst into life. The sudden blast of heat hit him square in the face, sucking the breath from his lungs. He immediately jumped backwards a few paces. As he watched the flames climb through the dead leaves, he thought he heard the distant ring of his front doorbell. But this was too important to leave. Anyway, Mel was in the house.

After five minutes or so of hot, arduous work piling on old branches, pruned shrubs and dead leaves, the victims of late autumn, Nick had built up the burning mass to a three-foot-high raging inferno. Despite the cold snap of the morning, Nick was now sweating profusely. He stepped back from the fierce heat of the fire and took off his warm, quilted cotton jacket. He wiped his brow with it, then hung it over the handle of the garden fork that stood in the ground beside him.

He picked up the handmade Persian rug that he had bought for eight hundred pounds only last summer. He was very proud of the purchase; he felt that it had made a statement in his house. It was going to break his heart to burn this exquisite piece of soft furnishing. And, in the circumstances, he thought it unwise to register a claim for it on his insurance policy.

As the rug landed on the inferno, a shower of brilliant orange and silver embers fired up into the chilly morning air.

CHAPTER 17

After Mel had finished clearing the table from breakfast, she took another look at the sitting room. Late last night she had cleaned that room inch by inch. She had scrubbed then replaced the holdall on top of the wardrobe, putting the contents back in their correct places. She'd then washed the back of the cream leather sofa, a large area of the ceiling and the surrounding oak wood floor where the incident had taken place. Now she wanted to make sure, in the cold light of the morning, that there were no other visible specks of blood or fragments of glass to be seen.

The chrome frame of the coffee table had been put away in the garage and replaced with an Indian table made of sheesham wood. It was dark, dense and heavily grained and of a similar size to the one that had been smashed. It had been stored in the garage ever since they'd moved into the house – Nick had bought the table when he lived in his bachelor flat but there had never been enough space for it in the sitting room. Mel now preferred it to the old glass-top table.

As she was wandering around the room, the doorbell rang. It gave her a start. 'Who the hell is that?' she whispered. She wasn't expecting anyone this morning. She crept to the window and peeked out from behind the voile drape. 'Oh, damn! Jo Major.' Mel had completely forgotten that she had invited her over to try on her overcoat. The last thing they needed this morning was a member of the constabulary walking around the house. She had to answer the door. Keep calm.

Mel took another quick look around the room then went to open the front door. 'Jo,' Mel said, in mock surprise. 'Hello. Do come in.'

'I hope it's not inconvenient? I just thought I'd pop round to try your coat on,' Jo replied.

'No, of course not,' Mel said, closing the door. 'Come upstairs.'

'Is Nick working today?' Jo asked.

'No, he doesn't work Sundays if he can help it. He's messing about in the garden.'

'Sort of busman's holiday,' said Jo, with a smile.

'Excuse me! Uh, yes. I suppose,' Mel replied.

The two women went up to the main bedroom. As Mel went to the wardrobe, Jo stood looking out of the rear window and down onto the garden.

'You've got a lovely garden. Oh, and Nick's got a bonfire going,' said Jo.

Mel realised immediately that she had made a mistake taking Jo upstairs. Stupidly, she had drawn attention to what Nick was doing. It was an innocent enough thing to start a bonfire, but Mel was gripped with an irrational fear that Jo would suspect something was wrong.

'Yes, he's just burning some garden rubbish,' Mel explained unnecessarily. *What else would he be burning in the garden? Stop being an idiot and relax,* she told herself. But her insides felt as if they were rolling up into a tight ball.

'I love bonfires. They remind me of when I was a little girl. Dad would always get one going in the garden on Guy Fawkes' Night,' said Jo.

Mel handed the coat to Jo. 'There you are.'

'Ooh, Mel, that's gorgeous! Just hope it's the right size.' Jo tried on the weighty, fur-collared coat. It was a perfect fit. Mel left the wardrobe door open to let Jo see herself in the full-length mirror that hung from the inside of the door. 'I love it,' said Jo. After performing a couple of twirls in front of the mirror, the sale was agreed.

Mel then led them downstairs and into the kitchen. Jo draped the coat over a chair and placed her handbag on the breakfast table. Mel was aware that she ought to act as a welcoming hostess and not appear to want to get her guest out of the house as quickly as possible. The invitation went against her every instinct: 'Do you fancy a cup of tea or coffee, Jo?'

'Yeah, that'll be lovely, thanks,' Jo replied. 'How much do I owe you, by the way?'

'Erm! It cost two hundred. Is fifty pounds okay? Sorry, was it tea or coffee?' Mel asked again, pulling two cups from the kitchen cupboard.

'Coffee, please – white, no sugar. And that's very generous of you. Thanks,' said Jo as she sat down at the kitchen table. She delved into her black leather handbag and took out her purse. As Mel turned, she noticed Jo looking at the piece of cardboard covering the window by the side door. 'Not a break-in, I hope?' she said, nodding at the broken window.

Mel couldn't believe she'd been so stupid again. She should have showed Jo into the sitting room and kept her out of the kitchen. She had to think quickly. 'Oh, that was me. I was sweeping up something from the floor and, uh, put the end of the broom handle through the window.' It didn't sound convincing and she knew it.

Mel sensed that Jo had registered her unease.

'That sounds like me. I'm the original Miss Clumsy from Clumsyland. I'm always breaking things,' Jo said. Mel realised that the detective was trying to paper over an awkward moment. She watched her pull fifty pounds from her purse and put the notes on the table. Jo then took out her mobile phone, checked it for messages and placed it over the money as a paperweight.

Then she stood up, walked to the rear of the kitchen and looked out of the back door window onto the garden.

Mel was aware that she was watching Nick once more and felt her heart rate rise. She hoped that he'd already put the rug on the bonfire.

She made two cups of coffee and placed them on the table in the hope that Jo would come away from the window and sit down again. 'So, are you busy in work at the moment?' she asked, trying to attract Jo's attention.

'Yeah, it's madness in the office. We've got a lot going on at the moment,' said Jo without turning round. 'I'll be polite, shall I, and say a quick hello to Nick? And maybe I can warm my hands on that gorgeous bonfire?'

'Yes, of course,' replied Mel. *It's only a bloody bonfire,* she thought. *What's so special about a bloody bonfire?*

Mel found a smile from somewhere and opened the back door. She had to warn Nick that Jo was coming down the garden. 'Nick!' she shouted. 'It's Jo, darling.'

Nick turned to see Jo waving as she made her way up the path towards him.

'Oh Christ! What's she doing here?' he muttered while putting on a welcome smile. Mel realised this was bad timing at its worst. She watched Nick glance at the smouldering rug and then at the oncoming police officer. Nick had thrown it on the fire face down, but the deep-red stain was still clearly visible from the back.

Mel stood outside the back door, looking helplessly at her husband over Jo's back, her hands pressing tightly to either side of her face. Her expression was one of impending doom.

Jo was halfway down the garden path when Mel became aware of the theme from *The Great Escape* drifting out from the kitchen behind her. She dashed back into the room and saw it was coming from the mobile on the kitchen table. This could prove to be a lucky break, but she had to act quickly. She darted to the back door. Jo was now only ten yards away from Nick. 'Jo,' she shouted, 'your mobile's ringing.'

She stopped and turned to Mel. 'Oh, bugger! I'd better take it.' Jo had been expecting a phone call all morning and she couldn't afford to miss it. She hurried back down the path to the house and picked up her phone.

Mel looked out at Nick and raised her eyes to the heavens. Nick just shook his head, put his hand over his heart and checked to see whether it was still beating. Hurriedly, he began to cover the rug, now giving off clouds of acrid smoke, with handfuls of leaves and twigs.

'Hello?' Jo said into her mobile. 'Hi, Rupert. Yes. Oh, great. That's fantastic. I can be with you in twenty minutes. Brilliant! Okay, thanks.' She switched off her mobile, put it in her handbag and turned to Mel with a beaming smile. 'Great news. There's a flat I really liked the look of that I saw in the estate agent's window. But when I enquired about it, I was told it had been sold. Well, it's just come back on the market. So I need to get over there now to view it. I hope you don't mind, but I don't want to miss it this time. I've already got a first-time buyer for my house so, fingers crossed, I could be moving soon.' Jo picked up her coffee and took a big gulp.

'That's great news. I hope it works out for you,' said Mel.

'Thanks. Right, I've got to shoot. All I seem to be doing at the moment is rushing around like a lunatic.'

Mel felt relieved. 'No, of course. You have to go. This is important for you. We'll catch up later.' Jo picked up her bag and headed for the front door.

'Don't forget your new coat,' said Mel, as she picked up the overcoat from the chair and handed it to Jo.

'See what I mean. I'd make a blue-arsed fly look sluggish.' The girls laughed. 'Bye then,' Jo said.

Mel stood at the door and watched Jo climb into her car and drive off. She closed the door and slumped heavily against the back of it. Her head felt as if it was in a brace. She thought she was going to faint. Deceit was definitely not her strong suit. There were serious doubts lurking in her mind as to how long she could keep up this pretence.

CHAPTER 18

Jack Jolley had endured a bad night's sleep. His wife, Karen, who lay next to him, had noticed.

As Jack pulled back the corner of the duvet to get up, she spoke, 'You have been really restless in bed – kept me awake half the night. What's wrong?'

Jack had not realised he had been such a disruptive bed partner. 'Oh. Sorry, darling. I've got a lot on my mind. It's erm... there's a problem at work.'

'Do you want to talk about it?' Karen asked, climbing out of bed.

'No. No, it's nothing serious.' Jack lied. 'But I just need to pop into the office this morning for a couple of hours.

It was a rare occurrence. As a rule, the supposed day of rest was exactly that for Jack. It consisted of sleeping in until nine o'clock, breakfast in bed followed by a leisurely scanning of the papers. At twelve thirty they'd walk to the local for a few drinks with friends for a couple of hours. The remainder of the day was spent relaxing in front of the television.

While his wife was taking a shower, Jack went downstairs to make himself a cup of tea. He stood waiting for the kettle to boil, staring deep into a picture of his family that sat on the windowsill before him.

He, Karen and his two children had lived in the four-bedroom detached house, situated in the more affluent part of Ashford for well over a decade. With the children gone they now lived alone in the house that, they both agreed, was too big for their needs. But it held too many important memories for them to ever think of moving.

Two years after they married, Karen had presented him with twins, one of each. At that time they were living in a small semi-detached in the centre of Ashford. A series of promotions had allowed Jack to move up the property ladder and install his new family into the impressive accommodation.

Their daughter, Penny, had married Tom, a young Canadian lawyer. Then, three years ago, much to Jack's regret, they moved with their baby daughter to live and work in Toronto near to Tom's parents. Outwardly, Karen had been more philosophical about the move. But she hid the pain well. As for Jack, communicating with Penny and his granddaughter by the wonders of webcam was a poor substitute for seeing them in the flesh.

Sam, their son, had opted out of college halfway through an engineering course to join the army. Bored with academia, he went in search of adventure. At the age of twenty-one his unit was posted overseas to Afghanistan. Five months later, while on a routine patrol, the vehicle he was travelling in drove over a landmine. Sam and his three buddies were all killed outright.

Six years ago, on a bitterly cold January evening, an apprehensive army chaplain wearing full service dress uniform appeared at the front door of Jack and Karen's home. He proceeded to read out the contents of a carefully written letter that contained the dreadful news of their son. It was an evening that would be etched on Jack's mind for the rest of his days. On hearing the devastating news, Karen's legs gave way as she fell into Jack's arms.

Karen's happy-go-lucky approach to life had been severely damaged. In its place was the stark reality of how dreams could be wrecked in the time it takes to issue a short statement.

Jack, too, had changed. Although he and Karen could still laugh together, it was never with the same sense of abandon as before. Their family cloak of invincibility had been ripped apart along with the body of their beloved son.

Jack turned away from the photograph, his jaw set, and focused on why he was going to work on this Sunday morning. At eight fifteen he kissed Karen goodbye, climbed into his Mercedes C200 Sport and drove the short distance to the office.

After he'd made himself a coffee, he sat behind his desk, studying Jo Major's last report. It made interesting reading. He noticed from the times she had entered on last week's surveillance sheet that she had worked a twelve-hour day on four occasions. The week before was the same. He was very impressed with her meticulous attention to detail and her industrious character. But it concerned him that she could be in danger of burning herself out if she continued with this tough schedule.

He had been head of the Ashford Drug Squad and Surveillance Unit for six years. During that time several of his officers had driven themselves to the brink of exhaustion. He had witnessed members of his team become so embroiled in an investigation that they had been dangerously unaware of their own state of health.

It was an easy road to go down. When after weeks, sometimes months, of surveillance, when an officer got close to a conviction, it was human nature to push hard for a result. Quite often that push would be executed a touch prematurely, then the quarry would become wary and go to ground. It was tough to take for the hard-working officers involved. Patience was paramount in this job and hard to employ when the target was lined up for the kill.

He had once driven himself to the point of illness attempting to build a sustainable case against a young West Indian drug dealer who was just setting out on what was to be a long and profitable career. He never managed to get a conviction on the streetwise hood, the frustration causing him to take on an unprecedented workload. His senior officer at the time had seen it coming and had given him, much to his annoyance, a forced period of sick leave for two weeks.

At the time he'd thought his boss was overreacting when he caught him napping at his desk one afternoon. It was only during his second week on leave, when his energy levels rose dramatically along with his powers of concentration, that he realised he had been running on empty for so long.

With that in mind, he decided to call Jo into his office to see, first-hand, how she was coping with the particularly stressful assignment she had been working on.

He picked up the report again. Her progress in this case had been admirable. Did he really want to stop her now and risk losing momentum in this investigation? A change of personnel could prove costly, awkward even.

He needed this thing cleared up as soon as possible. Jack had a difficult decision to make. However quickly and cleanly this problem was resolved the outcome of the investigation had the potential to tear the unit apart.

But his focus was on Jo Major. He was now beginning to doubt the wisdom of assigning the young officer to carry out surveillance and build a case against one of their own. Her boss. Detective Sergeant Nathan Ballack.

CHAPTER 19

Her excitement increased with every gear change as Jo drove out of Bourne towards her destination. It should have been a twenty minute journey but traffic on this Sunday was unusually heavy.

'Come on, come on,' she said to the queue of traffic in front of her. She wanted to see this flat. She hoped it wouldn't be a disappointment. Why were the roads so busy today? Perhaps there was a farmer's market in the area, thought Jo. There seemed to be one every week in some field or other. 'How many bloody farmers can there be around here,' she said, her fingers tapping the steering wheel.

While she was waiting to move forward she thought about her visit to the Summers' home. She couldn't get the sight of Nick's face, as she walked up the garden path towards him, out of her mind. For a split second she had seen panic in his eyes.

The look reminded her of when she had caught a ten-year-old boy pinching sweets from her local newsagent's shop. She had given him a severe telling off and a brief lecture on the virtues of honesty. She wondered whether Nick warranted the same treatment. Just then, the traffic began to clear. 'A-ha! Rupert here I come,' she said, with a tune of optimism in her voice.

Rupert was waiting for Jo outside the premises under the red and white FOR SALE sign that hung beneath the first floor window of the vacant flat. He'd been in the job a mere six months.

Whilst he waited for his client, he shifted from one foot to the other, checking his watch and mobile phone constantly. They had arranged to meet outside the premises at eleven thirty. She was already ten minutes late.

When Jo arrived, she looked at her watch. 11.42. She prayed that the estate agent had not got fed up and gone back to his office. She parked her car across the road from the address that she had been given. 'Ah! Good. He's still there,' she said, relieved. She climbed from her car and walked over to meet the dapper young man. The first thing she noticed about him was his gel-spiked hair with blonde highlights. *He can't be more than eighteen or nineteen,* she thought. *A baby trying to sell me a flat.* When she caught sight of the sign above his head her spirits plummeted. The two bedroom apartment was above a greengrocer's.

The details had stated that the apartment was over a private business. It had failed to mention that the business sold fruit and vegetables. A rather convenient omission, she thought. It stood in the middle of a row of small shops that served the basic needs of the residents in the charming village of Runcing.

Jo's first reaction was to get back in her car and drive off. But despite the flat's position, she resisted the temptation, deciding instead to view the interior before making a decision.

'Good morning,' announced Rupert as he held out a slightly shaky hand.

Jo ignored the gesture. 'Hi. I wasn't expecting the apartment to be over a fruit and veg shop.'

Rupert looked flustered, 'Oh! Was it not in the details?'

'No, it wasn't. But I'm here now so I may as well have a look at it.'

Jo had to admit that the location was a big plus. As she'd driven into the village it was impossible not to fall in love with the place. It was as if this sleepy, rustic piece of England had grown straight out of the soil and had been here forever.

A sixteenth-century church, with flint and ragstone walls, sat amidst a manicured lawn that had a scattering of grey and ginger mottled gravestones leaning in all directions like bad teeth. Further along the narrow high street, two sturdy, oak-and-red-brick pubs sat snugly beneath sun-bleached, pink-tiled roofs. The rest of the village fanned out into a hotchpotch of modest bungalows and chocolate box cottages. These dwellings housed the six hundred and thirty citizens of Runcing.

'You may want to have a quick look in here before I take you up to the flat. You might be surprised,' said Rupert, leading her into the shop with a glint in his eye. *Why would I,* thought Jo, as she followed him inside. The greengrocer's, on closer inspection, was a joy to behold, spotlessly clean and crammed full of character. The produce was displayed in white-painted wooden trays, stacked in order of size from top to bottom. Smaller produce like grapes, cherries and nuts sat in circular raffia baskets that hung from the ceiling at eye level from slim silver chains.

Twisted oak beams weaved their way through unconventional alcoves fitted with discreet lighting, presenting a range of normally unattractive vegetables in a fashion she had never witnessed before. This wasn't a shop; it was an Aladdin's cave.

Jo's first reaction to the prospect of living over a greengrocer's was one of distaste. But this was no ordinary greengrocer's. The instant black cross that had planted itself in her mind was rapidly promoted to a resounding tick.

To the left of the shop front was a newly gloss-painted black door with a shiny brass number 4 at the top. The estate agent produced a key. Behind the door lay a surprisingly wide staircase. Jo, encouraged by the fresh smell of a recently laid cream carpet, followed the estate agent up the flight of stairs to the front door of the flat.

Rupert, having got his client this far, now appeared to be far more relaxed. A smile swept across his face as he unlocked the door. He then turned to Jo. '*Voila!*' he announced rather dramatically and, like a circus ringmaster, he bowed and waved her into the hall. His display took her by surprise and it was all she could do not to laugh at his ridiculous gesture.

But the clown-like antics were soon forgotten. Whatever she had been expecting was not what she discovered. The original floorboards had been sanded and varnished, and at the far end of the huge living room were two enormous picture windows that suffused the flat with daylight, providing a spectacular and uninterrupted view of the Kent countryside.

'As you can see, this apartment has been recently decorated to a very high standard,' Rupert stated proudly. 'The owner has spared no expense with the fixtures and fittings, creating a fresh and contemporary feel. The property has only just come back on the market and I know that the vendor is looking for a quick sale.'

The words were straight out of an estate agents' manual. But she did not care. The apartment was a revelation.

Jo was impressed with how the interior designer had managed to blend old with new so tastefully. The result was a home that had style, character and every modern amenity you could wish for. She was not surprised when Rupert revealed that the owner of the shop also owned the flat. His flair and quality of work was written throughout the property.

If she had been wearing socks, this delightful accommodation would have blown them clean off. She offered the asking price there and then. Rupert, who looked like he'd just won the lottery, agreed the sale with the owner on his mobile phone and arrangements were made to pass on details first thing Monday morning.

Back out in the street, Jo took another look around at the charming village setting before bidding farewell to her estate agent. She shook Rupert's rather limp-wristed hand, then watched him drive off in his black BMW.

'Ooh! BMW, Rupert,' she called after him, finishing with a whistle, as he roared off into the distance. 'I'm in the wrong bloody job.'

As Jo sat in her car looking up at her new home-to-be, she could not have been happier. She put the key in the ignition and was about to turn it when her mobile rang. 'Hello. Oh, hello, guv... Yes, okay... Monday morning, eight thirty... See you then... And you... Bye.'

As she drove out of Runcing, her thoughts began to shift backwards once again. Despite her feelings of elation from her purchase of a beautiful new home, she had a voice twittering away in a small compartment of her brain.

There was something not right in the Summers household. The couple had appeared tense. Although Mel had gone through the motions of being friendly, she got the feeling she wasn't particularly welcome in their home. Then there was Nick and the bonfire. But it wasn't that.

It was that broken window, she thought... *No. It wasn't. It was Mel's reaction to it that worried her.*

CHAPTER 20

Sunday, as far as communication was concerned, was a disaster. Nick felt that the tension between them was as thick as a mattress. Neither of them seemed to know how to rectify the problem.

After Jo Major left their house, Nick came in from the garden. Mel was sitting at the kitchen table, her hands around a mug of tea.

'Well, that wasn't the cleverest thing to do, was it, Mel?' said Nick.

'I'm sorry. I should have kept her in the sitting room. But I'm still not happy in there. It gives me the creeps. And she just wanted to come out to see you and that bloody bonfire. How could I say no?'

Nick looked at Mel. 'Okay. I didn't realise. I'm sorry too,' said Nick.

'The trouble is, Nick, no amount of sorrys are going to put this thing right, are they?' Mel said, looking up at her husband.

Nick opened his mouth to speak. No words came out. An exchange of confused looks ended the conversation.

For the remainder of the day they immersed themselves in their separate chores around the house, each locked in a vortex of fear and bewilderment.

Nick burnt the rug along with his filthy clothes and then spent the best part of four hours cleaning the interior of his van. Mel spent most of her time in the kitchen, washing clothes and cooking the evening meal.

The dinner passed in virtual silence. Later, as they sat in front of the TV, Nick picked up the console. 'What do you want to watch tonight?' he said, flicking through the channels.

'I don't care. Anything you want.'

'Come on, Mel. This can't go on.'

'What can't go on? Really, I'm not fussed what we watch,' Mel said, as she lay full length along the sofa. Nick, tired of the one-way conversation, selected a costume drama. Both watched the entertainment only half taking in the programme's content. Occasionally, Nick looked across at Mel. She kept her eyes glued to the screen.

When the time came to retire for the night they had still hardly spoken to each other. The atmosphere between them was as if they'd had a serious row. Nick took Mel's silence as a punishment for his 'reckless' actions of the previous night. He wondered whether she felt scared of him.

When they were both in bed and the light had been turned off, Nick could not stand the awkward silence any longer. 'I didn't want this to happen, Mel. But it has happened. What was I supposed to do, ask him why he broke into our house? Ask him politely to leave and, by the way, please don't hurt us? You can never be prepared for a situation like that.'

Mel stayed quiet. Nick continued, 'I wasn't to know whether he was a thief or a madman who wanted to rape you or kill us both. How could I know that? I was scared shitless, Mel. I protected us. I hit him and I killed him.'

'Stop it. Stop it. *Stop it, Nick!*' Mel screamed. 'I don't even want to think about it. I didn't want this to happen either. I don't think we should talk about it any more.'

'After today I get the impression you don't want to talk about anything. Or maybe you just don't want to talk to me any more?' said Nick.

'That's not true and you know it.'

'I don't know what's bloody true and what's not any longer. Look at what could have happened, Mel. You could be lying here on your own, beaten up and raped, with me lying in the mortuary. Then you'd be wishing I'd been braver and killed the bastard who broke into our home.'

Nick was now in full flow. He had been holding this in all day. 'The country's graveyards are full of benign bystanders who didn't stand up to their assailants. We all feel sorry for them, but they are not here any more. And their poor loved ones have had their lives ruined. How many dead heroes are there who attempted to reason with a maniac holding a gun or a knife? Well, luckily, I'm not one of them. I'd like to think you're pleased about that.'

'Of course I'm pleased,' Mel replied, as her tears started to flow. 'I'm just struggling with how to handle this.'

Nick lay there looking into the darkness, his every thought strangled by uncertainty. He had nothing more to say tonight. There were no more answers that would give him the redemption he so desperately needed.

He hadn't meant to kill the intruder. He had been unlucky. He told himself he had acted as most men would have if placed in the same situation. He had to believe that, or he was a lost soul. And if his marriage was to have any future, he needed the woman he loved to believe it as well.

A feeling of isolation spread over him. Mentally, he was clinging to a sodden lump of driftwood floating aimlessly in the middle of a pitiless ocean. To cry out would have been futile; no one could hear him. Nick felt he was slowly drowning.

He squeezed his eyelids shut, hoping to release the pressure that was gripping his brain, starving it of a single clear thought. He was worn out. He turned away from Mel and let sleep claim his tortured mind. Tormented by a host of demons, it was another hour before Mel joined him.

CHAPTER 21

Monday morning's weather was as welcome as scarlet fever – exactly the kind of day that nearly sixty per cent of Britons, in search of the sun each year, spent fortunes holidaying in strange and foreign lands to avoid. Raindrops the size of walnuts were being discharged from low, menacing clouds as Jo left home for the office. A raw north wind sliced through her beige rain mac, blowing her sideways, as she hurried to her car.

The drive to work took a little under ten minutes, so by the time she arrived, the heater in her seven-year-old car had not really had time to do its job and warm her up. When she had dressed for work that morning, her mind had definitely not been thinking about the weather conditions.

A white short-sleeved blouse and thin cotton navy skirt suit were all she wore beneath her raincoat. When she entered the grey concrete building where she worked, her hair was still damp and the cold wind had penetrated her bones. In an attempt to warm herself up, she ran up the two flights of stairs to her office.

Jo was expected in at work by nine a.m., but she always tried to get there at around eight forty. It gave her time to carry out a small amount of preening in the ladies room, make a cup of coffee for herself and scan a few of her favourite pages of the *Daily Mail.*

This morning she was in at eight fifteen and was focused on one thing – her appointment with Detective Superintendent Jolley. She entered the economically furnished office where she worked slightly out of breath but still shivering and hung her mac on the coat stand behind the glass-panelled door.

She glanced across at Nathan Ballack's chair. It was empty. Her boss' timekeeping was getting worse. He always arrived after nine o'clock and more often than not it was closer to nine thirty. But today she was pleased that he wasn't in the office. It would make this morning's mission that much easier. Mark Smallwood and Colin Lynch, the other two guys in the pod of four, would come in just before nine. They were not the most dedicated of officers, it had to be said, but they did their job well enough and the three of them had enough laughs along the way to make the job more than bearable.

That could not be said of Nathan any more. He had become distant from his team and offered little in the way of support or active leadership. In her early days there, Mark and Colin would to try to make excuses for Nathan when Jo questioned his declining enthusiasm for the job. They had since given up covering for their boss. His lack of professionalism had become accepted as the norm and was no longer discussed amongst the three of them.

Jo checked her watch – eight twenty-eight. She got up from her chair, walked past three empty desks and along the stark, windowed corridor to Jack Jolley's office. She knocked on the imposing mahogany door. 'Come in,' Jack called from behind his desk.

'Good morning, guv,' Jo said as she opened the door and entered the room. The first thing she noticed whenever she entered Jack's office was the smell of freshly ground coffee. The next thing was the beautiful sapphire-blue carpet that covered the entire expansive floor area.

'Ah, Jo! Have a seat,' Jack said with a smile.

Jo nodded and closed the weighty door. She sat down opposite her boss in the proffered leather chair. The voluminous, mahogany desk was now level with the top of her shoulders. She should have felt small and insignificant, but she did not.

The desk sat in front of a large double-glazed window flanked by heavy indigo velvet curtains. Two ornately framed pictures on the wall showed wintry scenes of the Kent countryside. The atmosphere in the room was one of cool sophistication.

She was never sure whether it was due to the plush surroundings or Jack's easy demeanour, but a trip to the head honcho's office always left her feeling calm and assured.

A photograph of Jack, his wife and early teenage twins stood proudly in a silver filigree mount on his desk. Apart from the colour of his hair, which was now completely white, Jack had not altered that much. Her boss had aged well, thought Jo.

Jack rose from his black leather swivel chair and moved over to the coffee pot. 'Coffee?'

'Yes please – milk, no sugar,' said Jo.

Jack poured coffee from a glass percolator into two white bone china cups that sat on matching saucers. He added milk from a small silver jug and put them on the desk. *No chipped mugs here,* Jo noted as she admired the fine crockery.

'I've been reading your report and surveillance logs,' said Jack.

Jo nodded, crossed her legs, placed her hands in her lap and waited for Jack to continue.

Jack had two reports lying open in front of him - one from Jo and the other from the Department of Professional Standards. He lifted his frameless reading glasses from his face; his steel-blue eyes followed their deliberate journey down onto his desk.

'We need to put this whole affair to bed as soon as possible. This has been hanging over your pod for too long. That's not a criticism, Jo, it's an observation. More importantly, it's a necessity.'

'We're not far away, guv, but I want to tie all this up together. We need the main importer to show his face again. We got close a few weeks back, but the intelligence we received from the Medway Ports Authority was not as accurate as we'd have liked. We expected a delivery into Sheerness last week with the main man being there to pass it on to his dealer. But he and the delivery never showed,' Jo said.

'How about DS Ballack?' Jack asked.

'If we pull Nathan now we could scare off his supply chain. We've got more than enough on Ballack – who he buys from, who he sells to. We can take him whenever we want.'

Jo shifted in her seat and continued. 'He even took a delivery of Charlie when I was with him in his local on Saturday night. His supplier, a toe rag called Tony Scrivens, turned up. I clocked him across the bar. As soon as Nathan saw him, they both went outside. One of the DPS boys was staking out the car park. He saw Scrivens put a delivery into the boot of Nathan's car.'

'He's getting bolder – or careless,' said Jack.

'No, I don't think so. I don't think Nathan was expecting Scrivens to be there. He looked shocked to me. The thing is, we've been watching Scrivens in order to get closer to his supplier, but he's suddenly disappeared.

'When he left the pub that night he never returned home to his flat. The little weasel's either got nervous and done a runner or he's upset someone, probably by not paying his drug debts. If that's the case, there's a good chance he's joined the rest of the slime drifting around at the bottom of the River Medway,' said Jo.

'No big loss there,' replied Jack, glancing at the reports once more. He picked up his cup of coffee and took a drink.

'No, guv, but he was a useful lead to us. We're going to have to rely on tip-offs now from our other sources for the time being. It just makes the process more untidy and a bit more drawn out,' Jo replied as she took the lead from her boss and began to sip from her coffee cup.

Jack put his cup down and looked up from his desk and into the eyes of Jo Major. His expression softened somewhat. 'And how are you coping, Jo? It's not a simple task investigating a senior colleague – running this investigation parallel to the work you've been doing with your team. You've had to lie, carry out surveillance on him... and then his wife asks you to join them for a social evening. That couldn't have been easy?'

'I would be lying if I said I was enjoying this assignment, but it has to be done,' Jo said, narrowing her eyes. 'The hardest part, guv, is giving a hundred per cent to our team assignments whilst my focus is on helping to build a case against the bloody head of the team.'

For obvious reasons Jo had to write every report on Nathan Ballack in the privacy of her own home. Then the reports had to be delivered directly to Jack without arousing the suspicion of any member of her team. The deception was both stressful and time-consuming.

'Can I ask why you chose me to carry out this investigation on DS Ballack, guv? Normally, the investigation of a police officer is handled by the Department of Professional Standards alone.'

'I wanted someone on the inside to work with the DPS boys, and I'm afraid, Jo, it had to be you. I needed to know whether any other officer was involved. You've only been with this unit for a short period of time and I wanted a fresh pair of eyes. Smallwood and Lynch are good coppers, but they are, or certainly were, very close to DS Ballack – too close to investigate him. Do you see?' Jack was looking intently at Jo now.

'Yes, guv, I understand,' Jo said.

Jack picked up an expensive-looking gold pen that had been lying on a black leather-bound diary. He leant back in his chair and began tapping the underside of his chin with the pen. 'Putting you on this case was a risk. But one worth taking. You've worked well, but I'm still a little concerned with the size of your workload. I want this finished, Jo, but I need you healthy as well. George would never have forgiven me if I'd worked you into the ground.'

'I'm fine, guv. I just want to nail that Albanian importer. But he's not shown his face for a while. He's a right slippery bugger. I want to get this sorted and be part of a team again. A team that are all pulling the same bloody way,' added Jo.

'All right. But if you feel this is getting too much for you, you must tell me,' said Jack.

'Thanks, guv. But I'm good at the moment,' Jo replied dishonestly. At times this investigation left her feeling exhausted, but she didn't want her boss to think she wasn't up to the task. She was the only girl on the team and wanted to impress Jack Jolley – not just because he was the big boss but because he used to be her father's friend and colleague. What she really wanted was to impress her father, whom she so desperately missed.

'Keep me in touch.' Jack finished the conversation with a nod of his head. Jo got the message, downed her last mouthful of coffee and took leave of Jack's cosy office to return to the austere surroundings of her workplace.

When the door closed behind her, Jack turned in his high-backed chair and looked out of the window and into the distance. He was angry. He wanted Ballack out of the force and behind bars as soon as. He had worked doggedly to build a close-knit, hard-working team that he could trust. He was not going to let one renegade destroy it all.

He knew it was a risk involving Jo in this matter; he just prayed that it was one that would not end in disaster.

When Jo arrived back in her office, Mark and Colin were both seated at their desks. Mark was on the phone. She looked across at him and exchanged smiles. She got on well with DC Mark Smallwood. He was a big man with large rubbery features, married and the joker in the pack. He may have looked scary but in reality he was a big, soft lummox who brought a sense of flippancy to what was an otherwise serious job.

Colin looked up from his computer when he noticed Jo come in. A frown etched deep into his forehead. The two detectives could not have been more different. DC Colin Lynch, known as Merrill (after the investment bank) was dumpy with thinning, Hitler-straight, greying hair and lived with his retired parents.

'In the boss's office again, Jo? Not another pay rise?' Colin asked.

Jo was used to Colin's sarcastic remarks and knew how to handle him. 'Actually, yes, Merrill.' She knew he hated being called Merrill. 'The guv'nor's taking ten grand off your salary and putting it on mine. I pleaded with him but he wouldn't listen.'

Colin went to reply, then changed his mind. One-liners did not come easily to him, and he knew from experience that Jo always got the upper hand with him when it came to office repartee. So he nodded, made a short snorting noise and went back to his computer.

Half an hour later Nathan arrived. He said nothing and acknowledged none of his team. He walked in carrying a ham and coleslaw sandwich and a large plastic cup of coffee. He never ate breakfast at home: always ate his morning and lunchtime meals bought from the downstairs corner café. Jo believed that he would be happy to have his evening meals there as well if he could and never go home to his wife.

The first time she had spoken to his wife was shortly after she had joined the team. Cathy had called the office to speak to her husband. 'Hello. DC Jo Major speaking,' she had announced proudly.

'Is Nathan there, please?'

'No. I'm afraid he's out of the office at the moment. Can I ask who's speaking?' replied Jo.

'It's his wife. And you must be the new girl?' Nathan had complained to Cathy that the new addition to their pod was to be a female.

'Yes. I'm a mere two weeks old,' Jo replied.

'Well don't let all those men bully you in to submission,' she said, with a maternal ring.

Their relationship, carried out via phone calls, had continued in that manner ever since. Jo had found her to be a warm, friendly woman. Knowing now what she did about Nathan, she felt a degree of sympathy for her. She thought that her boss's wife deserved better.

She looked tentatively at her superior as he sat down at his desk. Jo felt proud that Jack had put his trust in her, but he had also put her in an impossible position. Her role, ultimately, was to ruin this man's imprudent life. She would be instrumental in putting Detective Sergeant Nathanley Ballack behind bars.

A small part of her felt that she was betraying him. A much larger part felt that she was betraying Cathy's friendship. There could be no winner here – no satisfaction of a job well done. Jo was a professional, but this matter gave her an uncomfortable feeling in the pit of her stomach.

CHAPTER 22

Three weeks later

Monday 14th December was a pivotal day for Nick Summers. It was the day he was going to sign a lucrative gardening contract with the local borough council. It was also his wife's thirtieth birthday.

Nick had suggested that Mel should take a day's holiday from work as she had complained of feeling tired throughout most of last week. She hadn't needed much persuading and had readily agreed.

At eight a.m. he sat alone at the breakfast table finishing his last mouthful of toast. He drained the remainder of his coffee from an enormous blue Chelsea mug, got up and went to the small cupboard under the stairs. There he pulled out an extravagantly wrapped parcel: Mel's surprise birthday present.

He had bought her a Catherine Malandrino dress from a designer fashion boutique in London. It was a silk-jersey mix in a stunning shade of violet and it was gorgeous. She had tried on the dress during the last trip they had made to the capital.

Mel had fallen in love with it, but at four hundred and sixty pounds had dismissed it as far too expensive.

Nick had thought his wife looked beautiful when she emerged from the changing room and had remembered every detail about the garment. He had travelled to London to purchase the dress on the Friday afternoon. Thirty was a special birthday, and after the recent events his wife needed a reason to feel special. When he handed over his credit card to the immaculately attired, heavily made-up female shop assistant, he had prayed that this milestone would see a change in fortune for them both.

Nick rose from his chair, cleared the breakfast things away and left the gift-wrapped dress, with a birthday card on top, in the middle of the table. In the card he had written:

You are not cooking tonight. We are out. Please wear the dress. Happy Birthday. I love you, Nick x. P.S. I'll be home early tonight.

He had booked a table at Terrazza, an Italian restaurant in the neighbouring town of Winsey. It had opened a year ago and the local paper had given it rave reviews. "Fine dining in an elegant and intimate atmosphere" was the line that had attracted Nick's attention. He had to find a way to rekindle their relationship. He hoped that tonight would be the spark to reignite the flame.

He certainly needed an injection of positive energy. The weeks following the break-in had been a test of their nerve and the strength of their relationship. There was still an underlying tension between them that, at times, made him feel as though they were strangers. The exchanges of romantic looks and the daily kisses and cuddles had been replaced by military nods and uneasy smiles. They hadn't made love since that fateful night.

Nick was at a loss as to how he could close the mental and physical gap that had opened up between them. He could hardly seek professional help or discuss it with either of their parents. The subject was a no go – even family.

Only last week Nick had brought up the question of how their parents would react if they ever discovered their secret. His mother and father had recently retired and moved to a cottage in Oxfordshire. Their life was now one of relaxed contentment.

Mel's blunt question had cut through him like cold steel. 'How would your parents take the news that their only child had killed a man and buried his body?'

Nick could only guess at their reaction. But whatever that may have been, their lives and how they regarded their son would have been tarnished forever.

'I dread to think,' he had replied. 'They would be forced to decide whether or not my actions were defendable, I guess. But I would hate to put them in that position. It's going to be hard enough for us to keep this terrible secret to ourselves – how difficult would it be for them?'

'How about your mum and dad?' he continued. Mel's parents had moved to Spain five years ago. At first Nick had been pleased to have the in-laws at such a safe distance. But in the light of their problems, children-wise, his attitude had changed. Nick now wished that his wife's parents had not moved abroad.

'My parents? God. They would find it incredible that their little girl was mixed up in something so outrageous – so devious. My mother still hasn't come to terms with the fact that I'm a grown woman who's old enough to marry and make

135

my own decisions in life. And Lord knows what she would think if her baby girl ever managed to bear a child.'

'Do you wish your parents lived closer? I know how isolated you feel at times as far as not getting pregnant goes. You haven't got your mother for support like most girls. I think...'

'Of course I do. But it doesn't change the fact that we haven't got any children,' Mel said, bluntly.

Nick felt the subject couldn't be discussed with anyone outside of family. It was far too personal. He also felt a sense of embarrassment about the whole issue. He believed there was a stigma attached to a man who failed to impregnate his wife. Amongst the male population it was regarded as less than masculine. One thing was certain in his mind. They were completely on their own with both of these issues.

He loved Mel dearly, but this was going to be a test of character for them both.

Getting his wife pregnant was important to them.

His biggest worry, after this last episode, was being around to see his children grow up.

CHAPTER 23

As quietly as he could, Nick closed the weathered oak front door of his house behind him. It was eight thirty. He had a nine o'clock appointment at the council offices where, after agreeing the conditions of a lucrative contract, he would put pen to paper.

He climbed into his van, angled the rear-view mirror downwards and looked at the reflection of his face. He had seen himself looking better. 'We,' he said forcefully to the mirror, 'are survivors. That's you and me,' he told his reflection through clenched teeth. 'So, we are going to bloody survive.' But who was he talking to? Nick Summers the murderer? The hapless victim? His guilty conscience? He readjusted the mirror, started up the van and drove away from his home.

The traffic on the roads at that time of the morning was always heavy, and what should have been a ten-minute journey took just over twenty. The municipal building, which luxuriated in seven acres of timbered countryside, lay on the outskirts of Ashford. As Nick drove up the long, tree-lined driveway, the modern, characterless, three-storey building finally came into view. It was a disappointment – a big concrete box with windows.

Peter Champion, the outgoing contractor, had been good friends with Nick for some years. He had rung Nick several months ago and told him to present his tender to the council before his retirement was common knowledge. He had also recommended him to his employers before he left the job. Nick realised he had been very lucky to receive all this vital inside help. He owed Peter a great debt of gratitude.

The contract was to design and maintain all hard and soft landscaping on open site projects. That included all council-owned parks and gardens for the entire borough. On Peter Champion's advice he had submitted a tender that was only slightly higher than Peter's contract. Peter felt confident that Nick's rivals would all come in too high. He was proved right.

But despite his friend's optimism, Nick had still not been convinced, initially, that he would be successful. Following his application, he had been invited by the horticultural committee to attend an interview. Nick had been used to relaxed, casual meetings when discussing the terms of new job assignments. But this was nothing like he had experienced before in his profession. As he had entered the imposing interview room the formality of the occasion drew beads of sweat from his tightened brow.

There, sitting in front of him behind an enormous solid teak desk, were three very severe looking council officers. They proceeded to fire rounds of questions at him like bullets from a Gatling gun. He had done his best to answer them, but due to their expressionless reactions, he hadn't held out too much hope.

'Thank you, Mr Summers,' was all one of them said as the interview was terminated. It was the secretary who told him on his way out that he would be contacted shortly if he had been successful.

When he had returned home to Mel that evening, he described them as the 'Botox Borough Brigade.' They had ended up in fits of giggles as Nick described the experience as 'like going before a prison parole board.'

The letter he received a few weeks later allayed his doubts. He was thrilled when they agreed to award him the job for the next five years. The Ashford council contract was one that would give his business a great deal of security. Nick could delegate this work to his employees while he busied himself with pricing new jobs and working on the better paid assignments.

Despite the fact that the rates paid by local government offices were not as high as the private sector, this agreement would provide continuous work for his sizeable team. Added to that, the civil service always paid their bills on time. It was the only occasion when this industry's regime of red tape and turgid rules received his seal of approval.

For the first time in over three weeks, he began to feel optimistic. As he climbed the grey concrete stairs on his way to meet the all-powerful horticultural officer with the soon-to-be-signed contract, he experienced a surge of enthusiasm race through his body. He allowed a smile to invade his face. It felt good.

When Nick reached the top of the stairs, his mobile phone pinged. A text message. He pressed the appropriate button. The message read: *The dress is stunning. Thank you, darling. I am surprised you remembered it. Very thoughtful of you. I'd love to go out for a meal tonight. Good luck with the contract today. Love Mel x.*

It was the first positive response he had received from his wife since that dreadful night. For some reason fate had dumped a massive dilemma on their doorstep, testing their relationship to the limit. Perhaps the picture was beginning to look brighter. Maybe they could put this ugly episode behind them after all, Nick thought. He realised his aggressive response to danger had put them through hell. But after this nightmare – what else could go wrong?

CHAPTER 24

Jo's office phone rang. It was Phil Ayres, one of the DPS boys. 'I don't know about you, Jo, but we're scratching around and disappearing up our own back passages here. 'We've watched Scrivens' flat night and day. There's still no sign of him. Nathan Ballack's supplier has disappeared in a cloud of smoke. The surveillance on Ballack has also been unproductive. He hasn't tried to contact a new supplier or taken delivery of any suspect parcels,' he told her.

Jo knew they couldn't move until he did. 'Same this side, Phil. How about inside Scrivens' pad?' Jo asked.

'Pad? It's a shithole, Jo. How people can live like that I don't know. When we broke into it the front room light was still on. We found a bit of puff, small amount of coke, thirty quid cash. And his passport's still there. We've left it as it is. I get the feeling he was definitely supposed to be going back there,' said Phil.

'I think you're right. But *I* get the feeling he won't be going anywhere ever again,' said Jo.

'Me too. Right, that was all – just a quick catch up. Must fly. Good luck,' he said.

'Thanks for keeping me in touch, Phil. Bye,' said Jo. This was not the best way to start a Monday morning. She turned to the rest of the team. 'That was Phil Ayres. He's come up with diddly as well,' she announced. *Coffee, that's what we need,* she said to herself. 'Drinks?' she asked the three other members of her pod.

'Skinny cinnamon caffé latte. And I'll have it black,' chirped Mark.

'Caffé latte black? Latte means milk, you fool,' replied Jo.

'I know, I know. I just like saying the word latte. It sounds posh,' said Mark. 'Laarrtteey,' he repeated, trying to emulate a Shakespearean actor.

'If there are two things you'll never be, Mark Smallwood, it's posh and skinny,' said Jo.

'Honestly! You try to raise the bloody tone in this place – waste of time. Okay, coffee, two fat sugars and no latte,' said Mark. 'Petit fours?' he added hopefully.

Jo tried to suppress a smile, gave him a withering look and shook her head.

Mark tried again. 'Petit threes?'

'There really is no hope for you, is there, Mark?' said Jo. It was not a question; it was a statement. 'Colin?' Jo asked her other colleague.

'Tea,' was his toneless, staccato answer.

Throughout the office banter between Jo and Mark, a hunched Nathan had been talking on his mobile phone. The low volume of his voice told Jo it was a personal call.

'Nathan?' Jo directed the question at her boss. There was no reply. 'Nathan, tea or coffee?' Jo said loudly to her boss. Nathan raised his head and looked quizzically at Jo.

'Tea or coffee,' she breathed with exaggerated mouth movements.

Nathan mouthed "coffee" and went back to his conversation.

Jo was about to get up from her desk when Mark called across. 'We've hit a brick wall with the Peckham case this morning, Jo.'

'Oh shit. Not again. I thought it was almost done and dusted,' Jo replied. The team had been getting close to nailing a major drug trafficker from the Peckham area of South London: a case they had all been working hard on.

Reports had been phoned in that two sixteen-year-old boys who lived on the notorious Dunwoodie council estate had been seen outside three local secondary schools selling drugs to the pupils at the end of the day's lessons.

The two juvenile dealers could be picked up anytime, but that was not who they wanted. The team were after their supplier and they knew who he was: a notorious street gang leader known as Rent. He was a vicious piece of work who ruled by bribes and threats. And he was clever.

More than once they had thought they had him, but he had a network of lookalikes and elaborate alibis that always allowed the drug dealer to escape the charges brought against him. This time Jo thought they had gathered enough solid evidence on him that would stick.

'What happened, Mark?' Jo asked.

'Uniform went to arrest him at his flat this morning – disappeared,' said Mark, shaking his head.

'Again? Bugger it,' said Jo. They were convinced that Rent must have a paid mole inside the force as he always seemed to know when they were getting too close to him. Jo was now beginning to think it may even be Nathan who had some kind of arrangement with him.

'I can't smell coffee, can you, Colin?' said Mark, sticking his nose in the air.

'Yes, okay. That's your fault, Smallwood, for distracting me with bad news,' replied Jo. She raised herself from her chair and walked through the office into the small kitchen to fill the kettle and prepare the beverages. She looked at her watch – five past eleven.

She leant back against the wall of the kitchen and watched the kettle reach boiling point as though it was at the end of a tunnel. She felt as if she had a thousand tasks to perform and sorting out their order of priority seemed impossible. The uncertainty of issues such as deadlines, unseen difficulties and changes of personnel was frustrating the hell out of her.

As Jo was stirring the milk into the hot drinks, she was suddenly aware of someone behind her. She turned to see Nathan standing in the kitchen doorway. She picked up his coffee and offered it to him. Nathan ignored the offer.

'A little birdie tells me you've been in Jolley's office again. It's becoming a regular thing, you and your meetings with the boss. What is it, four times this month?' Nathan asked.

Jo had not realised that every visit to Jack's office had been clocked. Most of their meetings had been arranged for early morning, before Mark and Colin got in. *There has to be a snitch from one of the other pods who's been reporting back to Nathan.* Jo had to think quickly.

'I don't know what the big deal is about me going into Jack's office, Nathan. It seems to be worrying Colin as well,' Jo replied dismissively.

'Well, no one else seems to be getting a fucking invitation to dine at the top table, Miss Major.' The line was delivered with a look of menace that Jo had never seen on Nathan's face before. It unnerved her.

The atmosphere in the small room had suddenly changed. Jo turned away from Nathan to put the cup of coffee back down on the ring-stained work surface. She was now aware of every hair follicle in her head as the skin contracted across her entire scalp. She turned to face Nathan.

'He just wants to know how I'm settling in with the team, that's all. He and my dad used to work together and were good friends. It's a bit embarrassing for me at times, but he's just keeping a fatherly eye on me. I'm sorry if it upsets you,' Jo said, defensively.

'I think I know exactly what you're doing in there,' Nathan said, moving forwards. He now had her trapped in the confined space which seemed to grow decidedly smaller.

'Well I'm not sucking his dick if that's what you think.'

'No,' Nathan said, a little surprised at the counter-attack. He then paused, set his jaw and stared right through her. He seemed to take an age to speak... 'I think it's far worse than that.' He leant forward, raised his right hand and moved it towards her neck as if to grab her by the throat. Jo froze.

As the claw-like hand got closer, it veered away at the last moment and picked up his coffee. With Nathan's face now just a matter of inches away from Jo's, he screwed up his eyelids, shook his head and tutted as if he was admonishing an errant schoolgirl.

'Jack and Jill went up the hill to fetch a pale of water,' Nathan said slowly. 'Jack fell down and broke his crown... Jill, trust me, will definitely come tumbling after.' He finished the verse with a cruel smile that ruled his entire face. 'Naughty, naughty,' he added, emphasising each word. He then turned and walked out of the cramped room.

Jo stood in the kitchen, her body taut, her head in a slight daze. The strange apocalyptic rhyme had sent shivers up her spine. This development was unexpected. She must not panic, she told herself. She had to think clearly.

If Nathan suspects he is being investigated it's going to make the ensuing days extremely uncomfortable. More importantly, it would compromise the chances of them apprehending the Albanian drug trafficker. Jo really wanted this catch. She had worked too bloody hard and long to end up with half a result.

None of this would affect the case they had built up on Nathan – they had gathered more than enough evidence on him. But would it mean that she would have to come off the investigation? Her feeling of being rattled turned to one of anger. She hadn't counted on Nathan discovering her involvement in the affair, at least not until after it had all been concluded.

Somewhat shakily, Jo gathered up the drinks and took them back into the office. As she handed the mugs to Mark and Colin, she scrutinised both men, looking for some kind of reaction. They appeared completely normal. If they knew what was going on and what had just been said in the kitchen, they were not showing it.

She was reasonably confident that they were not involved. Either Nathan was bluffing and trying to flush her out, or he had someone in the section passing him information. She had to inform Jack Jolley of their kitchen confrontation as soon as possible.

She sat back at her desk and busied herself on her computer. Occasionally, when she stopped to take a drink of her coffee, she looked over at Nathan. He was back on his mobile phone, head down, talking in hushed tones.

Jo was finding it impossible to concentrate on her work while her boss, whom she had been convinced was going to assault her in the kitchen, was in such close proximity. Part of her wished she had never been promoted to this position. The rest of the morning seemed to last forever.

At twelve thirty Nathan got up from his desk. 'Right, I'm off. I'm going to meet a contact who might be able to put us back on track with this Peckham case,' he declared. Without giving his team any more information, he strode over to the coat stand, grabbed his black, leather, knee-length coat and left the office.

Jo stood up as soon as Nathan had disappeared and announced that she was going to lunch. She then went straight into the ladies' toilet and rang the number of her contact at the DPS. The response was such that as soon as Ballack left the building there was an officer in position, ready to shadow his movements.

CHAPTER 25

As Nathan drove through the midday traffic in Ashford, he feared the worst. He had suspected, more than once, that over the past couple of weeks he had been followed. Then there was Jo. Her body language towards him had been growing increasingly distant. It was only when he paired that with her frequent visits to Jolley's office that he started to have doubts about her.

Janet, one of the admin support girls, was Nathan's eyes and ears when he was out of the office. Coincidentally, he had been chatting her up for the past few months and she had been flattered by the attention from the detective sergeant.

Janet had been the obvious choice to be his in-house spy. Nathan had invented a convincing story concerning someone in the office who had the knives out for him. The trouble was, he told her, he didn't know who. Janet swallowed it hook, line and sinker. She was more than happy to report back all movements and rumours in the office to the smooth-talking senior officer.

Nathan sat at traffic lights tapping two nicotine-stained fingers on the leather steering wheel. His constant use of cocaine was eating into his nervous system with increasing effect. When he wasn't feeling anxious, he was irritable, fatigued.

His shirt, damp with sweat, stuck to his skin. An increased heartbeat thumped through his head. Small bubbles of sweat glistened below his hairline, then trickled down his heavily veined temples. He wiped his forehead with the back of his hand and stared at the red light.

His reason for leaving the office today was not connected with work at all. There had been no arrangement to see his supposed contacts concerning the Peckham case; he just needed an excuse to have a long lunch break – get away from the office and work out his next move.

If his suspicions about being investigated were correct, he had a lot to be worried about. Not only was he going to be hunted down by the police but if Scrivens had revealed his identity to his supplier, he would be in serious trouble with them. He owed them a lot of money and these people were not the type to write off debts.

Then there was the body of Scrivens. If the police ever found that, they would surely trace it back to him. His DNA would be all over the corpse.

'Fucking cocaine. It's screwed up everything,' he said, as a stream of saliva shot out from the side of his pursed lips. He lowered the driver's window, searching for fresh air, as he waited for the lights to change.

His coke habit had started two years ago. He and his two-man team received a tip-off from an informer: the date of when a delivery of the narcotic would be arriving from Holland in the south-eastern port of Harwich. The cocaine would be hidden in a pantechnicon importing plants and flowers for UK florists.

They intercepted the enormous vehicle shortly after it left the docks. They found three hundred and fifty half-kilo bags of the drug hidden beneath a shipment of dwarf palmetto palms in four-inch deep compartments at the base of the plant pots. The haul had an estimated street value of over four million pounds.

His team were so pleased with themselves and the size of the haul that they decided to celebrate later that night. But Nathan also thought that he deserved some of the spoils. Five bags found their way into his overnight rucksack when his team were otherwise engaged.

He decided to sell the bags to one of his informants – a nice little bonus, he thought, for all the work he'd put in. But one bag never survived the evening intact. He had never taken cocaine before, but it had always been a hot topic of discussion. What was the big deal about this drug? What type of buzz did it give you?

That night, when he and his team hit the local town's bars, he had all those questions answered. In the seclusion of a pub toilet, the stale smell of urine was not the only thing that got sucked up into his nostrils that evening. The energy boost he got from the drug was a revelation to him; so much so that when he sold the cocaine to his informant, he arranged to get a regular supply for his own use. The informant was Scrivens.

As his habit increased, so did the need for more money. Dealing was the obvious answer. There were always plenty of takers amongst the lowlifes that he met in his job.

Three miles out of Ashford, Nathan arrived at his destination – an out-of-the-way pub in the tiny hamlet of Shear. He parked his car at the rear of the nineteenth-century tavern and entered the premises through the small rear garden door. He knew the place well: it was where he used to meet Scrivens when he needed another delivery. A few minutes later, a blue Ford Mondeo drove in and parked in the corner of the pub car park.

John, the ruddy-faced governor of the pub, knew him well. He was in his early sixties and whatever the time of year he always wore tan corduroy trousers, checked waistcoat, shirt and tie. John hailed from the south coast fishing village of Mevagissey in Cornwall and his accent was full of it. 'G'day, Nathan. What'll it be?' said John.

'It's been a fucking awful day, John. I'll have a pint of best and a large scotch and ice,' Nathan replied.

My! It *has* been a bad day.' John started preparing the drinks.

'And have one yourself,' added Nathan, easing himself onto a stool at the bar.

'Thanks. I'll 'ave an 'arf. So, do you wanna tell me about it?' said the landlord.

'If only I could, mate. If only I could.'

As he sat at the bar trying to drink away his problems, his immediate plans were muddled. But there was one thing certain in his mind. He couldn't ever return to work. The thought made him feel resentful. Someone was going to pay for it.

CHAPTER 26

The message from Mel had been a great start to Nick's day. The signing of the contract, subject to his approval of the terms, was going to transform his business. With Mel back alongside him, his negative thoughts were beginning to wane. He was now allowing himself to think of a positive future for them both.

Nick found the door marked HORTICULTURAL OFFICER. He knocked and entered.

Immediately in front of him sat a middle-aged secretary who looked as if she had been middle-aged all her life. She raised her head as if in slow motion and peered at him over the top of a pair of heavy-rimmed glasses.

Nick forced a smile. 'Mr Summers. I have a nine o'clock appointment with Mr Brown,' he said, slightly taken aback by his frosty welcome.

The secretary rose from her chair and pointed to a location behind his left ear. 'Take a seat,' she instructed, as she disappeared behind another grey door. It wasn't often he got to dress up in his navy-blue suit, white shirt and gold silk tie. He felt good.

After a few minutes the secretary appeared again. 'Mr Brown will see you now, she declared in a monotone as if she were announcing at which stations the Euston to Liverpool train would be stopping.

Nick stood and moved into the larger office. The room was tired. Reams of documents and official-looking papers were left, seemingly without thought or purpose, in haphazard piles that littered every available surface. Scarred, grey metal cabinets, some with half-closed drawers, lined two walls.

Mr Brown, the horticultural officer, stepped forward and shook Nick's hand. As far as Nick could make out, he was between thirty and fifty years old; it was impossible to be more accurate. His short dyed hair had the colour and lustre of an ageing hessian sack. He wore a jaded suit that crinkled at the crutch and back of the knees. But the sorry truth of the matter was he managed to blend in with the surroundings.

In less than fifteen minutes the formal proceedings were completed. The finer points of the contract were agreed and numerous signatures were scribbled on pieces of paper containing far too many rules of practice and regulations for Nick to contemplate reading. The process ended with another shaking of hands.

Nick was pleasantly surprised by the speed with which Mr Brown had concluded the official proceedings. Maybe his opinion of civil servants was misguided. But no. Now, Nick was informed, he was to be escorted on a tour around the grounds that surrounded the building and the parks in the borough. 'We are very proud of our borough, Mr Summers.

And I am confident, after today's visitations, that you will be too,' he droned.

Nick's tour was to be comprehensive. He would be instructed on immediate tasks, future projects and invited to put forward any of his own suggestions.

What he did not realise was that the overzealous Mr Brown was going to drag him around every council-owned garden and public park in the borough of Ashford. He should have realised which type of character he was dealing with when he introduced himself as plain Mr Brown. Maybe the poor man was never afforded a Christian name, Nick thought.

It had been a long, long day. Nick was beginning to think there wasn't much left of Kent to see. He was sure that Mr Brown had driven him around, in his tan Honda Civic, to every piece of land they owned and some they didn't. He was certainly a stickler for detail was Mr Brown. But that was where the trouble lay. Nick knew from past experience that when he was bombarded with so much information in such a short space of time he invariably ended up retaining virtually nothing.

Still, this bastion of democracy that held the tangled purse strings of our country, that had created more departments than a beehive, was prepared to pay him on a regular basis. So, who was he to complain?

'Just one more small plot to see, Mr Summers, and I think that's the lot,' said Mr Brown, checking his list.

Nick smiled weakly and looked at his watch. It was ten to four and it was already beginning to get dark. The little he could see in this light would not really be worth the effort, but he thought he had better keep his tour guide happy.

'Okay,' said Nick. 'I had better just ring the wife to let her know that I'm going to be a little later than expected. It's her birthday today. I'm taking her out for a meal tonight.'

'Oh! I am sorry if I've kept you,' Mr Brown replied, still studying his clipboard.

'Not a problem. I've thoroughly enjoyed my excursion,' Nick lied as he pulled his mobile phone from his jacket pocket. 'I won't be a second,' he added. Mr Brown nodded enthusiastically and climbed into his Honda as Nick walked several yards away from the car.

'Mel, it's Nick. You okay? … Good,' he said quietly. 'I was hoping to get home early today so we could relax together before we went out tonight, but I've got Mr I-NEED-TO-GET OUT-MORE Brown showing me every bloody flowerbed in the county. I'm cold, bored, pissed off and missing you, birthday girl,' Nick said as he looked back at his tormentor in chief.

'And I'm missing you, darling," Mel replied. "Thanks again for that beautiful dress. It's perfect. Try not to be back too late. I will have something warm waiting for you when you get home.'

The obvious sexual reference was picked up immediately by Nick. Mel had finished her period two weeks ago – the magical day fourteen had arrived once more. They had not made love since the break-in. In fact, neither of them had even mentioned sex during the last fortnight. Things were definitely looking up, Nick thought.

'Can't wait. Be home as soon as I can, darling. Bye,' said a partially revitalised Nick.

He walked back to the car, climbed in, and fastened his seatbelt. He turned to his escort. 'Sorry about that. Right, where we off to?' Nick said, summoning up his last ounce of enthusiasm.

'Okay. This is the last stop of the magical mystery tour,' said Mr Brown, trying to inject some humour in to the proceedings for the first time that day. 'It's a small area of garden that surrounds our wonderful technical college – not far away. It's in the area of Dunley Marsh. Do you know it?'

CHAPTER 27

After Jo had alerted the DPS of the possibility that Nathan was going to meet another supplier, she left the ladies room and headed straight for Jack Jolley's office. And this time she didn't care who saw her.

When she entered his office he was standing with his back to her looking out of his window. He turned his head. 'Yes, Jo,' he said, turning back to the window.

'Guv, Nathan knows we're on to him,' Jo said, unevenly, her nerves still strained from her confrontation with Ballack.

Jack wheeled around to face his detective sergeant. He was about to speak, then stopped. He stared into her face. 'You okay? You look a bit pale.'

'I'm fine, thanks. Just a bit frustrated, I suppose,' said Jo, surprised that her face had so easily revealed the turmoil inside her.

The conversation with Nathan that had just taken part in the small office kitchen was recounted in detail to her boss. She omitted how physically threatened she had felt by Nathan's body language: as a woman in a predominately male environment, she wanted to appear able to handle any office intimidation that came her way.

'I've also informed the DPS guys. They are, at this moment, shadowing Nathan's movements,' she added.

Jack listened in silence until Jo had finished. 'So we have a snitch in the office?' he said, sitting down at his desk.

'It looks that way, guv. If he believes we're on to him, well, it changes everything, doesn't it.'

Jack Jolley sat back in his chair and linked his hands behind his head. 'Yes, it does. Bugger! This is not what I wanted to hear. If, as you say, he thinks he's been rumbled, the chance of getting anywhere near his supplier has probably gone. But I'm tempted to forget about the main trafficker for now and just get closure on Ballack. I want that bloody poisonous character out of here as soon as possible.'

'So do I, guv, but can we just hold fire for a few days? If Nathan does suspect that he's under investigation and he panics, this is when he could make mistakes. He could still lead us to the bigger prize.'

'I don't like it, Jo. If he knows the game is up,' Jack paused, picked up his pen and pointed it at his detective sergeant, 'then we have a loose cannon on our hands. I'm inclined to get him off the streets without delay.'

'We're all over him now, guv. What harm can he do?' Jo said, hoping that one last plea would give her the time she wanted.

Jack pursed his lips, leaned forward and let his hands drop down onto his desk, lightly smacking the polished mahogany surface. He looked into Jo's eyes. She could not read the look on his face. Without realising it, she was holding her breath.

'You've got two days,' Jack said.

CHAPTER 28

Nathan never returned to work that afternoon. When he left the pub at four p.m. he had consumed three pints of bitter and four large whiskies supplemented by a line of cocaine inhaled, from the back of his hand, in the gents' toilet.

He left the pub the same way he went in: through the small rear door. He walked in a deliberate manner to his car and got in. He then sat at the wheel for a short time, weighing up his next move.

He was now convinced he had been rumbled as a drug pusher. He had got careless. Should he give himself up and hope for leniency? The thought did not sit easy with him at all. His only other option was to disappear from the radars of Jack Jolley and whoever else was after him. Australia, the Far East – somewhere far away from all these arseholes around him, he thought. That had to be the plan.

Anger began to mushroom inside his stomach, rising up into his throat. It was choking him. His past began to bore deep into his ribs, scything through his senses.

He felt that nothing had ever come easily to him. As an only child, he had been brought up on a tough council estate in Upminster, north-east London. His forty-fags-a-day mother finally succumbed to the nicotine, dying from lung cancer when he was ten years old. His Scottish father, who drifted in and out of labouring jobs, was a drunk. As he sat in his car, he tried to remember their faces. But he could not form one clear image of his parents.

He hated his time spent at the local comprehensive school. In his early years there, he had been the subject of much bullying. But by the time he reached the fifth year he had experienced a growth spurt. He was suddenly taller than most of the other boys in his class.

It was around this time that his unemployed father, who gave him regular drink-fuelled beatings, was kicked to death in a late-night street brawl. He had to move in with his frail, eighty-two-year-old grandmother and was now the man of the house. The transition from intimidated podgy boy to heavyweight bully was as unsurprising as it was effortless.

Everything from then on, he decided, had been down to his hard work. His jawbone tightened to its maximum. 'I owe no one,' he said to himself.

In that split second he realised that giving himself up was a non-starter.

'I hate this fucking country and the arseholes in it,' he slurred, as he pulled out of the car park and turned right onto the road that led back to his home. A few moments afterwards the blue Mondeo followed.

Fifteen minutes later, he pulled into the drive in front of his house and killed the engine. He got out of his car and entered his home. The man in the blue Mondeo decided he had seen enough and carried on past Nathan's house and headed back to the main road.

CHAPTER 29

Cathy arrived home having collected the children from school in her five-year-old green Renault Clio. It was not the most prestigious car that turned up every afternoon outside the school gates but she loved her little run-around. It was easy to drive, cheap on petrol and had a CD player that enabled George Michael to sing to her whenever she so desired.

Once in, the children headed straight upstairs to their bedrooms, as they did every day, to play on their games consoles and computers. 'Honestly, you kids and computers,' she shouted after them. 'Whatever happened to girls jumping over skipping ropes or twirling hula hoops around their waists? Boys playing football with jumpers for goalposts? I don't know.' But the kids had already disappeared behind their bedroom doors. It saddened her that youngsters hardly ever played outside the house with each other any more. Leisure time seemed to consist solely of insular activities such as texting, emailing and internet surfing.

Her focus on the children stopped abruptly. She sat at the kitchen table, the *Daily Express* laid out in front of her. She was turning the pages but her brain was not absorbing a single word. Even the comforting kick of her baby inside her did not detract Cathy from her new train of thought.

When she heard the front door slam, she was taken by surprise. She checked her watch – twenty past four. Why had Nathan come home so early?

'Nathan?' she called out. He appeared at the kitchen door and immediately Cathy knew he'd been drinking. She was scared of her husband when he was under the influence of alcohol, but this time she had to be brave. She had to make a stand. 'Why are you home so early?'

Nathan took a deep breath. Cathy could tell that he was trying to appear sober. 'I had to meet a contact, and by the time it finished it wasn't worth going back to work. They get enough of my time anyway.'

'I don't think they're getting much of your time at all lately. In fact, I'd like to know who *is* getting enough of your time. Is there something you want to tell me?' asked Cathy.

'What do you mean "is there something you wanna tell me"? What are you saying? That you don't believe where I've been?'

Cathy struggled up from her chair and shuffled over to a kitchen cupboard. She took out the cocktail shaker and placed it on the table in front of Nathan. 'How can I believe anything you say or trust you ever again? How long has this been going on?'

Nathan stared at the silver container on the table, taken aback. He tried to recover. 'So, you've been snooping around, have you?'

'No, I knocked the bloody thing over when I was cleaning your filthy drinks cabinet. And all these spilled out,' she said, holding up one of the dozen clear plastic bags filled with white powder. 'That's hardly the point, though, is it?'

She knew immediately what the white substance was. When she was seventeen she had taken the drug once at a party. At least half the girls in her class had dabbled with cocaine at one time or another. Most of them, including Cathy, had stopped as soon as they started. It was a peer pressure thing and no one wanted to appear "not cool" in front of their friends. But this was different. They were adults now, for God's sake, they were parents!

'This is not just about you, you selfish bastard. This is all of us: my life – your children's lives.' Cathy was now shouting at Nathan. 'You're not just taking cocaine, are you? You're dealing. If you're found out, that's it – your job, this house, your family. Everything.'

Nathan's face lost all form of expression for a moment. Cathy had never before seen this man lost for words. It didn't last long. The eyes narrowed, the nostrils flared. The colour surged up through his neck and into his face. 'Well, if you hadn't got pregnant to start with I wouldn't be in this fucking situation, would I?'

'Don't you dare blame me for your weaknesses. I'm beginning to believe that if I hadn't got pregnant you would never have even thought of marrying me. And maybe now I'd be married to an honest, hard-working man who had respect for himself and his family,' replied Cathy.

The words had hardly left her lips when Nathan took a step forward, raised his hand and slapped her hard across her face.

Cathy was caught off balance by the blow and fell backwards against the door of the refrigerator. Two china plates that had been sitting on the top of the appliance were knocked off by the impact. They smashed around Cathy's feet as she slid down to the floor with a thump.

She looked up at her husband, who was standing menacingly over her. She drew her knees up and crossed her arms over the heavy bulge of her unborn child in a protective manner. 'Get out! Get out, you bastard!' she screamed.

'I don't need this shit. I'm going down the fucking pub. I'll get more respect down there,' Nathan replied. He grabbed the cocktail shaker and made a beeline for his study at the end of the living room.

As he passed the stairs, he looked up to see his little boy and girl watching him from the top of the landing. They had heard most of the argument and had both left their rooms when they heard the loud crash as the crockery hit the kitchen floor. They knelt, looking down through the thin wooden banisters at their scowling father, their innocent eyes wide with fear. He ignored them and continued into his study.

Once inside, he snorted two lines of cocaine, poured himself a scotch and knocked it back. Then he left the study and walked out of the house into the half-light of the early evening. He needed some fresh air and time to think. His world was starting to crumble around him. He would take a walk and the local pub would be at the end of it.

As he traipsed through his housing estate, he was finding it difficult to formulate one clear thought, his mind a muddy pool of despair and resentment.

He decided to take the less direct route to the local pub. It would give him more thinking time. The wintry sun had dipped below the tree line, resulting in a quite dramatic fall in temperature. A spiteful wind whipped through the deserted streets of the estate, forcing the cold to drill into his bones. He pulled up the collar on his black, leather, knee-length coat, gathering the neck together as he laboured against the hostile conditions.

His change of journey, he admitted to himself as he walked on, was nothing to do with having more time to think. It was going to take him past the rear of Nick and Mel Summers' house.

CHAPTER 30

It was the first day that Mel had felt her confidence beginning to return. Although there were still lingering doubts, unanswered questions, she was starting the process of pushing them to the back of her mind. She was allowing herself, once again, to see a future for herself and Nick. But it was a slow process.

Yet, there were moments, in the still, black of the night, when she would get vivid flashes of the terrible scene she had witnessed in her living room. She prayed those memories would fade with time. But there had been many tears since that fateful evening. When she was on her own, without warning, they would return. There were times of dark despair when she thought she was near breaking point.

As a child, whenever she was frightened or upset, her mother would be there with a cuddle or a comforting word. Now that she couldn't share her worries, discuss her fears, she felt alone and vulnerable.

A party to murder and concealment of a body. It was a heavy burden. One she was struggling to carry.

But through that bleak tunnel she could see a light. And it was beginning to edge closer. She had witnessed how Nick, with each passing day, had appeared to get stronger. She knew he was still haunted by a guilty conscience, but her husband's efforts at trying to get their lives back on track had rubbed off on her. Gradually, she had drawn courage from his positive attitude.

When Nick called a short while ago to tell her he was running late, she had been excited to hear his voice. The reaction surprised her. It reminded her of when they were courting. Just to receive a phone call followed by the expectation of meeting up with Nick in those early days was enough to make her skin tingle. It had happened again.

Nick's suggestion to take the day, her birthday, off work had been a good one. She had dozed in her warm bed until shortly before nine o'clock, something she had not done since her teenage years.

Coming downstairs and seeing the effort and thought that Nick had put into her birthday surprise had caused a powerful wave of emotion. It had set up the day perfectly. The beautiful dress had made her feel feminine again. And when Nick phoned, her sensuality simply sparked back into life. She wanted him again, and when he arrived home she would have him.

But at that moment the dress was top of her priority list. She had thought about it many times since trying it on in the London boutique. She was thrilled that Nick had remembered and bought it for her birthday. Now, she could not wait to try it on and see which shoes and jewellery would best complement the garment. She got up from the kitchen table and hurried upstairs to her bedroom.

The exquisite piece of finery was lying across the bed, demanding to be worn. Off came the trainers, jeans and jumper as she slipped the sensuous, violet dress over her head. The silky material slid down her shapely body and dropped perfectly into place.

The design meant that one shoulder was completely bare. 'Mmm. One exposed bra strap is not exactly the look I'm after,' she frowned at the mirror. Of the few strapless bras she had, not one was right – the top of the cup was too high or the back of the bra was visible. There was nothing for it – she would just have to go braless. Her breasts were not small but they were still quite firm.

When she tucked herself into the dress she realised that she hadn't needed to wear a bra at all. She had forgotten how superbly fashioned the gown was. The built-in support gave her the lift and flattering cleavage she wanted without the aid of an undergarment.

Now for the sparkly adornments.

CHAPTER 31

As Nathan approached the Summers' house, he noticed that the lights were on. When he drew level he slowed his pace. His attention was drawn to an upstairs light. He could see the top half of Mel in her bedroom, posing in front of her wardrobe mirror.

He stopped and waited, hoping to see more, but she wasn't getting undressed, she was trying on different necklaces. He pulled back the sleeve of his leather coat and looked at his watch. It was four thirty. He wondered whether Nick was back home from work yet.

He made his way around to the front of the house and noticed that Nick's van was not parked in the drive. He was not sure what his motive was, but he felt the urge to ring the front doorbell. He wanted to see the lovely Mel but he needed an excuse.

She tried her hair up, tried it down and went through various combinations of shoes and jewellery. Finally, she was happy with her choice. She took one last look in the mirror. She felt great. She looked beautiful. Then the doorbell rang.

'Oh, damn! Who can that be?' Mel said. She was somewhat overdressed for late afternoon. *Hopefully they'll go away,* she thought. But the doorbell rang again, long and loud. She didn't have time to change; she would just pop her head around the door and get rid of whoever it was.

She kicked off her satin-covered shoes, hurried downstairs and opened the door a short distance. She was surprised to see Nathan Ballack standing in front of her. Her heart skipped a beat when she suddenly thought he was there to bring bad news. 'Nathan? Is there anything wrong?

'Cathy and I have just had a bit of a row and I was off to the pub. I just wondered whether Nick was in and fancied joining me? You know, bit of male support and all that.'

Mel realised instantly that he'd been drinking already and that he looked cold. Reluctantly, she opened the door wider. 'No, he's still at work.' Should she tell him that Nick would be home soon? If she did, maybe Nathan would persuade her husband to go for a drink with him. That would ruin everything. She had to get rid of him as soon as possible.

'Oh, that's a shame. Wow! You look great. Going somewhere?' Nathan said. Mel saw him taking in every curve of her body that was accentuated by the clinging dress.

'We're going out to dinner tonight. Nick shouldn't be long.' She forced a smile that she hoped would say *I'm busy, Nathan, goodbye.* But instead of making his exit he just stood rooted to the spot, looking past her into the house.

Nathan took a step forward. 'I haven't told Cathy, obviously. You know, about what happened here the other night,' he said, lowering his voice. The sentence was left hovering between them like a menacing spectre. Mel took it, not as a statement but as a half-hearted promise, a veiled threat.

She was now in a very awkward position. Because of recent events she was acutely aware that the detective had a commanding power over them. She could not afford to upset this man. She saw him shiver. She had no option. 'You look freezing; would you like to come in for a cup of tea?'

'That's very kind of you, Mel. Perhaps that would be better than the pub. I've already had a few.'

Mel showed him into the kitchen and put the kettle on. Nathan sat down at the table. 'Tea or coffee?' she asked.

'Coffee would be great.'

'Sugar?'

'Two.'

Mel made the coffee and turned to face Nathan, who was slouched back in a kitchen chair with his arms folded. She was aware that he not taken his eyes off her from the moment he arrived.

He was now staring at her cleavage as she bent forward to put the mug down on the table in front of him. 'I won't be a tick,' said Mel, aware of his prying eyes.

Nathan nodded as Mel hurried from the kitchen. She left him warming his hands on his mug of coffee. As she walked away, she could feel his eyes sucking in every movement of her tight, silk-covered buttocks until she disappeared up the stairs.

Even though he was a policeman, she did not trust Nathan. He was shady. Behind those cold, shark-like eyes lurked trouble, eyes that hid unpleasant secrets – corrupt thoughts.

The last thing she wanted to do was leave him alone downstairs, but she had to get out of that dress before her husband came home. More to the point, it was hardly the proper attire to parade around in while Nathan sat there ogling her. The fabric and cut of the garment left very little to the imagination.

Jo was annoyed that Nathan had interrupted her day off. She didn't want to tell him that today was her birthday – only to get rid of him, relax and prepare herself for when Nick came home from work. What was Nathan doing here? She wished she hadn't let him in. She began to feel very uncomfortable.

When Mel reached her bedroom, she closed and locked the door behind her. She had meant to remove the small bolt that the previous owners had fitted. She couldn't think of any reason why it was necessary. She was now pleased it was still in place.

She went over to the window, closed the curtains, picked up her shoes, put them back in the wardrobe. She would slip back into her jumper, jeans and trainers. She gathered the material from the waist of the dress and pulled it up and over her head. Her breasts swung free as she leant forward and laid the garment carefully on the bed.

As she did so, she heard the metallic sound of the door handle turn on its spindle. Mel wheeled round. She froze. She held her breath. All went silent. Time seemed to stand still as the only noise she could hear was the thumping of her heart against her chest.

CHAPTER 32

Nick sat in the passenger seat of the Honda Civic as if paralysed. He had never wanted to see this place again. He could barely turn his head to look at the location where he had hidden the body of the drug dealing thief. A cold sweat spread across his face.

Mr Brown turned to his passenger. 'Right. Here we are, Mr Summers. Oh! Are you feeling all right?' he enquired, seeing Nick's pallid appearance.

'Yes, I'm fine. I haven't eaten since breakfast; just a bit hungry, I guess,' said Nick, wiping a band of perspiration from his top lip. Mr Brown nodded his head as they got out of the car.

The familiar smell of the swamp was there again to haunt him. He immediately felt sick. He breathed deeply as he followed Mr Brown around the gardens of the featureless, pebble-dashed building.

Two circuits of the grounds had included every possible horticultural question he had ever heard. 'These flowerbeds here are, quite frankly, badly designed and lack any vibrant colour whatsoever in the summer months,' expounded Mr Brown.

Nick, by this time, was not taking in any of his employer's observations. He was only conscious of his shirt sticking to the sweat that was running down his back. He just wanted to leave this area as soon as possible.

But Mr Brown's suffocating fervour would not abate. 'So, what would your suggestion be, Mr Summers. How would you brighten up this dull corner of the campus?' he continued.

Nick did not reply. His eyes were looking into the flowerbed. His mind was peering into the distorted face of Scrivens. The only noises that were registering within him were the sounds of the thief's skull splitting on impact and the splintering of glass.

'Mr Summers?

'Excuse me?' Nick replied, as he jolted back to the now.

'Oh dear! I fear I have put you through a little too much today. Maybe we should go,' said the civil servant.

Nick's hollow expression said everything.

They were soon back in the car. 'Sorry it has taken so long, Mr Summers. I hope I haven't made you too late?'

Nick smiled and shook his head.

'If you're really pushed for time, we could take a shortcut though the marsh if you like. It's not the most attractive scenery, but it'll take five to ten minutes off our journey,' Mr Brown added.

All too quickly Nick replied, 'No! No. Erm, I'm in no particular hurry. The main road will be fine.'

'Probably just as well. It's a bit of a scary place. Wouldn't want to drive through there at night, that's for sure,' said Mr Brown.

'No,' said Nick quietly.

'Actually, I heard talk, via the government planning office, that the Wildlife Trust were thinking of converting a considerable part of the marsh into a bird sanctuary and wildlife observation site,' said Mr Brown.

Nick's hand tightened on the car door handle. 'Sorry?'

'Sectioning off a large area,' he continued. He turned his head toward Nick, whose expression was set in stone. 'Oh, yes. There's all sorts of weird and wonderful species over there, apparently. Lord knows what they'll find lurking among the bulrushes, eh?' Mr Brown added with a titter.

Nick forced a smile at his attempt at humour but his stomach, once again that afternoon, felt as if it was in a clove hitch. 'When do they plan on doing this then?' Nick asked tentatively.

'Oh. I'm not sure about that – just in the early talk stage, I think. Still, I for one would be very interested if it comes to fruition. I have to confess, I am an avid twitcher.'

Why doesn't that surprise me, thought Nick. He stayed quiet. He felt sick.

'Righty-ho! Let's be off then,' said Mr Brown.

Nick closed his eyes, breathed a sigh of relief and sat back in his seat.

When they arrived back at the Ashford municipal building, Nick shook hands with Mr Brown, said goodbye, and climbed into his van. He was cold and tired. *What a day. What a bloody boring day. Still, the contract's signed, and I'm still alive... just,* he thought.

He turned the key and the engine roared into life. He hit first gear and proceeded to drive out of the grounds, which were now in semi-darkness.

The black, shadowy pine trees that lined the twisting path back to the main road now appeared quite sinister in his headlights. For a split second he was back at Dunley Marsh, driving through the undergrowth with a corpse in the back of his van. He shivered briefly as the van gathered speed. But as quickly as the memory appeared, Nick forced the thought out of his head.

Having finally escaped the wrist-slitting voice of his new employer, the reality of the immense size and value of his new contract began to sink in. His feeling of exhaustion was now beginning to be replaced by one of satisfaction.

This contract, he thought, should give his wife and children the security he wanted. That, of course, was *if* he and Mel were lucky enough to have children. His enthusiastic plans were, all at once, halted by his recurring thought. *Even if we were to have a family, would I be around to see them grow up?*

The words of Mr Brown resonated in his head: 'Sectioning off a large area... Lord knows what they'll find lurking among the bulrushes...'

CHAPTER 33

The silence didn't last long. The wood-splitting impact against the door jarred Mel's senses as it was smashed open with terrific force. The small lock flew past her shoulder and hit the wardrobe behind.

Nathan stood in the doorway, a triumphant smirk dominated his sweat-covered face. Mel let out a fearful cry as her hands shot up to cover her exposed chest.

She took a step backwards. 'What the hell!' she screeched. 'How dare you. Get out!'

'You're beautiful, Mel,' Nathan said through clenched teeth. His eyes were slightly glazed as he spoke. It was as though he was talking to himself. He made no move to leave.

Mel tried to calm herself. She needed to try a different approach. This time she spoke more slowly. 'Nathan, get out of my bedroom. You shouldn't be in here. Nick will be home any minute.' Mel prayed that she was right.

His mouth twisted as he spoke. 'Nick? That lucky bastard doesn't deserve you.' Nathan took two paces towards her. He was staring at the front of her thin cotton panties as though he was in a trance. She suddenly felt very small; her eyes widened in disbelief as she looked into his face. It was unrecognisable as being human. It was of a predatory, wild animal.

A wave of terror coursed through her shivering body as her mind searched for a solution to this predicament – a phrase that would snap him out his lustful mindset.

'Nathan, you've been drinking. Don't do something stupid you'll regret later. Nick will be home any minute.' Her voice rose again, hoping it would shock him back to his senses.

'Stupid? I've already done fucking stupid. I've lost everything, Mel. It's gone. My marriage; my job...'

'What are you talking about?' said Mel.

'But I haven't lost you, Mel, have I? 'Cause you're here in front of me.' Nathan took off his leather coat and let it drop to the floor. He then stepped forward and put his hand on her bare shoulder. Mel tried to pull away but there was nowhere to go. She was now backed up against the bed.

Nathan pulled her close with both arms and smelled her hair. 'Don't, Nathan,' Mel said as she squirmed in his embrace. But he was immensely strong, and as much as she tried, she could hardly move. Her folded arms were now trapped between them.

'I've seen the way you look at me. You've wanted me for ages. Well, now you've got your chance.' He moved his head downwards and tried to kiss Mel on the lips.

The smell of stale alcohol flooded her nostrils. 'Get off me!' she screamed and pulled her head backwards in a violent motion. Nathan's immediate response was to pull Mel towards him again. Her head whipped back and struck the side of his jaw.

Nathan swayed back from Mel, looking momentarily shocked as he rubbed his injured face with his left hand. Then, gathering his senses, he let out a roar. 'You fucking bitch.' Nathan spat out the words. At the same time he swung his right fist and punched Mel full in the face.

The blow caught her on the cheek just below her left eye and on the side of her nose. Mel fell back onto the bed, stunned by the vicious act. Her vision blurred from the impact, blood started to seep from her nose.

Nathan lurched forwards, slid two fingers underneath the crotch of her panties and ripped them from her body. Mel was semi-conscious and only partly aware of what was happening. She was unable to move to protect herself.

The sight of her bleeding, vulnerable body produced not compassion but a stronger animal lust in Nathan. He knelt on the bed over her naked body, undid his belt and pulled his trousers and pants down to his ankles. He was already hard.

Nick pulled the van into his drive and turned off the engine. He sat there for a moment. He had stopped at a petrol station on the way home and bought a bunch of pink roses for Mel. He picked them up from the passenger seat and put them on his lap. Then he closed his eyes. He imagined Mel standing in the bedroom in that beautiful, sexy dress, waiting for him.

He was like a child with an unopened bag of sweets – putting off the moment for as long as he could before finally enjoying the treat. He was letting the thrill of expectation build inside his hungry mind.

Nathan pushed Mel's legs apart with his knees and thrust himself inside her.

'It was only a matter of time, my little darling,' Nathan whispered as he kissed her blood-smeared mouth. Gradually, Mel's faculties started to return and she let out a moan. Nathan's callous, drug-clouded mind interpreted this as one of pleasure. 'That's it, my little darling, you enjoy it. This is what it's like to be fucked by a real man. Not like your wimp of a gardener.'

Nick could stand it no more. He grabbed the flowers, got out of the van and walked up to the front door of his house. He put his key in the lock, opened the door and stepped inside. Hiding the flowers behind his back, he entered the sitting room, hoping to see Mel sitting on the sofa. The room was empty.

As Nathan continued to violate Mel's body he lowered his head to her breast and sucked her nipple into his mouth. He then bit down on it. The pain shot through her nervous system, jolting her brain back to full consciousness. Her eyes snapped open to see the full horror of her situation.

Nathan was holding her wrists above her head so tightly it was causing her hands to go numb. Bile rose in her stomach from the smell of stale sweat from his raised armpits as he pounded into her defenceless body. His naked buttocks were like a piston – relentless, unforgiving.

With fifteen stone pinning her to her bed, Mel realised her chance of escape was hopeless. In desperation, she released a protracted, agonising scream.

As Nick headed for the kitchen, his air of excitement turned to one of alarm as his ears were assaulted by the piercing shriek. It came from upstairs. And it was a cry for help.

'Oh my God!' cried Nick. The bouquet of roses tumbled to the floor as he turned and raced up the stairs. When he reached the top he noticed that the door to his bedroom was open. There were noises coming from inside. 'Mel?' he called, terrified of what he was going to find. He reached the door. The sight that confronted him sucked the air from his lungs. His legs buckled beneath him. His brain could not take in what he was witnessing.

Mel, who had heard her husband call her name, looked up at Nick from over Nathan's shoulder, her expression a mixture of despair and repugnance. 'Help me, Nick,' she pleaded.

Nathan, who was conscious of nothing other than his own pleasure, gave one huge thrust into Mel and orgasmed.

'You fucking animal!' Nick bellowed as he sprang forward and dragged the half-naked detective off his wife. Nathan tumbled off the bed and crashed to the floor. Shocked at Nick's sudden appearance, his face lost all colour, his mouth drooped open. Nick took a pace forward, aiming a kick at the detective's crutch. The toe of his shoe hit the target. Ballack yelped, doubling over in agony.

'You despicable bastard. What in fucking God's name do you think you're doing?' Nick raged as he lashed out once more with his foot, this time connecting with his ribs.

Mel curled up in a ball and covered her body with a pillow. Nick looked over at his wife. The pathetic vision that met his eyes tore him apart. This can't be happening, he thought.

Nick was suddenly aware that Nathan had struggled into a kneeling position and was attempting to dress the lower half of his body. Nick lifted his boot up to Nathan's head and kicked him back down.

The sight of catching Nathan in the act of raping his wife was almost too much to bear. His emotions became confused. Part of him did not know what his next move or reaction should be.

As he stood over the prone body of his wife's violator, his anger was mixed with hurt. 'How could you do this to us?' he shouted at Nathan.

But Nathan's surprise at being caught in the act of rape was starting to diminish. His cocky demeanour was returning. Once again he reverted to his only form of defence – aggression. He climbed to his feet, still holding his groin, and faced Nick. 'You should thank me. I'm doing you a favour,' he said with a smirk that twisted the corner of his blood-smeared mouth.

Nick could not believe what he was hearing. The rage began to build inside him again, but he remained speechless.

'You obviously can't service your wife properly, you can't give her fucking kids, so I've done it for you,' Nathan slurred.

As the final wounding insult spilled from Nathan's loose mouth, something exploded inside Nick. He stepped forward, a roar exploding from his lungs and swung a right hook that connected with the side of Nathan's jaw. It knocked Nathan clean off his feet. As soon as he hit the floor, Nick straddled his body, put his hands around his throat and squeezed with every ounce of his strength.

Nathan was now jammed between the bed and the wardrobe with his arms pinned under Nick's knees. His movement was severely limited. Nathan brought his legs up into Nick's back, trying to dislodge his assailant. Nick countered by crouching lower over Nathan's face and held his position, increasing the pressure around his neck.

Nick's usual self-control had deserted him completely. A red mist had descended between him and his wife's attacker. He had already killed a man, but it had been a dreadful accident. This was different. At that moment he didn't care about the consequences. Nathan Ballack suddenly represented everything that was going wrong in his life.

'Nick!' Mel pleaded. She had moved into a kneeling position on the side of the bed and was watching her husband strangle the life out of her assailant. 'You're killing him!' she said.

Nathan's face was beginning to turn purple. Part of her wanted him dead, but she could not just sit there and watch her husband murder this man. 'Nick! You're killing him!' Mel screeched. She dropped the pillow, leant forward and slapped her husband's face.

The blow stung Nick out of his cloud of destruction. He released his grip on the detective's neck and slumped backwards between Nathan's feet. He sat, mouth open, breathing deeply. He leant back on his arms, his head tilted towards the ceiling. The trauma of the last few minutes had drained him of energy.

Ballack stayed silent, not moving. Nick slowly looked down and into the face of the policeman. His bloated features bore no signs of life. The enormity of what he had just done began to seep into Nick's brain.

Mel looked at Ballack, then at Nick. 'You've killed him.' She stared at her husband in disbelief. Nick leant forward and grasped the policeman's wrist, checking for a pulse. He couldn't find one. Without thinking who it was or what this man had just done, Nick started pumping his chest. It was an inborn reaction.

He was not a cold-blooded killer. He wanted this man to live so he that could pay for his vile act. Just as he was about to commence mouth-to-mouth, the body on the floor convulsed, emitted a reverberating moan and sucked in a large amount of air.

The suddenness of the action broke the mood in the room. Nick and Mel jerked backwards. Nathan now began to groan and move his limbs. Mel breathed a sigh of relief as tears began to fall down her bruised and bloodied face.

Nick, aware that Mel was still naked, got up from the floor, unhooked her dressing gown from the back of the door and helped her put it on. He sat on the edge of the bed and put his arm around his trembling wife and held her close. They watched in stunned silence as Nathan regained consciousness. At that moment he felt powerless. He knew there was nothing he could say or do to take away the agony his wife had just gone through – was still going through.

Nathan lay on the floor, coughing, massaging his bruised neck. He opened his eyes and looked at Nick, expecting another attack.

Nick leant forward and pushed his fist hard against his cheek. 'You're lucky I didn't kill you, you filthy bastard. If it hadn't been for Mel, I would have. You're finished, Ballack. You are going down for this. A copper doing time for rape. You're going to suffer inside that prison. I'm *glad* I didn't kill you now.'

Nick moved around to the other side of the bed and picked up the phone from the bedside table. Nathan had managed to raise himself up into a kneeling position once more.

Nick looked across at the detective. 'You're going nowhere. Not until the police get here,' he said.

As Nick hit the first nine of the emergency service number Nathan made his move. He got to his feet and somewhat unsteadily moved towards the bedroom door. Nick reacted immediately. He dropped the phone and went to head him off, but before he could reach him, Nathan suddenly stopped in his tracks as though he had been shot.

His right arm moved slowly to his left shoulder. His mouth fell open. Nick stopped moving as well, not knowing what to expect next.

Then, as if in slow motion, he looked over at Nick. His eyelids widened, creating a puzzled stare. He tried to move his mouth to speak, then his eyes glazed over and fifteen stone of flesh and bone crashed face first to the floor.

As his body hit the carpet, it bounced back up almost a foot, then thumped down again and lay still. Nick and Mel turned to look at each other in astonishment. Nick moved to the detective and felt his neck for a pulse. He could feel nothing.

'Oh, shit, he's not breathing. He must have had a heart attack or something,' said Nick, now realising the implications of having a dead body in his house with strangulation marks around his neck.

Nick turned the body over and, against every natural instinct within him, he once again commenced resuscitation procedures. Part of him realised that his decision to try to save a life – this life – was bizarre in the extreme.

He started by pumping his chest, then, wiping Mel's blood from Ballack's mouth with his sleeve, he administered the kiss-of-life. He alternated these procedures for some minutes with no success.

Mel watched him carry out the life-saving methods. She too had mixed feelings. She despised the man her husband was trying to save, but she wanted him to suffer for what he had done.

Then it suddenly dawned on her. This episode would change her life irrevocably, whether he lived or died.

CHAPTER 34

Nick sat back against the bed, exhausted by his efforts. Despite his prolonged attempts at resuscitation, Detective Sergeant Nathanley Ballack was well and truly dead. Mel sat on the side of the bed holding the soft material of her dressing gown to her face. She was staring into the distance. Streaks of blood and mascara stained the white, fleecy collar of the garment. The dazzling Catherine Malandrino dress, which was to be her pride and joy for the evening's dinner, lay in a crumpled heap near her feet.

Nick was the first to speak. 'I can't believe this is happening to us again. This is another nightmare. A worse nightmare. God!'

Mel blinked twice and shook her head to release herself from her thoughts. She turned deliberately and stared at the lifeless body lying in her bedroom. Her jaw expanded as she clenched her teeth. She looked at Nick with a hardness in her eyes. Her attitude had changed and Nick noticed it.

'What?' Nick said, trying to read her thoughts.

'You've got to bury him,' Mel said without a trace of emotion in her voice.

'What?' Nick repeated.

'You've got to bury him like the last one. I don't think anyone saw him enter the house. The street was empty, and anyway, it was dark outside when he arrived.'

'You don't *think* anyone saw him come into the house? Jesus, Mel. Why can't we call the police? He's raped you, for pity's sake. That maniac assaulted you and raped you. Look at your poor face,' said Nick, who was close to tears himself now.

Mel moved over to the dressing table, sat down and studied her reflection in the mirror. Her face was a mess. Her left eye was bloodshot, the surrounding tissue badly swollen and she had an inch-long purple graze down the side of her bloodied nose.

She turned to her husband. 'I'll tell you why we can't call the police. First of all, we've got a dead police officer in our bedroom who was, most likely, well-respected in the force. Secondly, he's died from a seizure of some kind almost certainly brought on by attempted strangulation. How will the law regard that little misdemeanour? How do we know that they won't push for a custodial sentence? It's one of their own, Nick. That changes things. And all this because he raped me.'

Nick had rarely seen his wife like this before – demonstrative – tough. But he knew his wife and how her moods had become unpredictable since the break-in. They could change in the blink of an eye, and it worried Nick. He was concerned that this sudden hard edge was merely a dangerously thin layer between sanity and mental meltdown.

He went to speak but Mel got there first. 'I hate this bastard for doing this to me and I want him shamed. But even if you were found not guilty of causing his death, after what has happened to me, I couldn't stand all the attention it would bring. The media bloody scrum alone would be a nightmare. Can you imagine the publicity this story would attract? And what about the other man you got rid of? We're both guilty of covering that one up. Do we really want the police and the press asking awkward questions and snooping around the house?'

Nick had not thought of the ramifications of their position. He imagined the headlines: POLICEMAN RAPES LOCAL WOMAN THEN DIES OF HEART ATTACK AFTER BEING THROTTLED BY HUSBAND. It was a sensational story that would attract enormous interest.

Did he want prying eyes and hacks with eager-to-be-filled notepads waiting outside his door? And what if someone had seen him driving out late at night in his van, then returning in the early hours of the morning. A shocking story such as this would be just the thing to refresh the memory of that sighting. They could easily try to link it to tonight's incident. Neighbours love idle talk.

Mel continued: 'My life – our lives – would never be the same. It would be impossible to continue living anywhere near here for a start. I've seen how people regard someone who's been through an ordeal like mine.' Mel was on the point of crying once again. 'They stare and point, Nick. They gossip. Worse still, friends and neighbours avoid you. I've done it myself. It's human nature. I wouldn't be Mel, that nice lady at number 24 Bray Road any more. I'd be that poor bloody woman in the papers who was beaten up and raped – whose husband killed a policeman. I can't live like that, Nick. Can you?'

She turned back to look in the mirror. Then the granite face began to melt and was replaced with one of despair. Tears flooded her swollen eyes once more.

Nick sat cross-legged on the carpet, staring at his wife, trying to digest everything she said. He lifted himself up and walked over to where Mel was sitting. He stood behind her and put his hands on her shoulders. 'I just don't know if I can go through with it all again, Mel,' he said.

He too looked at her reflection in the mirror. He saw the injured, wretched face of the woman he loved and the anger in him returned. The words spoken by his wife were beginning to make sense.

Why should he let these bastards, who had ripped apart their sense of security, ruin their lives? If he and Mel were going to have anywhere approaching a normal life again, he knew what he had to do. Nick held Mel's head in his strong hands; he squeezed his eyes shut. 'Okay,' is all he said.

He did not want to have to do this, but Mel's reasoning left him with little option. He had to bury Nathan Ballack. And it was going to be in the same grave as Scrivens.

CHAPTER 35

Nick walked unsteadily downstairs and into the garage, his mind bursting with contradictory emotions. Tonight was to be the beginning of the healing process between them - intimacy, birthday celebrations, optimism – a positive step towards their future. Now those hopes and plans had been shattered.

He collected the other half of the plastic decorator's sheet and dragged it up to the bedroom. He unfolded it on the floor next to Ballack's body.

He was suddenly aware that the situation he found himself in was so shocking, so unspeakable, as to be almost risible. His brain was now labouring between reality and hysteria. He had to hold himself together.

But this was not going to be as easy as the last one. The dead body was upstairs for a start, and this time there was no strong policeman to help him carry the dead corpse from the house to the garage and into the back of his van. The well-built policeman was almost twice the weight of the stick-thin Scrivens.

His wife was on the landing, leaning against the wall outside the bedroom. She had dressed in her casual gear. 'I couldn't stay in the bedroom on my own. Not with him just lying there. I keep thinking he's going to get up and attack me again,' said Mel.

'He won't be attacking anyone ever again, darling. He's stone dead and we have a job to do.' Nick led his wife back into the bedroom. They began to wrap the plastic around the corpse.

'Hold on. Where's his coat?' Mel picked up the leather garment from the corner of the room and together they set about putting it back on him. It was not an easy task. When it was done they rolled the body over onto the sheet and wrapped it around the detective sergeant. As with the first body parcel, Nick tied the two ends securely with garden twine.

'You take his legs. They're not as heavy as the top end,' said Nick. 'We don't need to pick him up just yet. We'll drag him to the top of the stairs, then I'll bump him down from my end on my own. It should be easier to slide him along in the plastic.'

Mel bent down and picked up Nathan's feet. Nick lifted the other end. He noticed his wife looking at Nathan's blue-grey, swollen face that was still visible through the thin wrapping. It was a mistake. Nick saw her swallow more than once to avoid throwing up.

Mel kept her head turned away from the body as Nick started to drag it out of the bedroom and along the landing.

Simply the weight of his legs was enough to make her struggle. At the top of the stairs Mel let go of his feet. They dropped to the carpeted floor with a thump. Nick looked up at Mel once more and noticed the colour had drained from her injured face. He was worried that she might pass out. She was not the strongest of women and he could see that she was still feeling the effects of Nathan's vicious attack.

'You okay?' Nick said. Mel just nodded.

Nick, step by step, slowly bumped the body of their neighbour down the stairs to the bottom. Mel followed behind.

'Right! We slide him into the garage. Then you'll have to help me lift him into the back of the van,' said Nick. Once more he looked with concern towards his wife.

She was now sitting on the second step of the staircase, shivering. He couldn't start to imagine how the memory of the past hour's ordeal must be drilling through her brain. The assault on her slight frame, he could see, had left her weak. Then he noticed that something in the room had attracted her attention. He turned his head to see what it was. Mel had seen the pink roses scattered across the carpet in the middle of the room. She looked back at Nick and began to weep.

Nick sat down on the stairs next to his wife and put his arm around her. 'I am so sorry this has happened, Mel. I would do anything to turn the clock back, but I can't. I don't know why something terrible like this has hit us again, but it has. I love you so much. Nothing will ever change that,' said Nick, as he kissed her forehead.

He pulled her into his chest, trying to inject some of his strength into her battered body, but he had never felt so emasculated in his entire life. 'Are you alright to do this, darling?' Nick asked gently.

Mel looked at her husband. She was not all right, Nick could see that. She must feel wretched, savaged. He prayed that she could just hold on to her sanity.

Mel wiped her eyes and once more the expression on her face changed. 'Yes, I'm all right. Let's get rid of this bastard before I cut him up and feed him to the rats. I want him out of my sight,' she said in a lower register than was normal for her.

It was what Nick needed to hear, although, once again, he was concerned by Mel's conflicting mood swings. But he couldn't manage this task by himself.

Mel picked up the policeman's encased legs, Nick once more took the head end and together they dragged the package across the sitting room and into the garage. Nick opened the back doors of the van, which was fast becoming a makeshift hearse.

The first two attempts at hoisting the heavy body into the back of the van failed. Mel could not hold her end of the body up high enough. The corpse simply slid back down onto the garage floor.

The second time this happened, Nick lost his grip on the plastic cover, the heavy torso slipping from his sweat covered hands. Ballack's head hit the concrete surface of the garage with a sickening crack. The two of them exchanged looks of horror in silence.

This was the man with whom he'd recently been drinking. He had always been suspicious of the detective and his motives, but it still pained him to know that his dead body was wrapped up in plastic in his garage. He suddenly felt sorry for him. *What terrible, twisted kind of past possesses a man to carry out such a heinous act?* he thought.

Then, just as suddenly, he remembered that Ballack had just beaten and raped his wife – a vulnerable, trusting woman who had invited him into her house. He had to retain this thought. That image was the only thing that was going to give him the strength to carry out tonight's deed.

They sat on the floor next to the body exhausted by their efforts. 'This needs some thought,' said Nick. After a few moments, he came up with the solution. He swivelled the body around, took hold of Nathan's feet and dragged him close to the van doors, then hooked his legs over the inside of the rear of the van. Together, they tried to lift his heavy torso up. It was a back-breaking job. After the first attempt they had to lower him back down to the garage floor.

Nick had another idea. On the second attempt Nick, using all his strength, lifted the torso up on his own to a height of two feet and got Mel to wedge a wheelbarrow underneath it. He then rested the top half of his body back down onto the temporary platform. The weighty corpse was now suspended halfway towards their goal.

After pausing to recover his energy levels, Nick, along with Mel, raised the detective up the remaining distance and slid him all the way in. Drained, they both sagged down onto the back of the van, sitting either side of the human package.

The couple looked at each other, waiting for the other to say something. Neither of them spoke. Once again their world had become a place they did not understand or wish to be part of.

After Nick threw the shovel in the van and closed the doors, they left the garage and its gruesome contents in the dark. Now all Nick had to do was to wait until midnight again, when there would be fewer people around to witness his movements. It was six p.m. The next six hours would be the longest of his life.

CHAPTER 36

Jo arrived home just after six p.m. It had been a long and difficult day fending off querying looks from her two male colleagues and persuading Jack to keep her on the Ballack case. At times during this investigation, she had carried forward a small amount of compassion toward her boss for reasons she couldn't really put her finger on. But after the episode in the office kitchen, those feelings had ground to a halt.

Jo was still relatively new to the section. She wanted to be respected by her colleagues, not regarded with suspicion. She had not yet become as battle hardened as she would like. This latest episode was going to test her resolve to the limit. She just hoped that when this was all finished she could work in a close-knit, friendly team again.

She placed her hands behind her back, linked her fingers, stretched her tight shoulders and yawned. She was hoping to move into her new apartment before the end of the year, but she knew from experience that solicitors were not famed for their urgency. She had to find time to keep on her solicitor's case, and then encourage all other parties in the chain to do the same. Then there was the telephone company, electric and gas suppliers, the post office and countless others to inform of her move – the list just went on and on. With everything that was happening at work, Jo realised that the timing of this house move was, at best, unfortunate.

She reached down to the doormat, picked up two circulars offering cheap home insurance, kicked off her black, low-heeled shoes and padded into the sitting room. She stopped by the telephone answering machine. The illuminated red number two was flashing.

The first message was from Mary Shortcliffe, the solicitor handling her house move. There had been a small hitch, she said, involving the vendor of the flat. He had suddenly decided to take his family away to Tenerife for ten days.

'Bugger!' Jo whispered as she listened to the apologetic solicitor. 'Bugger,' she shouted at the small piece of machinery. 'What a time to take a sunshine holiday – lucky sod!'

The second message was from the ever-keen estate agent, Rupert, basically repeating the same information. He hoped it would all go through within a few weeks.

'Thank you, Roop, but I'll believe that when I see it,' Jo said as she erased the messages. She decided not to acknowledge them tonight; she would do that when she got to work in the morning.

Instead, she poured herself a liberal glass of a heavily fruited cabernet sauvignon, sank into her mother's favourite armchair and turned on the telly.

Rupert Whatever-His-Name-Was and Mary Shortcliffe could both wait until tomorrow. Tomorow for Tony

Scrivens? Something told her there were no more tomorrows for that character. And Nathan Ballack? His tomorrows were soon going to be very different from what he was used to.

CHAPTER 37

Shortly after midnight, Nick drove his van out of his garage, down the drive and out onto the road. This time he would take a detour around the grid of minor roads that formed the skeleton of the housing estate to avoid going past the late-night hamburger bar. He did not want a repeat of the incident he had encountered the last time he made this trip. Tonight he prayed he would have a trouble-free journey to and from his destination.

The police, thankfully, had not contacted him concerning the stabbing outside the eatery, but his car registration number would surely be on a CCTV tape somewhere. If they were still monitoring late-night traffic in the vicinity, he did not want his number coming up on their records twice in two weeks and at the same time of the evening.

The traffic that late at night was fairly light so the reappearance of his van could well bring him unnecessary attention. The local paper had reported that three men were being interviewed in connection with the incident. But until there was a conviction and the case was closed, he felt he could not relax.

This time Nick had wedged Nathan's body against the side of the van with a large bag of sharp sand. Hopefully the heavy weight would stop it sliding around like the last one. It was bad enough having a dead body in the back of his vehicle; he didn't want to hear it shifting about every time he braked or turned a corner. It spooked him. It was as though the corpse was struggling to escape from the suffocating polythene shroud.

After weaving his way through the minor roads of his housing estate, he arrived at the far side of the shopping precinct. There, he turned onto the long main road leading to Dunley Marsh. He was just commending himself on his decision to bypass the high street and avoid prying eyes and CCTV cameras when the clouds opened. Down came the rain – raging rivers of it. His windscreen was immediately awash.

This was the last thing Nick wanted. Traversing the narrow strips of land through the boggy terrain of the marsh had been tricky enough on the first occasion, but this time it would be hazardous. There was now the very real danger of his van skidding off the snaking, muddy pathways and dumping straight into the swamp. It would also make the exhausting job of burying a body much harder and extremely messy.

Nick switched on the wipers but still struggled to see the road in front of him. He moved them on to the fastest speed, which just threw more of the deluge across his line of vision. The orange tail lights of the car in front of him were now just a blur.

He moved down into third gear and slowed the van to fifteen miles an hour. Just as he did so, he heard a screech of brakes behind him. He gripped the steering wheel and braced himself for an expected impact. The contact from behind was, mercifully, fairly light, shunting his van forwards a few yards.

'Sod it,' he said. He would now have to pull his vehicle over, get out and check the damage to his car. As much as he would have preferred to ignore the minor collision and simply drive on, he knew it would appear suspicious to the other driver.

Nick cursed his luck as he pulled his van into the side of the road and applied the handbrake. He kept the engine running to prevent the front windscreen misting up. He sat in his car for a few moments, peering through a wall of cold December rain, hoping it would let up before he had to get out. But the heavens were still throwing everything they had at him. Just as he was about to give in to the torrent there was a tap on the front passenger window. Nick pressed a button on the inside of the door and the rain-spattered piece of glass slid slowly down.

'I'm terribly sorry. I couldn't see a bloody thing, and all of a sudden there you were, right in front of me.'

Nick looked up to see an elderly gentleman dressed in a brown checked sports jacket and gold corduroy trousers. A striped club tie over a plain white shirt completed the smart but dated outfit. It struck Nick that this man had probably attended a social function that evening. He was sheltering beneath a large, multi-coloured golf umbrella.

He leant forwards through the open window, closer to Nick. 'I've had a quick look at your bumper and there only appears to be a very slight dent. No other damage that I can make out, but it's pretty filthy out here,' he continued. 'I think you ought to check it out for yourself. I have a rather large umbrella here that should do for the both of us.' Nick detected a faint smell of alcohol on the gentleman's breath as he spoke.

'Uh, Okay,' Nick agreed, somewhat reluctantly. The old gentleman walked around to the driver's door of the van and waited for him to get out.

Nick had been driving for over fifteen years and he could not remember the last time he'd had an on-road confrontation. The fact that he'd had two in two weeks and at times when he was ferrying dead bodies about in his vehicle was beyond belief. He could feel his pulse tripping across his forehead from one temple to the other as if it were on a telephone wire.

He turned towards the back of his van. The body was still securely anchored under the weight of the sandbag. Even if part of the bundle was visible from where the gentleman was standing, the dismal conditions and torrential rain would make it impossible, surely, to determine what it was.

'I'm sure the damage will be minimal; it was only a slight nudge,' Nick said as he climbed out of the van under the shelter of the elderly man's umbrella. They walked towards the rear of the vehicle. All around them bullets of rain were exploding against the tarmac, bouncing up over their shoes and peppering the lower half of their trousers.

As they reached the back of the van the old gentleman produced a torch from his jacket pocket and shined it on the bumper. The dent was hardly noticeable. Nick looked at the front of the other man's car.

It was an old Volvo Estate, the nearest thing on the road to a tank. Unsurprisingly, there appeared to be no visible damage at all. The front bumper of the Volvo was sturdy and lined with rubber and looked like it could have demolished a brick-built outside toilet without causing so much as a scratch.

'I'll fetch my insurance details for you. Just in case you find more damage in the daylight,' the old gentleman declared. He moved the torch up the rear doors of the van and onto the two small windows at the top of the doors to check for more damage. The light was now shining straight through the square windows and into the van.

'No, please. That won't be necessary. It's an old van, and to be honest that dent could've been there before.' The plastic-sheeted body was now clearly visible to both of them. *Please put that damn torch out,* Nick pleaded silently.

'No damage to anything inside, is there?' The man was looking straight at the wrapped corpse of Nathan Ballack as he spoke.

Nick froze. He prayed that the shape of the bundle did not resemble a human body. He looked the smartly attired gentleman in the eyes. 'No, there's nothing in there of any real worth,' he said. And he was telling the truth.

'Right, okay. Now, are you sure you don't want my details?' the gentleman repeated. The last thing Nick wanted to do was to swap insurance details and names and addresses. He wanted this incident forgotten as soon as possible. And if the old fella had been drinking, he was sure that he too would want as little fuss as possible.

'No. Absolutely sure,' Nick replied. He looked through the front windscreen of the Volvo and for the first time he noticed someone sitting in the passenger seat. It was a very distinguished-looking lady of a similar age to the gentleman –

presumably it was his wife. The poor lady was looking very worried, as if she was expecting Nick to punch her husband on the nose. He waved at her and forced a smile.

'Well, that's very decent of you,' said the gentleman as he walked Nick back to the van door. 'Maybe you should let me go off first. You'll feel safer that way,' he joked. 'Okay, cheerio,' he said, as he walked back to his tank.

Nick sat in his van as the rain drummed a frantic beat on the metal roof. He took the gentleman's advice and waited for the Volvo to pull out onto the road. He watched it disappear into the rain-washed murky distance. Then he let his head fall back onto the headrest. 'Fuck me!' he said to the ceiling of the van. 'This is killing me. What are the chances?' He squeezed air out through his teeth that made a loud hissing noise. 'If this is all a dream, please, please let me wake up,' he added, with a shake of his head.

CHAPTER 38

Throughout the rest of his journey, Nick lapsed into a semi-trance-like state. His brain had reached the precarious stage of overload and the only way he could cope with the reality of his position was to recall the sight of Ballack drilling into his beaten, defenceless wife. But even that image could not erase the terrible guilt that engulfed him.

As he sat behind the wheel with the detective's body lying behind him, he felt as if he had been transported into a life that he had only read about in crime thrillers. He was the main protagonist – he was the killer. The thought made his heart feel weak. The fact that he had defended his home and his wife from attack should have made him feel, if not proud, at least worthy. But he felt none of these things. Now, he was tainted. He was unclean.

His actions, though not premeditated, scared the hell out of Nick. *Most people have a pretty good idea of who they are, however inaccurate their assessment may be. They have an innate sense of identity. I'm losing mine fast,* he thought.

More than once he angled down the rear-view mirror in his van and looked at his reflection. His face had changed. It was cautious, sickened, defensive. What he saw in his reflection emanated from the dark recesses that had taken up residence behind his tortured eyes – eyes that had witnessed more than any benign soul should ever see – recesses that harboured untreatable wounds. The grievous events of these recent weeks had tilted, forever, his perspective of right and wrong.

As he drove on towards his destination, he watched the cars through the teeming rain as they approached and passed on the opposite side of the road. Each time, they threw up a wave of rainwater that battered the side of his van, every splash making him flinch. He wondered how many of these road users had terrible secrets such as his. How many times had he driven past vehicles that concealed a dead body, a hostage, an illegal immigrant, a massive consignment of drugs, an arsenal of weapons? He used to believe that most people led ordinary, guilt-free lives. Tonight he questioned that belief.

Then the sign jolted him out of his self-analytical state: *DUNLEY MARSH 1/2 MILE.*

The heavy rain continued to fall as Nick once again made the right turn onto the road that led into the stinking swampland. This was the third time in a matter of weeks that he had visited the unsavoury location. He promised himself it would be his last. As he struggled to see through the rain-lashed windscreen, policed by the frantic, mind-numbing rhythm of the wipers, he was suddenly gripped by uncertainty.

Would he be able to find the same spot where he had buried his intruder? It was only a fortnight ago that he had driven to this destination, but as he proceeded slowly along the road each gloomy left turn appeared to look the same as the previous one. He should have counted the turnings from the main road when he was here before. But that's ridiculous, he thought to himself. He was hardly expecting to return here with the same task in mind.

He was painfully aware that part of this extensive area of marshland was to be declared a wildlife sanctuary, according to Mr Brown, drawing more people to the location than before, but he had no choice. He knew of no other place of such desolation at which to perform his ghastly operation. And there was less chance of one grave, rather than two, being discovered.

Thinking he recognised the narrow track he had taken on his first visit, Nick turned down the unlit route only to arrive at a dead end after fifty yards or so. With no room to turn his van around he had to reverse all the way back along the winding, muddy track. Turning his head around, he tried to avoid looking at the wrapped corpse as he peered through the small rear windows.

Due to the constant rain, his vision through the water-streaked glass was greatly restricted. The delicate manoeuvre was made more difficult by the fear-induced tension in his body that constricted the movement of his spine. The muscles across the top of his shoulders felt like blocks of wood. It was a slow and tricky process making it back to the minor road.

Now hopelessly confused and close to panic, Nick took the next left turn and just prayed that this was the correct one. When, after a short distance, the track split into two he felt sure he had guessed right this time. He took the narrower left fork.

Once more, he had to negotiate the slender, twisting pathway to reach his destination. The persistent rain confirmed Nick's worst fears – the mud and slime had increased twofold since the last time he was here. Crawling along in first gear with his face inches from the windscreen, he guided his small-wheeled, hopelessly inadequate van along the treacherous strands of earth. Never in his life had his powers of concentration been put under such enormous pressure.

The stinking water from the swamp had risen an inch or two since his last visit and was now beginning to lap over the muddy path that he was crawling along. It suddenly became apparent to Nick that if this downpour did not stop soon, the winding route back would have disappeared completely.

The journey to the clearing where Nick had buried Scrivens' body seemed never-ending. Just as Nick began to question whether he had indeed taken the correct path, the route took a sharp bend to the left, revealing the very glade he was searching for.

Nick breathed a deep sigh of relief as he momentarily relaxed. It was a big mistake. With his vision now locked on to his destination some fifty yards away, he lost concentration on his immediate surroundings, failing to see the enormous pothole in front of the van. The right front wheel plunged and twisted into the deep hollow, wrenching the steering wheel from his grasp, causing two of the fingers of his right hand to be forced violently backwards. 'Ow, shit!' Nick yelped in pain.

Now out of control, the rear of the van slewed to the right towards the quagmire.

Nick grabbed the wheel again, turning it hard right to counteract the skidding vehicle. The van straightened for a few yards, but before he could turn the wheel left again, the front of the van lurched right and headed straight for the swamp. His right foot hit the brake. It had no effect as the van kept sliding forwards across the sludge-covered surface of the causeway.

Just as he was convinced he was going to plunge into the filthy water, something astonishing happened. The van, still only travelling at ten miles an hour, came to an immediate stop with a bone-shuddering thump.

The sandbag and the body in the back slid forward at speed, hitting the rear of the driver's seat. This time Nick was ready for the impact – he locked his arms and braced his spine. The only real pain he felt was in his two sprained fingers that gripped the steering wheel.

Nick put the gear stick into neutral, applied the handbrake and left the engine running. Without knowing what damage the van had sustained, he feared that if he turned the engine off, he may not get it to start again.

Thankfully, the rain had eased to a fine drizzle as he got out of his van and walked to the front. There it was – his salvation. A dead but sturdy tree stump on the margin of the swamp had halted his journey into the dark depths of the stinking quagmire. 'Jesus! How lucky was that?' Nick whispered into the cold, dank air. He watched his breath turn to vapour and disappear up into the black, wet blanket of the night.

He bent down and checked the van for damage. The front bumper and number plate had been dented but nothing, as far as he could see, had broken off in the collision. He bent lower and scoured the ground beneath the front of the vehicle. He did not want to leave any evidence of his presence in this hellhole.

Nick climbed back into his van and put it in reverse. After an initial scraping sound, the van responded to his commands as he positioned the vehicle in the middle of the path once more. He pushed the gear stick forwards, drove carefully towards the clearing, turned the van full circle and switched off the engine.

He shook his head, puffed up his cheeks and expelled a noisy wodge of air. 'Well, that's the easy part over,' he announced, rolling his eyes.

Nick moved round to the back of the scrub, switched on his torch and inspected the burial site. Apart from the added rain across the surface, it was exactly as he left it. When he went to collect his shovel the rain increased in volume once more.

'Thanks! Thank you very much. That's all I bloody need.' He was not sure whom he was thanking when he spoke, as his belief in God had dissolved substantially during the events of the past fortnight. And if God did exist, he certainly did not want to be having a conversation with Him during this evening's proceedings.

With his torch wedged between the tree branches once more, he removed the bracken from the saturated surface and got to work digging out the loose earth from the recently dug grave. Within a few minutes he was soaked to the skin. The rain-drenched earth had turned to cloying mud and was getting heavier to shift by the minute. The handle of the shovel became difficult to control as it twisted and slithered through his slippery, mud-spattered hands. Each time he thrust the slime-covered tool down into the deepening grave it caused his sprained fingers agonising pain.

Nick was aware that using the same burial plot as Scrivens was going to be a particularly objectionable task; knowing that the rotting remains of the thief were lying in wait for him. But apart from one grave being the safer bet, the earth would still be loose and easier to remove, and the spot he'd found was by far the best he'd seen and unlikely to be stumbled upon.

After an hour and a half of relentless digging Nick's shovel hit an immovable object. There was an abrupt snapping sound as the blade sliced through two of Scrivens' ribs. It was then that the putrid stench hit his nostrils. His head jerked away from the decomposing body – an instant reflex action - his stomach muscles tightening as he fought the urge to retch.

Suddenly, the enormous mental and physical strain of what he was doing took hold and exploded inside his chest. He let out an anguished cry into the rain-lashed night, the intensity of which could have been heard by anyone within a mile of the locality, but never could it have been attributed to that of a human – it was the sound of an animal in torment, a cry of a soul in pain pushed to the limit of endurance.

The emotion was so powerful that it surprised Nick. He looked up into the grim night sky and, with the rain blinding his vision, he began to weep – openly, loudly. The volume of rain could have represented his tears such was the powerful release of grief and regret that bled from his battered spirit.

It was a good few minutes before Nick regained his strength of will. It took another ten minutes to clear a space next to the body of his intruder large enough to house the second occupant within the muddy tomb. Every so often he had to turn his head away from his task as the acrid smell of Scrivens' remains wafted up and attacked the lining of his nostrils. The odour was so pungent his taste buds were clogged up with it. It was as if he had just eaten part of the putrefying corpse. It sickened him.

He now had to get out of the slippery-sided hole to complete his mission. Using his shovel as an aid, Nick scrambled out of the pit, exhausted, and headed for the body of the detective. With cold, stiffening hands, he pulled Ballack's heavy corpse from the van and dragged it to the graveside. He then rolled him out of the plastic sheet and into the hole. The body landed partly in the gap that Nick had created and partly across Scrivens' legs.

'Damn it!' he said. Not happy with the position of the second corpse, Nick climbed back down into the open grave with the two bodies. And, whilst standing on top of Scrivens, he shifted Ballack's mud-spattered head and shoulders, using every last ounce of his strength, across and into the narrow gap. Then, using his feet, he wedged the policeman's body down and in line with the one he was standing on.

As he did so, he looked into the policeman's face. It was impossible to equate the dough-like, lifeless visage with that of the overbearing, animated personality in the pub just a fortnight ago. A swarm of emotions tickertaped through his brain. He hated what he was doing; he despised what had happened to his beautiful wife; he detested standing in the rain on two muddy, rotting corpses. They, alone, had taken the decision to go beyond society's accepted rules of behaviour. But in retaliation, so had he.

With that thought in mind, he struggled, once more, from the slimy tomb, turned and stood on the edge. He looked down at the grey, odious corpses. This was their tragic fate. *What will be mine?* he thought, as he trembled by the graveside.

CHAPTER 39

It took another hour of muscle-tearing labour to fill in the grave and cover it over with the surrounding bracken. Finally, Nick climbed, exhausted, into his van and pulled forwards ten yards. He killed the engine, got out and walked back to inspect the scene once again.

There were a few deep sets of footprints and tyre marks he could not completely remove from the sodden earth. He hoped the continuing deluge would eventually wash them away. He had done all he could to minimise his presence there. Now it was time to leave this wretched place of gloom and never return.

He sat at the wheel of his van, soaked from head to foot, coated in foul-smelling sludge. Once again he had to negotiate the greasy, gnarled fingers of land where every twist and turn threatened potential disaster. He switched on the ignition. Good! No screaming birds this time. Then, just as he was about to leave, a small orange light on the dashboard caught his eye. It was the low fuel warning indicator.

'Petrol. Oh, shit!' His mind had been in such turmoil that he had not even thought to check that the van had enough petrol on his departure. How long had the light been on? That was the vital question.

If he had been driving his Jaguar, a warning light would have appeared and a short beeping noise would have followed to alert him when the fuel had dropped to a certain level. In addition, a gauge on the dashboard would have shown how many driving miles he had left before it ran out. The van had no such modern technology. The fuel was low but he had no way of knowing how low. The light could have been on for miles without his knowledge.

If he ran out of petrol on his way back through the muddy paths of the swamp, he was done for. There was no way he could push the vehicle through the narrow, slimy passages back to the main road, and ringing any call-out service was obviously out of the question. He would have to leave the van there and head off in the pouring rain to find a service station. The only one he knew of that was open was the one he had used a fortnight ago and that was eight miles away.

He pulled back the saturated sleeve of his jacket. He looked at his watch – three twenty a.m. If or when he found somewhere to buy a small can and fill it with petrol, by the time he made it back to the van it would be daylight. His van would surely be seen and someone was bound to remember seeing a drenched figure trudging along the roadside in the early hours of the morning.

This was not good.

'Not clever, Nick,' he said to himself. His cold, partially numb hand pushed the gear stick into first and, edging his vehicle forwards, he left the gloomy scene and headed off through the swamp.

The journey back to the main road was slow and nerve-shredding with his van sliding perilously close to the crumbling edges of the watery bog at every turn. As he feared, dips in the path were now overflowing with swamp water. This made it impossible to see clearly the margins of the way ahead.

Keeping the mud-clogged wheels on the track through some of these large, murky puddles was pure guesswork. He was also aware of driving the van's engine constantly in first gear – the worst possible way to proceed as far as fuel economy was concerned.

On three occasions, each for just a split second, he allowed his eyes to leave the route ahead to glance at the fuel gauge that was nudging closer and closer to the "empty" pin in the glass-covered dial.

His overtaxed body had withdrawn into a ball of taut muscles and strained tendons as his breathing became shallow. He dared not move in his seat as he drove on. He held the irrational thought that if he kept stock still, he would make the van more stable and therefore cut down on fuel consumption throughout its undulating journey.

After a ten-minute mud-splashed safari from hell, to Nick's immense relief he reached the main road without serious mishap.

He desperately needed petrol, but the detour to the twenty-four-hour service station to clean his van would have to be abandoned this time. Nick realised that the sight of him and his vehicle pulling up on the forecourt in such a state would draw too much attention to himself, even in the early hours of the morning.

At least he had made it to the main road. Now he just hoped that he could make it home with whatever fuel he had left in the bottom of his tank. He would give his van a thorough scrubbing later that day, but it would have to be in the confines of his garage.

As Nick drove towards the village of Bourne, his wet clothes started to chill his bones. But he dared not turn the heater on in case that used up more fuel. 'Too many things to think of,' he said to himself, 'too many bridges to cross.'

He knew he had to unearth reserves of mental strength, an ounce of positive thought, to get him through this. His sanity had been tested to the limit – he was not sure he'd passed the test. Was it really him that had carried out these mind-shattering operations?

He suddenly thought of the pregnant Cathy Ballack and her two small children. If Nathan had survived, she would have had to live with the knowledge that her husband had raped her best friend and had gone to prison. Nick's confused mind could not decide whether or not his disappearance had made it less painful for Cathy. But the reality was, she no longer had a husband and three small children will have lost a father. An unbearable feeling of remorse swept over his shivering body as he wept once more.

Just then, the rain stopped beating down on his van. As the deluge ceased so his mind was able to view his own personal journey ahead more clearly. Would he feel like this for the rest of his life? Christ! That could be fifty years. The possibility was too much to contemplate. He wondered if his conscience would one day grant him peace of mind. At that moment, he didn't hold out too much hope.

CHAPTER 40

Nick made it home just after four a.m. The dregs of petrol had done their job - luck was on his side. As he drove up the road towards his home, he was thankful that the surrounding houses were in complete darkness. Mel had not waited up for him this time and, considering her mental and physical state, he had not expected her to.

After he had driven his mud-covered van into the garage, he closed the external door. He stood shivering in the utility room as he stripped naked and bundled all his clothes into a black bin liner. Then he took them out again, realising that the sodden garments would be impossible to burn in the morning.

He returned to the garage and draped them across the steaming bonnet of his van. Tomorrow, after he had cleaned the vehicle, he would start another bonfire and burn the evidence once again.

Exhausted, Nick climbed the stairs, shuffled quietly past the closed door to his bedroom, and headed for the bathroom. As he stood beneath the shower, he allowed, for the second time that night, a torrent of water to splash over his upturned face. But on this occasion it was hot, thawing and welcome. Never did he think a shower could feel so wonderful, so cleansing.

He reached out his right hand to grab the shower gel from the steel, wall-mounted tray; a sharp pain shot through his two injured fingers. He winced in agony as he examined the damage. They were badly swollen and caused him great discomfort whenever he made a gripping motion with them. He decided he would be delegating any physical aspects of landscaping to his workforce over the next week or so.

Then he noticed it. While he was holding his right hand his attention was suddenly drawn to his left. Where his wedding ring used to be there was now just a white band of skin. His jaw gaped open. 'Oh no! Oh Christ! Where did I lose that?'

His mind raced through the night's proceedings. He came to the conclusion that because his hands were so cold and slimy, it had to have slipped off when he was digging or filling in the grave. It had probably been buried along with the two corpses.

He decided to tell Mel that he had lost it a few days ago, whilst working in a local garden. To tell her the truth would have only added to her worries. He was annoyed with himself; he loved that ring. It was so unusual, with the beautiful oval diamond set in the top. He knew Mel would be upset.

More to the point, he thought, it was an incriminating piece of evidence. If those bodies were ever discovered in the bowels of Dunley Marsh there was a fair chance they would also find the ring. Once again he recalled reading that everyone makes mistakes, however small, when a crime is committed. He had just made a huge one.

He stepped from the shower, towelled himself down and left the bathroom.

When he entered his bedroom, Mel was in a deep but restless sleep. He slipped in quietly beside her. She was lying away from him in the foetal position; strangled moans were coming from deep within her throat. God knows what nightmares she was having to endure; in which menacing, grim pantomime she was an unwilling player. He realised that he had many similar dreams to come.

He pressed the side of his unshaven face deep into the soft cotton pillow. It felt good. His skin, which had been so cold for much of the night, was now tingling from the hot water of the shower.

Every component of his body seemed to ache. He could not remember ever feeling so totally drained, mentally and physically.

As he lay in the darkness, a muddle of thoughts, once again, whirred around his brain like autumn leaves in a vortex: it would be impossible to ever tell anyone their terrible secret – even their closest family. They could not pretend that it never happened. It had happened. But he asked himself repeatedly, *was he wicked?*

He supposed, in the eyes of the law, he was. But he hadn't planned to play the leading role in this macabre drama; to break into someone's house; to rape a friend's wife. He was now searching for some scrap of redemption, scrabbling around in his brain for a not guilty verdict. It remained elusive.

Tired and confused, Nick closed his eyes and prayed to join another world. One in which he was happily married to a beautiful woman, with two healthy children and a long and disaster-free future ahead of him.

On the edge of sleep, Nick's disturbed brain started to recall the graphic images of his Uncle John's lifeless body lying in the blood-drenched gutter. He had no idea that day how that seminal incident would infuse him with an almost unnatural sense of survival. It was two years after his beloved uncle was killed that those seeds of guilt and anger first sprouted shoots. The day, that was an imprint on his mind, started to roll.

*

Seventeen years earlier

Hungry eyes looked up intermittently, gauging the progress towards freedom. There it was – one more, hardly noticeable, downward twitch. Off went the high-pitched siren.

Thirty bottoms lifted off identical chairs in a cacophony of noise. The excitement in the room that would be evacuated in less than thirty seconds was almost palpable. It was twelve thirty – lunch-time.

The navy blue procession of boys and girls, struggling through the fourteenth year of their lives, poured out of the classroom and hurried down the grey stone staircase boasting and gossiping their way towards the playground. The area was a sixty-by-sixty yard square of concrete standing in the shadow of the three-storey Edwardian building that housed the school.

Nicholas left his stampeding Year Nine classmates at the top of the stairs. He turned left and hurried along the corridor to the toilet. For the last ten minutes he had been struggling to cope with a bulging bladder that felt as if it was the size of a cow's udder – a consequence of too much cola consumed during mid-morning break.

His mission complete, he headed back to the stairs where he bumped into Mr Millis, the history teacher from his last lesson. A worn briefcase dangled limply from one arm, a pile of textbooks cradled in the other.

Mr Millis was now eyeing Nicholas Summers. 'Summers. Why aren't you in the playground?' enquired the teacher.

'Just going now, sir,' replied Nicholas.

'Hearing promising things about you, lad. Flying high. But don't forget: the measure of a man is the way he bears up under misfortune,' said Mr Millis with a tight smile.

'Yes, sir. Thank you, sir,' said Nicholas. He turned and hurried down the stairs, confused as to whether or not the teacher had just given him a compliment.

By the time he reached the playground it was already swarming with eleven-to-seventeen-year-olds. Some stood in small groups talking, others were playing ball games. The area was enclosed by an eight-foot high wood-panelled fence with a ribbon of grey wire mesh that ran along the top.

Nicholas headed for a circle of friends who were throwing a rugby ball around between them. He walked past two girls from his class who were sitting on a low wall that ran along the back of the school. The girls checked out Nicholas and giggled.

He smiled politely at them and continued his journey.

Above a fresh and slightly freckled face sat a mop of casually styled, deep brown hair that fell across one eye in a deliberate attempt to look cool. Although he appeared rather coy, Nicholas enjoyed the attention he received from some of the girls in his age group.

'Ooh, Nicholas! We love you,' shouted one of his mates, noticing the female attention he had attracted. Nicholas looked up just in time to see a rugby ball hurtling towards his face – he caught it an inch from his nose.

He grinned and, with mock anger, threw the ball back at his friends. Constant teasing amongst the boys was not the most enjoyable part of school life. But being popular with a few schoolgirls was a taunt he could happily live with.

When he joined the circle, the rugby ball continued to be propelled back and forth between the lads. Then, as the ball was on its way to Nicholas again, he was barged sideways by an overweight fifth former. The lout intercepted the oval missile in flight.

'Whose ball is this?' asked the intruder. He stood in the middle of the crowd, pushing his chest out like a prize cockerel and scouring the apprehensive faces before him.

The intruder was one Bruno Doyle. He stood just short of six feet, his large head set deep into round shoulders, his unkempt hair straw-like, the colour of butterscotch. He and his three followers badgered and stole from any unfortunate boy who happened to be in their ear-twisting proximity.

The gang of four, all Year Eleven students, were considerably bigger than Nicholas and his friends.

The once animated, ball-playing group was suddenly motionless as if turned to stone. They said nothing.

'It wouldn't be yours, Summers, would it?' asked Bruno, locking his cruel eyes onto the young schoolboy. He moved closer. 'I've been hearing things about you. Top of your class in exams, little star in the rugby team. You flash little wanker. Mr Perfect Pants. Bet you're a little mummy's boy as well, eh?' said Bruno, slapping him around the side of the head.

Nicholas blinked and tried not to appear hurt. 'Can we have our ball back, please?'

'Okay, I'll give it back. Here you go,' glared Bruno as he leant back and threw it clean over the school boundary fence. 'Happy now, Summers?' said Bruno, his eyebrows disappearing into his unruly fringe. The three other members of Bruno's gang cackled excitedly.

'And you call *me* a wanker,' Nicholas said quietly.

Bruno lurched forward, grabbed the lapels of Nicholas' school blazer and pushed him up against a nearby wall. 'What did you call me, you little shit?' The bully spat the words out inches from Nicholas's face. Immediately, the leader's trio of henchmen surrounded Nicholas like ravenous hyenas around a cornered gazelle.

Bruno took hold of Nicholas' tie, pulling him forward with a sharp jolt. He rapped him hard on the top of his head with his knuckles. This time Nicholas winced, crying out in pain. One of the gang kicked him on the left shin bone, another did the same to his other leg. Bruno, enjoying the pain he could now see on his victim's face, started to tighten the tie around Nicholas's throat.

Nicholas was on his own and this assault was becoming serious. At that moment he became terrified. All at once, he was his Uncle John, surrounded by a gang of feral youngsters.

Visions of his distraught auntie weeping over the crumpled figure of her husband's body flashed in front of his eyes. This time he couldn't stand back and watch helplessly. It was then that his brain responded to his position of danger.

He managed to reach his right hand across his chest and into the breast pocket of his blazer. There he found what he was looking for – his fountain pen.

As he pulled it from his pocket, he received a vicious punch to his left arm. The pain shot through the whole left side of his body. He very nearly dropped the pen. The blows were beginning to drain his strength. It had to be now, before it was too late.

With his right thumb he flicked off the top of the pen. He slid his arm from between him and his assailant. Then, with all his strength, he stabbed Bruno in the face. The upward motion of the sharp nib penetrated the bully's cheek and drove clean through to the inside of his mouth. The weapon came to a halt only when it collided with his first upper molar.

Howling like a baby, Bruno leapt back in agony. His cowardly cohorts, seeing the blue-black, bloody facial wound, retreated as one with similar haste.

There followed a few seconds of stunned silence. Eventually, someone spoke. 'You're a fucking maniac, Summers,' was all one of the gang could say as they led their bleeding fallen hero away. The young boy's desperate action had the desired effect – the confrontation was instantly terminated.

The incident was never reported to the authorities, much to his surprise. Bruno Doyle had an awesome reputation throughout the school. His pride would not allow him to whinge to the teachers that he'd been attacked and defeated by a mere Year Nine student. He pretended for the remainder of his school education that the incident meant nothing to him.

But stories such as this: that occur within school walls – whispered down endless, resonating corridors – spread like petrol fires. For the remainder of his time at school, he was never threatened again. For a good while afterwards, he was the playground hero. It was a tag he did not enjoy.

*

Recalling from so many years ago the instantaneous defensive reaction to the threat of attack suddenly had a pivotal effect on Nick. At that moment, as he lay in bed, it made him realise that his uncle's death had left him with a thick seam of scar tissue hidden deep within his personality. Its two main components – guilt and anger – were like an ulcer waiting to burst.

In light of his current predicament, Nick had just learnt two important facts about himself: he could be irrational, but he wasn't a coward. Regrettably, unlike most individuals who attempt to make a stand against life's dark forces, his actions, this time, had resulted in disastrous consequences, he had turned two terrible accidents into full-blown crimes.

He turned over, away from his wife. The eighteen inches that separated them, at that moment, may as well have been eighteen miles. His eyes closed. Seconds later, his body drifted off into a storm-tossed sleep full of despair and regret.

CHAPTER 41

Jo Major was deep in thought as she sat behind her office desk on the morning of Tuesday 15th December. She looked at her watch for the fourth time in under an hour: it was ten fifteen. Nathan had not turned up for work and there had been no phone call from his wife to say he was sick. His time-keeping had not been too good recently, but he had never been this late into the office.

Mark and Colin were busy on their computers. They had their hands full working on the Peckham case, trying to locate the whereabouts of the illusive Rent. Neither of them had commented on Nathan's absence. More to the point, neither of them seemed to care. Detective Sergeant Nathan Ballack had long ceased to be the respected boss he once was. But Jo sensed something was wrong.

She had already made contact this morning with the DPS, who had informed her that, after a lengthy session in the pub, Ballack had driven home. That was when the surveillance had stopped. Jo had not been happy about that; at this crucial point in the investigation she had wanted him watched twenty-four seven.

She had made it clear to them that she thought things were coming to a head. But she knew the DPS lot were a law unto themselves. They made the decisions on how, when and where they carried out their enquiries, and Jo had to respect that. But it appeared that the same level of respect, much to Jo's frustration, was not reciprocated.

During the conversation, the subject of budgetary restrictions had emerged as a contributory factor in their decision to limit the tail after the subject had been housed. It was an argument that was difficult to contend.

But she had an uneasy feeling in the pit of her stomach that would not go away; a suspicion that something significant had gone on last night and it had been missed.

By eleven o'clock there was still no word from Ballack.

'Has Nathan called in sick?' asked Colin eventually, looking up from his computer.

'No. Well, not that I'm aware of,' Jo replied.

'He must have pushed the boat out last night then,' said Mark, as he walked back from the kitchen with three cups of coffee.

'Yeah, well, it's a shame he couldn't get the same bloody boat into work this morning,' said Jo. The remark got a chuckle from her two colleagues, but Jo was in no mood for light-hearted banter. She was worried.

She wanted to let Jack Jolley know that Nathan had not turned up for work, but she decided to phone Cathy Ballack first. She hoped there would be an acceptable explanation for his absence and thus avoid having to go into Jack's office again.

Jo dialled the number. The phone rang, unanswered, for a good thirty seconds. Then, just as she was about to hang up, a barely audible voice at the other end spoke.

'Hello?'

'Hello. Cathy?' said Jo.

'No.' There was a pause. 'This is Tom.'

'Hello, Tom, darling. This is Jo Major. No school today?'

'No. Mum says we don't have to go today. She phoned the teacher.'

'Oh, you lucky boy. Is your mother there, please?'

'I think she's upstairs in bed. I'll go and get her.'

'No, don't worry if she's...' But it was too late. Jo heard Tom put the receiver down and call out to his mother. The alarm bells started to ring in Jo's mind. If she had kept the kids off school because she wasn't feeling well, where was Nathan?

After a short pause she heard Cathy's distant, shouted voice. 'You can put the phone back on its cradle now, Tom.' Then she said into the phone, 'Hello?'

'Cathy, it's Jo. I was wondering whether everything was okay? Nathan hasn't come in this morning.'

There was another pause, then Cathy replied, 'I don't have a clue where he is, Jo, and I don't care.' For a moment Jo was stuck for something to say. She had not been prepared for such an answer. She was now torn between apologising for ringing her at home and delving into the reasons for her unexpected reply.

The decision was taken away from her as Cathy said, 'We had a terrible argument yesterday when Nathan came home.' She began to cry as she struggled to continue. 'He walked out immediately afterwards and I haven't seen him since. He said he was going down the pub. He's a violent, selfish bastard, Jo, and if it wasn't for the children, I'd be happy never to see him again.'

The word *violent* did not come as a shock to Jo. But now she was concerned. 'Are you okay?' she asked.

The immediate reply she got was increased sobbing down the telephone line. 'Mmm... I think so. He hit me, Jo,' Cathy replied after a short while.

Yes, I know he's a selfish, aggressive bastard only too well, thought Jo. She had witnessed in the office kitchen his threatening behaviour towards her and the evil look in his eye, but she had never actually seen the violent side of Ballack. She just hoped that her drug-dealing boss had not caused any lasting damage to his wife and her unborn child.

She realised immediately that this latest development had added another dimension to the investigation. She had to find out exactly how much Cathy knew of her husband's misdemeanours. Any extra information could help the enquiry and may provide a clue as to his whereabouts.

The time for diplomacy had passed. 'Cathy, we have to speak. There are certain things I think you need to know.'

'I think I may already know what you want to tell me,' replied Cathy.

'Can I come over, please?' asked Jo.

Jo heard Cathy sigh deeply. 'Yes, okay.'

'I've just got to run a few things past my supervisor, but I should be over in the next hour. Bye, Cathy.' But Cathy had already hung up.

Jo got up from her desk, grabbed her jacket from the back of her chair and headed straight for Jack Jolley's office. Colin and Mark were now looking over in her direction, aware that something clandestine was going on. She could not worry about their suspicions any more; she had to let her boss know of this latest development.

Jack listened to the details of Jo's phone call to Cathy Ballack. Jo noted the look of frustrated anger on his face when she told him of Ballack's attack on his wife.

When Jo had finished her account, he stood up from his imposing chair. There was no meditative chin-tapping with the pen routine this time. 'Right. Pay Cathy Ballack a visit and see what else you can find out about Nathan's whereabouts. What were the bloody DPS doing, ceasing surveillance on him last night.'

Jo was about to speak but Jack continued, 'I'll inform them of this latest development. If he has gone AWOL, there's a good chance he's warned his suppliers. So that's probably gone down the Swanee for the moment.'

Jack picked up the phone from his desk and began to dial. Jo watched him as he leant forwards and stroked his nose while waiting for someone to answer his call. It reminded her of her beloved father, who had the same habit whenever a problem arose. It was then that she realised why she so enjoyed her visits to Jack's office.

As Jack started to speak on the telephone, he looked up to see Jo still standing in front of him. 'Just a second,' he said. He put his hand over the mouthpiece. 'Well, go on. What you waiting for?' he said to his DC.

'Oh! Okay, guv,' said Jo, not realising her boss had finished with her. She turned to leave.

'And listen – Ballack's wife. I know she's just been given a right hander, but she's got two young children and one on the way by that so-called husband. A woman can be very protective of their children's father, however much of a bastard he is. She may know more than she's letting on,' Jack said as Jo reached his office door.

'I don't think so, but I hear you, guv,' said Jo, as she left his office.

CHAPTER 42

After five hours of troubled sleep, Nick's eyes snapped open as if he'd been stung by a hornet. It was just after ten. Ordinarily, it took him a good few minutes to wake up fully, but this morning it was as if he had never been to sleep. His weary body had demanded rest, but throughout his short period of slumber, part of his mind had been on constant alert.

Regrettably, it had not stopped the dreams. A labyrinth of haphazard nightmares had bled in and out of each other, filled with threats and whispers, rain and mud, shame and indecision, shovels and staring faces. Distorted images of his mother and father pleaded for mercy as he threw them, one after the other, into the stinking swamp that was thick with rotting human carcasses. Muffled screams of the damned continued to resonate inside his head.

It was a shocking picture; a vivid string of lurid dreams that taunted his guilty conscience. Nick shook his head as if, like an Etch-a-Sketch screen, doing so could erase the lingering graphic images. Gradually, they began to fade as he tried to focus on the day ahead. Despite his fatigue, he was grateful that he was awake and free, if only temporarily, from the disturbing visions that haunted his subliminal mind.

The cold space next to where he lay told him that Mel had risen earlier. What mental state would she be in this morning? He prayed that this last horrific episode would not further erode his wife's faith in human nature. He now had to summon every ounce of strength that he possessed to give her the positive support she was going to need.

Nick dressed hurriedly and went downstairs to the kitchen. Mel was sitting with her back to him, staring out onto the rear garden. A weak sun was shining in a cold, colourless sky. A heavy frost during the night had decked the shrubs and trees with glistening, platinum frills.

Nick moved forwards and laid his hands on her shoulders. It made her jump. 'It's only me, darling,' he said as he bent over and kissed the soft curls on the top of her head.

Mel continued to gaze out onto the wintry scene. 'Look at that. It's beautiful. But what does it matter? Who bloody cares?' She paused, 'What are we doing?'

'What do you mean?' said Nick.

'Why are we here? What's all this about?' Mel was not really addressing him; she was talking aloud to herself. 'I don't know who I am any more. And I'm not sure I care.'

For the first time in their relationship Nick did not know how to answer Mel. She was rambling but somehow it made sense. He remained behind her with his hands still resting lightly on her shoulders.

'When you left last night I went and had another shower. I still felt dirty. I've showered this morning and I still feel dirty. I've been up since seven o' clock and that's the only thing I'm certain of, Nick. I don't know who I am, I don't understand people – relationships – any more. Are you the only person I can trust? Can I even trust you?' Mel said as she got up from the kitchen chair and headed for the stairs.

Nick put the stinging rebuke aside for a second. 'Mel,' he called after her, 'I'm sorry, but I have to ask you this. What if you are pregnant due to this assault?'

Mel stopped dead and without turning around, she replied, 'I'll handle it.'

'What do you mean, *you'll handle it*?' said Nick.

'You don't have to worry. I know what I'm doing. Now, I'm going back to bed. I'm tired,' she added. But he was very worried.

Can I even trust you. The phrase sliced him in half. A suffocating feeling of loss descended as he watched his wife leave the room. The vacated chair was pulled back as he sank down. Stretching his arms in front of him, he put the palms of his hands on the wooden table. It was his turn to stare out of the kitchen window. What *was* out there? And was it worth fighting for?

He tried to imagine how Mel would be feeling this morning. To be punched senseless and brutally raped. That sudden, unexpected attack – stripped of dignity; self-esteem; confidence. She had suddenly been faced with a life-threatening situation in which she was helpless to respond.

He had read that many victims of rape felt, in some way, responsible for the actions of their violator. The thought angered him. Could there be a more horrific, degrading ordeal for a woman to suffer? Nick sat there for five minutes lost in thought, surrounded by indecision. At that moment, hope was his only tool available for a positive future. And yes, it was worth fighting for. But Mel's poignant words remained parked in his head like a neon warning sign. He could only guess where her mind was at this point in time.

He had to admit that he was not far away from being in a similar place. As he sat at the table, on his own, he felt himself being dragged down into the same dark hole in which Mel appeared to be descending. He couldn't let that happen. It was an abyss from which they would surely never escape.

CHAPTER 43

Jo was shocked by the sight of Cathy when she opened the door to her. She had three finger-shaped bruises just below her left cheek and the left side of her mouth was swollen to twice its normal size with a cut across the lower lip. She attempted a smile. 'Hello, Jo.'

'My God! Cathy! Did Nathan do this?'

Cathy raised her bowed head and made eye contact with Jo. Her effort at bravery suddenly failed her and she dissolved into tears. Jo stepped forwards and put her arms around her. There was nothing she could think of to say at that moment that would alleviate the pain that she saw on Cathy's face. Jo stood in the hallway, not attempting to move, happy to be of some small comfort as she let her cry on her shoulder.

Jo's heart responded with sympathy but her brain was elsewhere. The overriding emotion that was spreading like a forest fire inside her was one of intense anger. At that instant she could not have cared whether Nathan Ballack was dead or alive.

As Cathy's tears subsided it was she who spoke first. 'I'm so sorry. I didn't want to break down in front of you.'

'You don't have to apologise to me – or anyone, for that matter. You've every right to be upset.' Jo motioned to Cathy's extended belly. 'Are you, you know, okay in there?'

Cathy produced a hanky from the sleeve of her powder-blue cardigan. 'I'm fine, Jo. The children are upstairs. Let's go into the kitchen. I'll put the kettle on.' Jo followed Cathy into the kitchen and sat on one of the raffia-slatted chairs.

The kitchen appeared very dated with pale-green laminated cupboards and drawers that had long since given up sitting on the horizontal. The floor was covered with yellow and tan checked linoleum scarred with two cigarette burns and beginning to curl at the edges. Whatever Nathan had made from his career and his illicit earnings, it was evident that he had not spent it on the house.

Jo sat at the small kitchen table. As she watched Cathy pull two mugs from the overhead cupboard, she wondered, when faced with a crisis, how many people decided that the best form of comfort was to put the kettle on for a cup of tea.

She looked at the body language of the woman standing in front of her; *she needed more than a cuppa to heal her troubles*, she thought. Nathan's wife appeared defeated, wrung out. Her compassion grew as she witnessed Cathy's pain.

During the next hour, Jo got the painstaking, unexpurgated story of Cathy's marriage to Nathan. It was not a children's bedtime read, that was for sure. It was full of greed and physical and mental abuse. The shock of finding her husband's drugs cache in the cocktail shaker and the ensuing quarrel brought the account to a tearful end.

At this point Jo decided that Cathy deserved to know the extent of Nathan's involvement with drugs. There was a small risk that it could compromise the investigation, but she was pretty sure that Nathan had lost, irretrievably, any lingering respect and support from his wife.

'Cathy, you have to know that we have had Nathan under investigation for some time now. We don't know when it started exactly, but he's been a coke user and dealer for – well, it may be years.' Jo watched Cathy for a reaction.

It was not shock that registered on her pathetic face but utter defeat – the realisation that the man she had married and who had fathered her children was a stranger to her. There could be no greater pain in a marriage than finding out that your partner is a liar and a cheat.

'I suppose you have no idea where he may be?' Jo asked gently.

Cathy shook her head.

'Relatives?'

'He's never kept in touch with any relative as long as I've known Nathan. I wouldn't even know whether any still exist,' said Cathy.

Jo believed her. 'Will you let me know if he contacts you?'

'Yes, I will,' replied Cathy. 'You don't think he will do something stupid, do you? I mean, he wouldn't harm the children, would he?'

'I'm pretty certain he wouldn't. But I think he knows he's been found out, so we can't predict his next move. We'll have an officer watching the house twenty-four seven. We won't let anything happen to you or the kids, Cathy. You have my word.'

Jo just hoped her word would be enough.

In her business, Jo met many men and women who were skilful liars, good actors. If Cathy was hiding anything concerning her husband, she was worthy of an Oscar.

When she left the house, she was certain of one thing. The future for Cathy Ballack was going to be a massive uphill climb.

CHAPTER 44

After Mel had gone up to bed, Nick set about cleaning his much-abused van. The exterior of the vehicle was caked in mud with dried streaks of bronze and aubergine slime running up the bonnet and across the side windows. Remnants of weeds ripped from the narrow, overgrown paths of the swamp clung to the wheel arches and were wedged in the cracks by the door hinges. The inside was still damp and smeared with dirt and silt from his filthy, rain-soaked clothes.

After hours of scrubbing, spraying and polishing, his tired body screamed for him to stop. When he finally finished he stood back to check on his labours. It was impossible to imagine the foul task this small vehicle had been party to a few hours previously.

He then set about burning last night's clothes on a disobliging garden bonfire. It was not easy to light in the damp, frosty conditions. But with the aid of carefully added petrol, the pile of leaves, twigs and logs from his garage finally burst into flame. Once the small fire had grown into a sizeable inferno, the still-damp, heavily soiled garments were thrown on top.

Once again, clouds of thick smoke from the moist, fetid garments billowed upwards and wafted over the surrounding properties. He was lucky that it was not spring or summer when the gardens would be swathed with lines of drying clothes. Lines of irate housewives at his front door, asking awkward questions, would surely have followed.

While he carried out these chores, Mel was nowhere to be seen. He assumed she was still upstairs in bed. When she did not make an appearance at lunchtime, Nick became concerned. He climbed the stairs and entered the bedroom to check on her. She was sleeping. He left quietly, not wanting to wake her.

He continued to make regular visits to her throughout the afternoon, on each occasion she was either asleep or was pretending to be. Either way, she did not want any company.

Nick had to believe the old adage that time was a great healer. He just wished that he could fast-forward that precious time to heal his wife's battered face, her defiled body and her disillusioned spirit.

Surely, after what they had both been through, no other calamitous event could be skulking in the weeds, conspiring to threaten their happiness together. They just needed time.

CHAPTER 45

Cathy said Nathan was heading for the pub when he stormed out of their house. That's where Jo was now.

She soon ascertained that the governor of the pub knew Nathan well. 'Yes, he's one of my regulars is Nathan,' he said. She could see that he was surprised that a police officer was enquiring about another. She couldn't let that worry her.

'Was he in here yesterday, late afternoon?' she asked.

'I was working all day yesterday and he didn't come in. Hang on, I'll check with the other staff,' he said, as he walked through to the other bar. 'Nope. Not yesterday,' he informed her on his return. 'Is there anything I should know?' he added, looking concerned.

'No. But thanks for your time,' she said, as she took her leave. *So, where did he go,* she said to herself, as she headed back to work.

The first thing Jo did when she arrived back at the office was make sure the DPS had put in place immediate full-time surveillance outside Cathy's house. Then it was straight into Jack's office.

'There's nothing that Nathan's wife can tell us, guv. I'm absolutely sure she's an innocent party in all this. Excuse my French, but he's been treating her like shit for years. Last night, by accident, she found his store of coke. They argued; he knocked her about, then buggered off down the pub, or so he said – she hasn't seen him since. I've just checked with the landlord. He didn't turn up there,' Jo told a contemplative Jack Jolley.

'She's pregnant, isn't she?' asked Jack.

'Yes, guv.'

'Is the baby okay? Does she need hospital treatment?'

'No. She's bruised facially and mentally she's a wreck; but physically, I think she's all right.'

'Okay. Arrange for an officer from the Community Safety Unit to drop in on her. Apart from her own problems she's got two kids that need to be looked after,' Jack said.

'I'll get onto it straight away.'

'Check his friends and relatives; he may be holed up with one of them,' added Jack as Jo got up to go.

'Cathy has already told me she doesn't think he has any living relatives in this country. He's never visited relatives and hardly ever mentioned anything about his past as far as his family goes. That's very strange in itself. I'm guessing there are some dodgy old skeletons rattling about in his family closet. The more I learn about Nathan Ballack, the more I realise what a dysfunctional character he is,' said Jo.

'Friends?' asked Jack.

'Hardly any of those, I'm afraid. Socially, he's fairly insular. He mainly drinks with one or two colleagues,' Jo said. She paused, then added, 'Outside of work the only friends I know of are Nick and Mel Summers, who were at the pub with us the other week. I'll drop in on them on my way home after work. But I think it was the women who initiated that friendship – I didn't get the impression that Nick and Nathan were particularly close mates. I'm pretty sure Nathan won't be staying with them, but I'll check it out anyway.'

Jo was opening the door to leave when Jack spoke again. 'Uh! Jo, you'd better ask Mark Smallwood and Colin Lynch to come in here. They've got to know what's going on with Ballack now. That is, of course, if they don't know already.'

'They know something's going on, that's for sure. I've been getting odd looks and sarky comments for weeks now. It'll come as a relief, guv. I'll send them in,' said Jo as she left Jack's office.

As Jo reached the door to her office, she noticed that Colin and Mark were in deep discussion. As she entered the room they stopped talking and looked up at her. They both wore an expression that told Jo they were anticipating bad news.

'Yes, I've been in Jack's office again and very shortly you'll know why. He wants to see you both straight away,' said Jo, trying not to sound too authoritarian.

The reaction of the two officers could not have been more contrasting. Colin Lynch suddenly wore the face of a condemned prisoner on death row who had just been asked which ingredients he would prefer to make up his last meal. Mark Smallwood had a twinkle in his eye and put on an expression of mock horror. 'Oh no! It's because I haven't done my homework again, isn't it? Trousers down round me ankles, bent over the boss's desk. I just hope it's the cane this time!'

Jo giggled. Trust Mark to come up with the line that sliced through the tension that was building inside her. It was exactly what she needed. 'Rogered by the boss,' she added. 'You should be so lucky.'

The two men got up from their chairs and headed for the door. Mark turned his head to Jo. 'This is to do with Nathan, yes?' he asked, suddenly looking more pensive.

Jo pressed her lips together to answer Mark, and then changed her mind. 'I'll see you two when you get back. Coffee's on me.'

It was only after she had left work that evening and was driving to their house that she started to think seriously about Nick and Mel Summers. On their first meeting she had warmed to them both. Mel was open and friendly, if a little nervous. Jo had put that down to the old chestnut of "meeting a female copper syndrome". Sometimes, when Jo introduced herself as a police officer, especially in a social environment, the odd person's behaviour would instantly change. It was a natural reaction that she had got used to. Some would become self-conscious, some guarded, others slightly awestruck.

Then there was Nick. He was handsome, humorous and possessed a relaxed confidence. What Jo particularly liked about him was that he didn't take himself too seriously, unlike some of the supercilious coppers she worked with.

In that first meeting in the pub, it had been obvious to Jo, via their body language, that this couple had a very close relationship. But when she had recently visited their house to try on Mel's overcoat, there had been a noticeable change in their characters. There had definitely been something on Mel's mind other than selling the coat to her. Although Mel had been a touch uneasy at their first meeting, this was different. The atmosphere had been tense, unnatural, from the moment she arrived.

To add to the intrigue there was that broken window. When she'd asked Mel how it was damaged the explanation about the broom had not been convincing. She had noted that the position of the broken pane was next to the latch on the main window. It had appeared to Jo to be the handiwork of a professional thief. But Mel had denied that it was an attempted break-in. Had she been hiding something?

Then Nick had not exactly looked overjoyed to see her coming up the garden path either. And as far as she could see, he had appeared to be burning a perfectly good rug on the bonfire.

All these seemingly innocuous incidents didn't really matter at the time. But being in such close proximity to the unfolding drama of Nathan Ballack now evoked suspicion in Jo's mind. Ever since she had worked at Ashford nick, apart from a few unsavoury incidents in the local park, nothing worthy of police attention had occurred in the small town of Bourne. Now it was playing host to mystery and intrigue. Was it a coincidence? Was it possible that Nathan's clandestine activities could be connected, in some way, to Nick and Mel Summers?

She juggled with the implausible notion that pinged around in her head as she drove towards the outskirts of Bourne. 'How could they possibly be linked? Am I being ridiculous?' she finally said out loud.

Maybe it was merely her detective's brain - her overactive imagination - that saw something from nothing. But there remained more than a morsel of doubt. There was definitely an air of anxiety in that house; she could feel it, she could smell it. One thought was prominent in her mind. Would that uneasiness still be there? If so, she wanted to find the reason for it.

CHAPTER 46

It was a few minutes after six p.m. when Jo arrived at the Summers' home. She parked directly outside but did not get out immediately. Sat at the wheel of her car, she looked across at the attractive dwelling. She'd never looked at it in detail before.

The solid oak front door was set in the middle with four windows in perfect symmetry slotted into each quarter. It was every child's first drawing of a house, Jo thought. The cottage was dressed with copper-edged ivy leaves that merged with primrose-yellow flowers sprouting from a mature winter jasmine. A pale-grey slate roof sat amongst the jade-green needles of three Norwegian spruces.

Jo's pulse slowed as she warmed to the sight of this charming early twentieth century home. For a few seconds she imagined herself living in such a house. It was a long held dream. She was determined that, one day, it would come true.

Her thoughts transferred to the interior of the dwelling. Maybe on her first visit she had interrupted a row between them. Perhaps Nick had spilled red wine on that rug and Mel had thrown something at Nick in frustration. That could account for the smashed window. It was not beyond the realms of possibility that Mel had been simply too embarrassed to admit it to Jo. Why would she? They were hardly the best of friends.

Jo got out of her car and approached the entrance to the cottage. If this couple were having some difficulties in their marriage, it was no concern of hers. If the odd behaviour was due to something else...

CHAPTER 47

After the day's exertions, Nick had showered and dressed in tracksuit bottoms and sweatshirt. On his third visit of the afternoon to their bedroom, he had woken Mel and left a cup of tea and a sandwich on the bedside table.

One hour later, he had checked on her once again. The food and drink had remained untouched.

Mel had stayed in her bed all afternoon. Standing in the bedroom, he was now determined to get a response from his wife. She needed to eat, but more importantly, they had to talk. He approached the side of the bed and sat down next to her. She lay curled up in the middle of the bed. He nudged her shoulder. 'Darling, come on,' he said softly.

Mel opened her eyes, looked up at Nick, and began to cry. Her pleading, pathetic tears tore him apart. He felt powerless seeing his wife's unceasing pain. He slid his powerful arms beneath her shoulders, lifted her up and held her soft body close as she sobbed into his chest. Her skin was warm but he felt no warmth from the woman within. There was nothing left but hurt. He had to find a way to help Mel regain her mental strength. Without that there was no hope for them.

Nick laid his wife down and kissed her forehead. 'I love you and no person or thing will ever change that,' he said. His eyes suddenly felt twice their normal size. As he gazed down at her a tear fell onto the white pillow beside her head. He touched the silky curls of her blonde hair, fighting the overwhelming impulse to break down. He had to show his wife that he was the rock she so desperately needed.

Nick wiped his eyes, set his jaw and spoke. 'We will get through this. Believe me, we will. If you want me for anything, just call. I'll be downstairs. Get up when you feel you're ready, darling.'

Nick picked up the cold cup of tea and left the bedroom. The bag of sand he'd used to weigh down Ballack's body in his van now felt as if it had wrapped itself around his shoulders. As he descended the stairs, his every step was taken on ponderous legs.

At the bottom he turned and headed for the kitchen, where there was a chilled bottle of Sauvignon Blanc waiting in the fridge. It was the same bottle he had put there yesterday for Mel's birthday celebration.

He opened the fridge door and pulled out the bottle of wine. He needed a drink – some escape.

Then the front door bell rang.

CHAPTER 48

Nick swung around and looked in the direction of the ringing bell. 'That's the last thing I need right now. God! Who's this gonna be?' Reluctantly, he replaced the wine, closed the fridge door and walked towards the front of his house. When he opened the door, he was confronted by the last person he wanted to see – a police officer.

'Jo! Hi,' he said, hoping that he appeared surprised and not shocked. 'To what do we owe the pleasure?'

'Hello, Nick. Sorry to drop in on you unannounced, but, uh, can I have a quick word?'

Nick felt himself tense as he forced a smile. 'Of course, come in. If you've come to arrest me am I allowed one last cigarette before the cuffs go on?'

Jo looked around at him and laughed. 'Only if you give me a written confession. I want to know everything. Get it?' she replied.

Nick breathed out. His droll opening line had achieved the desired effect of easing the tension he was feeling. He led her into the kitchen.

'Coffee?' Nick asked.

'That'll be lovely, thanks. Milk, one sugar,' Jo said as she pulled out a chair and sat down at the kitchen table.

Nick filled the kettle and pulled the cups from the cupboard.

'Mel not in?' Jo enquired.

Nick hesitated for a second. Should he lie and say she was out? No. That was a stupid idea. If she started to move around upstairs and Jo heard her she would definitely suspect something was wrong. Tell her the truth – well, half the truth.

'She's not feeling very well, Jo. She's upstairs in bed,' Nick said with his back to Jo whilst spooning the coffee into two cups. He tried to say it in a way that meant it was no big deal.

'Oh! Nothing serious?' Jo enquired.

'No, no. She's just got a slight headache – feeling a bit out of sorts. I think it's women's, erm, you know.' It was another lie, but Nick thought it to be a plausible reason for Mel to take to her bed. In addition, he knew that any mention of problems concerning menstruation evoked immediate sympathy amongst other women. And it was certainly not a subject that was going to be discussed in a casual manner with a man.

'Ah! Okay,' Jo said.

Nick breathed a sigh of relief. Jo's short reply told him that she was happy to let the matter rest. But he knew that there was only one reason that Detective Constable Major was here.

Jo said nothing more until Nick had made the coffees and joined her at the table. 'Nick, Nathan never showed up for work today. And no one knows where he is,' Jo said. Nick swallowed; he realised Jo was watching his face for a reaction. Apart from raising his eyebrows, his face remained passive.

'Look, I may as well tell you,' she continued, 'he's in a lot of trouble. It's an in-house matter. I can't give you any details, I'm afraid, but it's a very serious police matter.' Jo's news, instead of alarming Nick, gave him an unexpected amount of satisfaction. It afforded him a degree of solace. Not only was Ballack a rapist, he was a bent copper.

Nick's heartbeat slowed a few beats. He knew that Jo worked in the drug squad and that Ballack was her boss. *In-house* could only mean one thing, surely. 'Jesus! You mean he's been caught taking drugs?'

'As I said, I can't say any more at this point,' said Jo.

Nick assumed he had hit the nail on the head. 'Bloody hell, Jo!' Nick sat back in his chair, genuinely shocked by Jo's revelations. Maybe that went some way to explaining Ballack's sickening behaviour with Mel. It may be a reason, thought Nick, but it was no vindication.

'The first reason for my visit was to ask whether you or Mel had seen Nathan in the last thirty-six hours. But I guess that's a no from you, going by your reaction.'

Nick nodded in agreement, thankful that he did not actually have to speak the lie. 'How about Mel?' Jo added.

Now he had no alternative, 'No. If she'd seen him she would have told me. As I said, she's not been feeling too well. She's not even been outside the house for the last couple of days,' Nick replied.

'No, I thought as much. Secondly, I thought I'd better inform you of the situation. If he does try to contact you, please phone me immediately.'

'I would be surprised, in the circumstances, if Nathan does contact us – we're not particularly close friends. It was Mel and Cathy that struck up the relationship,' said Nick.

'Yes, I know. I'm pretty sure he won't get in touch with you. But we have to cover every possibility. We don't know what frame of mind he may be in. I'm not necessarily saying he's dangerous but he almost certainly knows we're on to him. That could make his movements, well... let's say... unpredictable.'

'Okay. Thanks for letting us know,' said Nick. He now wanted to move off the subject.

'Mel tells me you've found a new flat.'

'Yeah. Really pleased with it and I can't wait to move in. It's even got a small rear garden. It's a bit of a mess. Maybe you could give me some ideas after I get in?' asked Jo.

'Be pleased to,' replied Nick.

Jo finished her coffee and stood up to go. 'Right, I've taken up enough of your time. Oh! Let me just jot down my number for you.' She dipped into her handbag, pulled out a small notepad and pencil, wrote down her office and mobile number, ripped the small page from the pad and handed it to Nick. As he reached out his left hand to take the number, he saw Jo looking at the white band of skin where the wedding ring should have been.

'Where's that lovely gold wedding ring of yours?' she said. The question caught him off guard. He felt his face grow hot. He had to think quick.

'It's, erm, in the bathroom. It came off when I was having a shower. I think I must be losing weight,' he said with a weak laugh. 'I'm going to take it to the jeweller's to see if I can get it made smaller.'

He knew that he hadn't sounded very confident with his explanation. He saw that Jo noticed he was uneasy. But her next reaction surprised him. She too appeared flustered. Whether she realised she'd asked a personal question, that was none of her business or not, Nick could only surmise, but they were now facing each other in a shared degree of embarrassment.

They stared at each other for a few seconds as time came to a halt between them. It was Jo who spoke first. 'I'm only jealous – you know, wedding ring.' It veneered over the sticky moment. Nick smiled in response.

'Okay, I'm off. Sorry to have bothered you with this, but I thought you ought to be aware, you know.' Jo left the phrase hanging in the air and made her exit.

Nick noticed the awkward look on her face as she turned and walked down the path. As she neared her car she looked back. Nick was still standing at the open door.

'Oh! Give my regards to Mel – hope she feels better soon. Bye!' she called.

Nick's head was filled with mixed emotions as he watched Jo climb into her car and drive off. He stood there until she was out of sight, closed the door, and walked back into the sitting room.

CHAPTER 49

'What did Jo want?'

The voice startled Nick. Sitting at the bottom of the stairs, wearing her dressing gown, was the hunched figure of his wife. The plum and indigo welts around her bruised eye stood out in stark contrast against her pallid face. The marks were now so vivid they looked unreal – like face paint.

'She wanted to know whether we had seen Nathan because he hadn't turned up for work today,' Nick replied.

'She also told me he's in trouble with them. It has to be linked to drugs, Mel.'

'Oh God! I can't take much more of this, Nick.'

'Mel, you wanted me to bury him.' Mel's mood swings were becoming of great concern to him.

'I know. I know. It's the deceit, the lies, the wondering when someone like Jo will discover our crimes,' said Mel.

'Crimes? Is that what we've committed? Nick announced. 'How about the victims of crimes? Crimes that threaten innocent people's safety. Look at you. When those victims fight back are they criminals too? If we're not allowed to feel secure in our homes without worrying if we are using excessive force, we have nothing.'

Mel watched the anger rise in her husband - a husband from whom she had rarely heard a shouted word since the time they had met. He walked over to the window by the front door.

Nick looked out and addressed the tiny part of the world he could see though that small window. 'Reasonable force. Huh! Don't make me laugh. What the fucking hell is reasonable force when someone breaks into your home in the middle of the night? When you come home to find your wife being raped?

'I've got to live with what I've done for the rest of my years, and believe me, it will always be there, whether I'm in jail or not. I will never be able to sleep peacefully in my bed ever again. The two people, who have brought misery to us and those around them, have lived and died by the sword. I'm not proud of it – in fact I hate myself for what I've done. But who is really to blame here? Me or them?'

Nick turned to look at his wife. 'Don't you see, Mel. If we didn't have these *soft on criminals* laws we wouldn't have even thought of trying to hide these unfortunate bodies. It's all gone arse about face. It's crazy! We may as well just set up bloody sanctuaries across the country where misunderstood offenders can have counselling, tea and sympathy?'

Mel looked at her husband; a smile eased its way onto her face. Nick was always at his most amusing when in the middle of a rant. But the smile was a release; her emotion was close to tears. She had a choice – delirium or laughter.

Thankfully, Nick saw the farcical side of his rhetoric as he turned to look at Mel. He raised his eyes to the ceiling. 'Well! For fuck's sake!' he added.

'Do you know, you've sworn more in the last three weeks than in all the time we've been together,' said Mel, blowing her nose on a tissue.

'No shit?' Nick replied, as he approached Mel and pulled her up to a standing position. He drew her towards him in a tight embrace where confused smiles and tears intermingled like soul mates.

CHAPTER 50

When Jo arrived home, she felt drained. It had been a long and disturbing day. Her mind was full of questions with no satisfactory answers. She entered her house and went through her nightly routine. She picked up her mail from behind the door, kicked off her shoes, went into the kitchen to make herself a cup of coffee. She then changed into jogging bottoms and a sweatshirt, retired to the sitting room and checked her answer phone. Nothing.

She sat down, cradling the mug of coffee on her lap. Her visit to the Summers had not convinced her that all was happy families in that house. She had enjoyed her time talking to Nick but he appeared nervous when she enquired about his missing ring. Or was it merely embarrassment? Perhaps their marriage was struggling – no wedding ring on his finger – could they be on the verge of breaking up? *Who knows what goes on behind closed doors?* she thought to herself.

And her reaction had come as a surprise to her. She had been embarrassed for him. In her line of work, making enquiries was never a straightforward exercise. But she had felt self-conscious in front of Nick, uncomfortable even. Was it fear or attraction?

But a few doubts still remained. There was Mel's absence. Nick's account of his wife's condition was plausible, but it only added to her suspicion that all was not right between them. And when she had told him about Nathan being in trouble it was if he was expecting the news. Maybe Nick's intuition had detected something bad in DS Ballack from the moment he met him. She had already sensed that the brash police detective was not really Nick's cup of tea.

There were periods, she had to admit, that he had appeared relaxed and confident during her time there. But, beneath that pretty cottage roof, the smooth flow of marital harmony had hit an unexpected and menacing obstacle. She was certain of it.

CHAPTER 51

The following day, Jo and her team were sitting at their desks, tired and frustrated with the investigation into Ballack's disappearance. Annoyingly, despite their combined efforts, they had disappeared up more blind alleys than a stray cat. The small pod were now engaged in amalgamating their findings – or rather, the lack of them.

Mark Smallwood had been assigned to check out the local area, taking statements from Nathan Ballack's neighbours.

'How's it going, Mark?' asked Jo.

'It's not. Disappointingly, no one saw Nathan on the afternoon in question. And I have to say, from the tone of some of his neighbours' replies, he was not the most popular of residents in the area. Accounts of loud music and quarrels, being overheard at all times of the day and night, were not uncommon. He hardly ever spoke to any of them either,' replied Mark. 'Not someone I'd choose to live next to, that's for sure.'

'Well, I've got no further than you, Mark,' said Jo. 'I've tracked down and bent the ear of three of our local dealers.

Despite the fact that it has cost me a fortune in beers, not one of them has seen or heard of Nathan themselves or through their network of associates.

'Merrill?' Mark asked his colleague, who was typing away at the speed of light on his computer. Colin Lynch had been digging into his boss' financial dealings.

'It's *Colin*, Mark,' he replied, dismissively.

'Oooh!' chorused the other two detectives.

Colin ignored them. 'Anyway, I've been in contact with Ballack's bank, NatWest, and no money has been withdrawn on or since the day of his disappearance. His credit card company gave me the same information. And no large sums of money have been taken out of his account for over three weeks. If he's still alive, someone is paying for his upkeep,' he concluded.

'What did you just say?' asked Jo.

'I said...'

'Never mind. I know what you said,' she replied. 'We know he's got a mole in the office, right. And my guess is that it's a woman. It never dawned on me before; he could be holed up with her.' The three of them looked at each other. Mark shook his head. 'That's the only other explanation,' he declared.

'*Other* explanation?' said Jo. 'What's the first?

'He's dead. Of course!'

CHAPTER 52

Christmas and New Year's Eve was a time for celebration. Nick had seen it come and go with hardly a flicker of acknowledgement from him or Mel. Without children, the festive season was not something that they particularly looked forward to. Nearly every splash of television and newspaper marketing in the lead up to December 25th was geared to young expectant children and their pressurised parents. It left them feeling isolated.

With the recent traumatic events still raw in their minds, the end-of-year celebrations had been even more subdued than usual. Reluctantly, Mel had phoned Cathy. Nick realised it was an attempt to give the woman some comfort, but Mel told him that she thought Cathy had detected the insincerity in her voice. Mel wanted to tell her the truth – that her dead husband was a bully and a rapist and was well rid of him. But, of course, she couldn't.

It was after that phone call that Mel descended into a dark place once more. No amount of words or actions from Nick could lift her spirits.

'I don't want a Christmas present this year. It's a complete waste of money buying things we don't need. And the prices are a rip-off. I won't be buying you one either,' said Mel. Nick hadn't argued. Christmas dinner was haddock, mashed potato and peas, the same as every other Friday's meal.

He said nothing when Mel had politely declined the few invitations received from neighbours to join in their family festivities. He was pleased they didn't have to pretend to be jolly at such a difficult time. They spent the entire week at home on their own. In effect, they had put their relationship and their social lives in a holding account.

Late December had seen a drastic temperature drop. High winds and freezing conditions had turned the earth to something resembling concrete. Nick, apart from keeping his paperwork up to date, had been unable to work over the entire Christmas period.

An enforced work-break was not something he would have chosen. His mind cried out for a distraction. He needed to escape the stricken environment of his home and once more immerse himself in the business of creating beauty throughout the Kent countryside.

Today, he was busy trying to keep his home warm. Despite central heating having been installed many years earlier, the hundred-year-old property suffered from draughts that seemed to have no locatable source.

He reversed his van, packed with logs and kindling, up the drive of his house, stopping just short of his open garage door. As he stepped out of his vehicle, he was careful not to slip on the icy surface of the paving stones.

After he had stacked all the logs in a corner of the garage, he carried as many as he could manage into the sitting room to start a fire. Mel, who was wearing an Aran crew neck sweater, was on the sofa reading a book.

'Soon have this place like toast,' Nick said, dropping the bundle of chopped logs in the hearth. Mel continued to read. The atmosphere in the Summers' household, similar to that of the temperature, was not as warm as he would have liked. 'Then you can take that jumper off and relax,' Nick added.

'I like this jumper. And I am relaxed. For God's sake, Nick! I don't see any need for a fire. It costs money and just creates mess. And I'm the one who normally has to clean it up in the morning,' Mel said, with her head still stuck in her book.

Over these past few weeks he had learned to stay silent. Any extended conversation was inclined* to end in an argument. He started to place the kindling in the grate.

Every Christmas the small firm of event organisers that Mel worked for closed for two weeks. The two partners of the firm, who each owned a villa on the island of Gran Canaria, packed their suitcases and took their families out of frosty England and off to the sunshine.

Consequently, he and Mel were confined to their house when the weather was at its worst. The only plus, as far as Nick could see, was that when the company resumed business in the New Year, Mel's facial injuries would have healed. And, hopefully, she would feel strong enough to go back to work. Moping around the house was not going to do either of them any favours.

He attempted to communicate with Mel once more. 'I know things are really tough for you at the moment, but I want you to know that I really miss you next to me in our bed at night. I feel like I'm half the man without you beside me. And I'm not talking about making love – just your presence.'

Shortly after the day of the rape, Mel had decided to sleep in the spare room. It was a decision that cut Nick to the bone. Their sex life was not important for the time being. He knew it would take time for Mel to even think about sex after her ordeal. It was the withdrawal of her physical and emotional presence that really hurt him. The woman he loved no longer lay close to him at night when he most needed her.

'I can't, Nick. Not yet. It's too soon,' she replied, avoiding his eyes.

'I understand, darling. I will never push you to do anything you're uncomfortable with. I just wanted you to know how I still feel about you. Nothing will ever change that.'

But Nick was worried. Mel had become distant, immersed in a deep depression. At first, he tried to coax her out of her detached state of mind, but whenever he attempted to discuss her feelings, it only seemed to push her further away from him.

He was sure she blamed him for all that had occurred in their lives recently. Whether that was true or not, he had been cast aside by the very person he adored and was trying to protect. The situation was becoming unbearable and he could see no immediate way out of it.

Against every instinct he possessed, he had decided to change tack. He chose to go about his daily life and leave his wife to get on with hers. He hoped that by giving her more space and time to heal, she would eventually soften and come back to him.

He began arranging the logs in the grate when the phone rang. Mel didn't move. He got up from the floor and hurried into the kitchen. 'Hello?'

'Hello, Nick. It's Jo Major.'

'Oh! Hi,' Nick replied, pretending to be pleasantly surprised by the call.

'Just following up on our meeting the other week. We've had no luck, so far, this end with our enquiries. Just wondered if you had heard or seen anything that may be of interest concerning our missing detective? However innocuous it might be. You know, a rumour here, a word out of place, there,' said Jo.

'Nothing I'm afraid,' he replied.

'No other acquaintances you know of that he mixed with – down the pub, maybe?'

'No one I can think of. So, you've got no idea where Nathan is?' asked Nick.

'Not yet. I've been in touch with Cathy a few times but he hasn't tried to contact her. He seems to have vanished into thin air. Taking into account the time he's been missing, Nick, we are now concerned as to his wellbeing,' she added.

Nick was really struggling with this conversation. Until recently, he'd never been seriously deceitful in his entire life. Now his whole existence was one of deceit. He said nothing.

'Anyway, sorry to have bothered you. Oh! By the way, how's Mel?'

'Yes, she's fine, thanks,' Nick said, hoping she wasn't going to ask to talk to his wife.

'Good. Okay then, bye,' Jo said.

'Bye.' Nick placed the phone back in its holster. Then he picked it up again, wiped the sweat from the surface on his jeans and put it back. He was spooked by the call from Jo. Was it simply an update to the enquiry or a ploy to test his nerve? He thought he detected something in the tone of her voice. An edge. Was she just doing what coppers do, or was she using her friendship to entrap him? She knew something. He was convinced of it.

CHAPTER 53

Jo had been looking forward to this weekend for what seemed a lifetime. Her solicitor had completed on both her sale and purchase, contracts had been signed and she had taken possession of the keys to her new apartment this Saturday morning at the estate agent's office.

Every item from the house had now been packed, apart from one; she left the picture of her father 'til last. As she took it down from her office wall, she stared at the image in the wooden frame. George, a rotund, happy figure, was the epitome of the jovial bobby on the beat.

It was on her sixteenth birthday party when her father, then aged fifty-three, had brought the celebrations to an abrupt end in front of an assembly of stunned teenage revellers. In the middle of an enthusiastic jive with her, his body suddenly went rigid. In an instant, his loose, florid complexion turned to one of alabaster. He suffered a massive heart attack and was dead shortly after his unrestrained head hit the floor.

Jo's grip on the small frame tightened as the memories returned of how that evening changed her life. Her remaining teenage years disappeared almost overnight. In a short space of time, she'd had to assume the man's role in the house. Maturity arrived all too soon for this fun-loving girl.

When Jo locked the door of her home for the last time, she experienced a sudden wave of sadness. A house full of memories was being left behind, but that was exactly where they needed to be. There was now only one direction in which Jo wanted to go: forwards.

By the time she had reached the village of Runcing, her melancholy was replaced by a swell of excitement. She parked her car outside the greengrocer shop that sat below her stylish apartment. The shop was closed but she had met the proprietor on two occasions and instantly liked him.

He was a mirror image of his shop – interesting, immaculate. On both meetings he had been dressed in highly polished burgundy brogues, just visible beneath navy-blue cords that had a crease down each leg you could cut a finger on. He seemed genuinely thrilled that Jo had fallen in love with her flat.

When she entered her new apartment the feeling was indescribable. The novelty of owning her own home lock, stock and barrel was going to take a long time to wear off.

The dimensions of the place were more than adequate for one person. As she breathed in her new purchase, the thought entered her head that her home was, in fact, more than adequate for two people.

It was longer than she cared to remember that she last had a boyfriend. Since her mother's death, not once had she allowed herself the conscious thought that she was now free to do whatever she wanted – to date *men*.

There had been three semi-serious relationships in her life, but they hadn't lasted long. Each had been with a police officer from her place of work. They had all been a disaster. Her hope was that a different world existed outside of the police force – one of sensitivity, of thoughtfulness.

By early Saturday afternoon all of her belongings had been moved in. Despite all the removal team's hard work, Jo knew that the real drudgery, as far as she was concerned, had yet to be addressed. Huddled together in a tight circle in the sitting room, like a wagon train expecting an imminent attack from Red Indians, was box after box of pictures, kitchen utensils, clothes and assorted knickknacks, all waiting to be unpacked. They would have to wait until tomorrow.

Now, for the first time, she was on her own in her new apartment. The faint smell of fresh paint was still evident as she wandered throughout the spacious flat, deciding where to place her collection of worldly goods. She stopped by the sitting room window.

Jo stood in awe as she took in the magnificent panoramic view of the wintry countryside. She had a lot of time to make up for. This, she told herself, was it. The beginning of her new life.

CHAPTER 54

Monday 4th January arrived through the Summers' bedroom window like an invitation to dine at The Ritz. A distant sun shone in a vast, pale-blue sky, the wind had dropped and the temperature had risen enough to get a spade in the ground. It was to be Nick's first day back at work.

Mel noticed the look of relief on her husband's face as he spoke. 'The council-owned park, you know, where I go for my morning runs, needs three large flowerbeds to be cleared and prepared for early spring planting. Looks like, at long last, I can get started on that today,' said Nick, pulling on his work clothes. It was a two-day job that he could manage by himself.

Never before had Mel seen him look so pleased to be going to work on a Monday morning. She sat, sipping tea, watching Nick bolt down a bowl of porridge. It had been weeks since she last ate breakfast – her appetite operating on half-power. Mel offered her cheek as Nick leant over the kitchen table to kiss her goodbye. He left the house at ten to nine.

Mel rose slowly from the kitchen table and walked to the window. She stood and watched her husband drive off in his van. She hated herself for not sharing his bed. But she could not bring herself to reveal the reason that she felt it necessary to sleep apart.

Ever since her body had been violated, she had been scared to death of the most unwanted irony – that Nathan Ballack may have made her pregnant. The day of her attack had been day fourteen of her cycle.

Apart from the brutal act taking away any immediate desire for sex, she could not bring herself to show any physical warmth towards her husband, not whilst there was any possibility of her carrying another man's baby. A rapist's baby.

Her fears were now growing by the day – she was almost a week overdue. She knew she could have gone to the doctor to get the morning after pill. Two things had stopped her. Her doctor knew she was desperate to have a baby; she had visited him more than once for various related tests. How would she now explain away such a request?

She had read that these pills could be purchased over the counter, without a prescription, but the second reason prevented her from doing so. And it was a personal one. It was set deep within her religious beliefs. She could not live with the fact that she had aborted a healthy child, however it had been conceived.

When Nick had brought up the possibility of her getting pregnant by Ballack, she told him she would handle it. Thankfully, he hadn't mentioned the subject since. He trusted her. She was now doubting whether she was worthy of that trust.

Mel had put off using one of the pregnancy kits she had in the bathroom, terrified that it would confirm her worst fears. With all the difficulties she was having getting pregnant, she wouldn't let herself believe that one isolated incident could alter her condition.

She had read a few years ago that some women who experience an emotional ordeal can miss a period completely. As she stood in the bathroom looking at her reflection in the large mirror, she prayed that one of those women was her.

She had the house to herself - now the time had come to find out. She opened the door of the wall cabinet in front of her and took out a small cardboard box marked with the words CLEAR BLUE. She had used the kit numerous times before, longing desperately on each occasion for a positive result. This time her hopes and dreams were reversed.

She had to hold one of the small devices provided under a stream of her urine for five or six seconds. Within minutes a message would appear on the device: PREGNANT OR NOT PREGNANT. The test, so it claimed, was ninety-nine per cent accurate.

Mel took one of the units from the box and held it in front of her with a trembling hand. 'Let's get this thing over with,' she whispered to herself. She moved to the toilet, carried out the procedure, dressed herself and returned to stand in front of the mirror. Then she waited.

She held the device behind her back for a good few minutes, praying that it would be a negative result. As she stared deep into the mirror, she did not recognise the person looking back at her. The sophisticated, confident woman, the person she thought she knew, had evaporated. In her place was a frightened child – the child who used to be scared of the dark, terrified of dogs, afraid that she would never find a boyfriend.

How would she react if it was positive? The question hovered above her head. But her mind was incapable of providing an answer. Every muscle in her body strained against every tendon. She started to shiver. She had never felt so utterly alone.

Mel breathed deeply, closed her eyes and brought her hand round in front of her face. Slowly, she raised her eyelids and read the result.

CHAPTER 55

Jack Jolley sat at the large white-oak table that dominated the centre of his farmhouse kitchen. His wife, Karen, stood behind him, wearing a lavender towelling dressing gown with matching slippers. She was washing up the breakfast plates and humming along to a tune on the radio.

Jack was perusing the sports pages of Monday's *Daily Telegraph*, which lay open in front of him. A mug of coffee sat on one corner of the page. He had read the opening paragraph of a football report three times without any of the contents being absorbed by his troubled brain.

'Where are you this morning?' said Karen.

Jack glanced up at his wife over the top of his glasses. He was surprised his body language had, so easily, revealed his innermost thoughts.

'How's that problem at work going. The one you can't talk to me about,' she added, with a hint of mischief.

'I can't go into too many details, but one of my officers has gone missing. He's been a stupid boy and we need to find him,' replied Jack.

'Oh dear. That's not good, is it?' said Karen.

'No. It's a disruption to my workforce and will attract a lot of bad press when this all comes out.' He paused. 'You've been urging me, recently, to think about retiring. Well, I was going to tell you that I was planning to do just six more months. Finish end of June. But with this hanging over the station, and it could go on for God knows how long, what's it going to look like? I don't want to quit with people thinking that I left under a cloud – that I didn't run a good ship. I've worked too bloody hard for that,' said Jack.

'That's ridiculous Jack. You can't think that one officer's misdemeanours will ruin thirty years of unblemished service. A copper has gone bad. He won't be the first or the last. And it's not your fault. How can it be?' said Karen, sternly.

Jack sighed. 'I know what you're saying. But I can't leave with a nasty taste in my mouth. My career has meant too much to me.'

'I understand that. And I'm thrilled you've decided to retire, Jack. But please, don't let this issue affect your decision,' said Karen, praying that her husband would heed her words.

With the aid of his team, Jack had investigated every avenue that he could think of to locate the whereabouts of DS Ballack. It was never easy investigating a fellow officer. He could not be sure how hard some of his team were trying to pursue one of their workmates. Most of them hated the idea of a bent copper giving the police force a bad name, but there was the possibility of a sense of misplaced loyalty in these cases. It was human nature to protect your own.

The general feeling amongst his pod, though, was that Nathan had become unpredictable and therefore a danger to the drug barons at the top of the supply chain. And he almost certainly owed them money. It was an extremely precarious position in which to be, thought Jack.

He was now of the same opinion, shared by the majority of his cohorts, that there were two main probabilities. The first was that, despite not having taken his passport, Ballack had managed to flee the country. If that was the case, it should only be a matter of time, having little money and no job, until he was picked up by Interpol.

The second and most popular theory was that he was dead. To save his family pain and embarrassment and allow the department to function once more as a close-knit team, Jack hoped the latter was true. He had no sympathy for a copper that abused his position of trust in such a shameful fashion. It reflected badly on his colleagues, the force in general and Jack's managerial credibility.

He had an uneasy feeling in his stomach. It was caused by the nagging worry that this case may never get the closure vital for the ongoing morale of the team.

He rose from the table, scooped up the charcoal-grey Gieves and Hawkes suit jacket from the back of the kitchen chair and put it on. A royal-blue silk tie knotted perfectly over a starched white shirt completed the ensemble.

He then turned and patted his wife's towelling-covered bottom. 'Thanks for your support and good sense. I needed that,' he said.

What he really needed was to tie up the Ballack problem as quickly and cleanly as possible.

He kissed Karen on the lips and left for the office.

CHAPTER 56

Mel stared at the word on the small device that she held inches from her face: PREGNANT. The word reverberated through her like a pneumatic drill. Stunned by the result, she repeated the process only to get the same damning verdict.

The term she had longed to use to describe herself, one that should have evoked a feeling of euphoria, instead filled her with disgust. Suddenly, those eight letters represented everything that was wrong in her life. It was the message from hell.

Mel sank to the floor, still clutching the now alien contraption in her clenched fist. She looked at it once more in the hope that it may have changed its message. But there it remained in clear characters, piercing her eyes like two hot needles: PREGNANT. Now there was no doubt. She was carrying Nathan Ballack's bastard child.

She lay with her cheek on the cold tiles of the bathroom floor, slowly opened her mouth and emitted a long, whining scream. It was not a scream from a frustrated or angry woman, but from a brutalised soul that had been pushed to the very edge. Why had this happened to her? What had she done wrong to deserve this pain? She could not comprehend the cruelty of being denied a baby by the man she adored only to be impregnated by a vicious rapist.

Wearily, she raised herself up into a sitting position, propped up against the base of the toilet. She spent the next ten minutes staring at the bathroom cabinet in front of her, recounting the horrors of the past few months. How had their comfortable lives been ruined in such a short space of time? That two such contemptible individuals should choose them as their victims was beyond belief. At that moment she hated her life. She hated the world.

Eventually, she found the energy to get back to her feet. She threw the Clear Blue devices into the small, suede-covered bin, dabbed her mascara-streaked eyes with a handful of toilet tissue and went downstairs into the kitchen. She opened the cupboard that housed the tea and coffee and stared at the containers. Then she had a change of mind.

Instead of reaching inside, she closed the cupboard door, bent down and opened the lower cupboard that contained their supply of alcohol. She had not had a drink for weeks, not even over the Christmas period. But today she needed one. She had to have something to help her escape the mind-shattering reality that was now her life. Her hand went straight to the bottle of gin. A large bottle of tonic was the next to be pulled out along with the ice bucket.

She filled the bucket from the freezer and poured herself a very large drink into one of their best cut-glass tumblers. Mel sat down at the table and drank the contents in two gulps. She poured herself another one, brought the glass to her lips, then stopped and looked at her watch. The day was young.

CHAPTER 57

Nick arrived at the park just before nine a.m. Its appearance had changed dramatically in the weeks since his last morning run around its boundary. The warm colours of autumn had tumbled from the trees and shrubs to form slimy carpets of pulp across the floor.

His first observation was how the grounds had become so one-dimensional. Nature had become introspective in order to triumph against the invasive elements of winter.

It was now a stark canvas of gnarled tendrils – bony fingers reaching out for the promise of another spring. Swathes of coral-tipped lilies had vanished from the surface of the lake; giant reedmace and gypsy wort that had embellished the margins were withered, gone. The tranquil sweep of water now appeared defenceless against the pitiless season.

Still the lone, imperious swan remained in the centre of the lake, guarding her territory. The low sun glinted off her powerful white wing feathers, a thin silver streak bisecting the smooth surface of the water. Nick was aware that swans usually remain loyal to one partner, yet this small pen always swam alone. He wondered briefly whether she had lost her mate in battle or to disease. But this was a magnificent, sublime creature. Far too impressive to be left on the cygnus shelf.

Nick gathered his garden tools from the back of his van and headed for the largest of the overgrown flowerbeds. Clearing the dead, sodden remains of the year's growth and forking over wet, clammy mud was not the most pleasurable part of Nick's job. But it had to be done. The fruits of his labours would be there for all to see in the following seasons.

Suddenly, his positive thoughts of new, emerging life began to turn as the atmosphere in the park changed. Just as he commenced his back-straining task amongst the surrounding dead foliage, the sun was swallowed by a bloated, mushroom-coloured cloud. It was immediately followed by an icy cold, scything wind that skidded across the lake, tearing at his clothes, stinging the skin on his face. Just as rapidly as the weather had altered for the worse so did Nick's mood.

His attention was drawn to a sudden flurry of movement nearby. He looked up to see two magpies land on a low, spindly branch of a young silver birch – the thin, jagged limb bending beneath their bloated bodies. They stood together, motionless. Silent. Watching him. Four small black eyes boring into his conscience.

He turned away from them, eager to get on with the job in hand. But as he started to dig, ghastly visions began to form in front of him. An involuntary shiver climbed his spine as his spade sliced through the wet earth that seemed to pulsate of its own volition. Distorted images of the rotting corpses of Scrivens and Ballack bore deep into his soul from within the agitated folds of the cloying mud. Nick struggled in disbelief as the murky soil pulled and sucked at his spade as if trying to wrest the implement from his hands. Muffled screams echoed inside his head; tormented moans appeared to seep through the clay and sludge that clung to his slowly sinking boots.

Spooked by these menacing images, he lurched backwards out of the flowerbed. His reaction was so violent that it caused him to lose his footing on the wet grass that lay behind. His legs went from beneath him and he landed with a thump, flat on his back, knocking the wind from his lungs.

Nick wheezed, trying to catch his breath, as he peered wide-eyed up at the cloud-infested sky. Slowly, and in some pain, he turned his head sideways towards the silver birch. The magpies now had their beaks stretched open in anger, but still no sound came from the two predators. Their hostile presence frightened him. He could feel his heart pulsing though the back of his head and down through to his fingertips.

At that moment he was at the mercy of the land. The power of what lay beneath his prone body overwhelmed him. It was if all the elements of nature around him were giving him a warning sign, an indication of its displeasure. How long was this going to continue, he asked himself. Were these dreaded phantoms going to haunt him for the rest of his life? Was this his punishment?

Nick remained in his unceremonious position for a short while, part of him resigned to his fate and part of him trying to gather his composure and his scrambled senses. As the rhythm of his breathing began to return to normal, he raised himself up into a sitting position and scoured his surroundings. The magpies were nowhere to be seen.

Fortunately, he was the only person in the park that morning. The only other creature present to witness his embarrassment was the swan on the lake. She had left her position in the centre of the water and moved closer towards him, and, with her head extended to its apex, she was regarding him with superior disdain.

Then the heavens opened. The cold rain arrowed down, bouncing off the lake, causing the glass-like surface to suddenly appear electrically charged. Nick pulled up the collar of his jacket and hurried towards the shelter of his van.

Although he enjoyed most aspects of his profession, there was always going to be a downside to landscape gardening – days like today.

CHAPTER 58

Nick had not achieved as much as he would have liked in the park due to the appalling weather. A third of the day had been spent in his van reading the daily paper and drinking coffee from his thermos flask. Despite the conditions and his current state of mind, he still felt relieved to be able to work outside again.

Feeling cold and wet, he decided he could do no more work that day and headed for home. He arrived just as darkness fell over the quiet housing estate. Unrelenting rain, highlighted by the streetlamps, slanted down over the cluster of indistinguishable slate rooftops.

He climbed wearily out of his van, the musty, citrus smell of wet pine trees filling his head as he made his way up the front path. Although the surrounding temperature was only a few pips above freezing, the rain-soaked cypress trees exuded a damp warmth from their sagging, weighty branches as he passed beneath them on his way to the front door of his home.

Once inside, he kicked off his shoes, hung his saturated 'shower-proof' jacket on the hook in the hallway and entered the sitting room. Mel was sitting in front of the television, staring at the screen. But the TV was not turned on. The next thing he noticed was the glass and half-empty bottle of gin on the table next to her.

'Mel! You okay?'

As if in slow motion his wife raised her head, with eyes half-closed she tried to focus on Nick, she then wound slowly back to the blank screen. It was the first time he had ever seen his wife drunk. He didn't need her to speak to confirm it.

'Right! Let's get you upstairs. Come on,' he said, as he helped Mel to her feet and led her up to the bedroom.

Thirty minutes later, after Nick had showered and changed into dry clothes, he was sitting in the same chair in front of his television. This time the box was turned on. A programme was playing but nothing registered in his brain apart from Mel's mental condition. He was hoping that as time passed she would begin to get stronger, but she appeared to be retreating even deeper within herself.

The following morning, Nick rang one of his team to tell him he wouldn't be in that day. He thought he should be at home whilst Mel was in such a low moment. By nine o'clock she hadn't appeared and her bedroom door was still closed. Twenty minutes later he was standing at her bedside holding a tray that contained tea and toast. Without moving her head, his wife looked up at his offering, her face remained passive.

'Breakfast in bed? Only five star hotel service in this place,' he said, cheerily.

'I'm not hungry,' Mel replied, her eyes moving back to the horizontal. 'I'm tired, Nick. I just want to sleep.' She turned over in bed, away from him, pulling the covers up higher. Only the top of her blonde hair was now visible to Nick as he stood, disconsolate, still holding the breakfast tray out in front of him, hoping she'd change her mind. He tried once more. 'Mel, please.' But his words were met with silence.

Twice over the next few hours he brought her tea. Both drinks had remained untouched. By midday the situation hadn't changed. Nick had spent the morning deeply regretting his reckless actions over the past few months. He blamed himself for Mel's condition. It was up to him to find a way to help her through this. Maybe in desperate circumstances desperate measures are needed, he thought. Once more he climbed the stairs.

'Right, come on,' he said forcefully, as he strode into her darkened room and threw open the curtains. 'It's time you got up, Mel. You've got to get yourself out of this. I'll give you all the help you need but it's got to be down to you.' He moved forwards to pull the duvet down to her waist but just as quickly she grabbed it and pulled it back up.

'I will get up when I'm ready,' she shouted back at him. 'Just leave me.'

Her reaction shocked Nick. 'God, Mel. I don't know what to do for you any more,' he said. He opened his mouth to say more, then changed his mind. He simply shook his head and left the bedroom. Sitting downstairs, his mind was in turmoil. Why had she suddenly gone plummeting downhill so rapidly? Once again he felt like a useless onlooker as he witnessed his wife's decline. More worryingly, she was becoming more and more distant from him.

Mid-afternoon, Mel suddenly appeared downstairs fully dressed and with her overcoat on. 'I'm going out for a walk,' she declared to a surprised Nick.

'Do you want me to come with you?'

'No. I just need to get out of this place for a while and get some air,' she said as she walked to the front door and left the house.

After Mel departed, Nick moved aimlessly from room to room, numb, wishing he could turn the clock back to that night – wondering how he could have handled it differently. Still wandering around his home deep in thought, he reached the kitchen. He opened the back door and walked out into the garden. Despite the chilly weather, he lingered, for an age, in shirtsleeves, staring into the grey ashes of his bonfire. Was that all that was left of his life, his marriage?

Whilst he stood looking down into the remains of the material casualties from his night of hell, a spiteful wind whipped past his body, sending a cloud of embers spiralling into the air. Nick shivered and went back inside the house. He looked at his watch. Mel had been gone for over an hour and the early season sun would soon be casting a lengthening shadow over the small village of Bourne. Nick was concerned. He put his coat on and left the house in search of his wife. After twenty minutes of walking around the streets of the local neighbourhood, he caught sight of her. She was standing outside the perimeter fence of the local junior school, watching the children play in the playground.

'Mel. Thank God, I was getting worried,' he said as he drew close. On seeing Nick, Mel went to speak, then stopped, as though she had something caught in her throat. Her shoulders dropped as she broke down in tears, sobbing whilst Nick held her in his arms.

A few of the children turned and watched, curious – then confused – as Nick led his distraught wife away from the school and back home.

Once in the house, Nick again tried to reach his wife. 'Will you talk to me, darling? Just let me in. Please.'

'I can't, Nick. There's too much,' she said, not meeting his gaze.

'What do you mean, too much? Too much what? Mel, I realise what you've gone through. And I know I can't imagine what it must have been like to be attacked in that way by that bastard Ba...'

'Don't, Nick,' she said, forcefully, 'just... don't... I don't want to think about... hear his name in this house ever again,' she declared, with clenched fists, her eyelids screwed tight shut.

'Maybe that's exactly what we need to talk about; get this ugly incident out in the open, to allow it to heal,' Nick said, softly, hoping she could find the strength to share her innermost thoughts and fears with him. But Mel merely shook her head and made her weary way back upstairs. Nick heard the distant thud of her bedroom door as it was pushed closed. He stood by the window, hands in pockets, looking out at the trees, cars, people, neighbouring houses but focusing on nothing, aware of one thing only. His reserves of strength were seeping fast from his shattered spirit. There seemed to be no escape from this perpetual nightmare. He could find no release.

CHAPTER 59

Jo Major was woken by her alarm. She turned, reached out an arm and switched it off. She had to get up for work but as she lay on her bed, her mind was fidgety, bouncing from one subject to the next. She was disturbed once more by her mobile ringing on the bedside table. It was 7.25 a.m. Who…? She pressed the button marked with the green phone. 'Hello?'

'Hi, Jo. It's Nick. I've not got much work on today. I wonder if you'd like me to come over and sort your little garden out for you?'

Jo wiped her eyes. 'Oh. Uh, yes. Yes please, if that's not too much trouble,' she replied, surprised at the early call.

'Okay. Give me the address and I'll be over in half an hour,' he said, sounding quite eager to start.

When the doorbell rang shortly after, Jo had just finished showering. Hastily, she threw on a light blue dressing gown over her naked body and hurried downstairs. She was surprised how nervous she felt as she opened the external door. He was standing there, a smile on his face and a handful of garden tools. 'Hi, Nick. Come in,' she said, as she led him up and through the apartment and down the back stairs to her garden.

'Can I leave you to get on with it? I've got to get ready for work,' she said, aware that Nick was staring at her breasts partly exposed by the loosely gathered towelling robe.

'Yes, of course,' he replied, with a broad smile.

Without adjusting the garment, she paused then turned and went back up the stairs, flushed and excited by his attention. A flame started to burn in her belly and was moving downwards. It had been a long while since she had experienced these feelings. She closed her bedroom door and looked at herself in the mirror. Her hair was still wet, it was pushed back from her face. She opened her dressing gown wide. Her breasts, she decided, were quite large for her small frame but still firm. She looked good. For the first time in ages she was aware of her sexuality, something she had filed away and forgotten. Then there was a knock on her bedroom door. Her pulse raced through her system. Now her whole body was on fire.

Without adjusting the robe, she turned and opened the door. Nick stood, mouth open, and took in all her nakedness. He looked back into her eyes, stepped forward, took her in his arms and kissed her hard on the lips, their mouths opening to each other, exploring. The gown fell to the floor as Jo ripped off Nick's clothes and pulled him to her bed. She took one last look at his fit, muscle-defined body before she guided him into her.

Nick pushed her breasts together in his strong hands, brushing his thumbs over her nipples as he thrust himself deep inside her. Frantically, they made love. They didn't make love, they fucked. They fucked fast, furious, sweat-covered, animal, explosive.

Jo lay on her back, breathing heavily, mouth slightly open, legs tightly pressed together, her hands clasped between them. Her mind was free, floating on waves of pleasure, drifting across sun-bleached sands. That was until the unexpected sound of the alarm stung her consciousness once more. She blinked her eyes open. It was 7.25 a.m. She was alone. The garden had been untouched by Nick – as had her body.

CHAPTER 60

The solo performance of a blackcap mimicking the tunes of a flute drifted through the open window of Nick's bedroom. It was the first sound to meet his ears as he returned to a conscious state. He raised his head from the pillow towards the bedside table, the clock showed 7.10. He had awoken before the alarm.

After showering, he dressed and went into the adjoining bedroom, where Mel slept. The bed was empty. Nick's brain switched into alert mode as he hurried down the stairs and into the sitting room. It was also unoccupied. He heard movement coming from the kitchen.

Mel was sitting at the table, a mug of coffee in front of her.

Nick breathed again. 'Morning. Couldn't sleep?' he asked, as matter-of-factly as he could manage.

'I've only been down for a few minutes. Anyway, I could ask you the same question,' Mel replied. She looked up at her husband. 'Listen, I appreciate you being at home yesterday but you don't have to stay off work for me again. I'm feeling much better today,' she added, confidently.

Nick was surprised by the change in his wife's state of mind. Maybe yesterday's outpouring of emotion was the release she needed. 'Are you sure?' he said.

'Honestly, I'm fine.'

Twenty minutes later, after Nick had changed into his work clothes and prepared a packed lunch, he stood at the open front door of his house. Mel was beside him. 'Okay, darling. I'm off. I'll pop in to see you lunchtime,' said Nick, as he kissed her on the cheek.

'You don't need to. I'll be all right. I'm a lot better today,' she repeated.

'I know, but the job's only five minutes away so it'll be nice to have a fresh cup of tea with my lunch for a change. It's never the same from a flask,' he said, in an attempt to appear unconcerned.

Mel shrugged.

'Right. See you later.'

As Nick drove away from his house, he pondered on how Mel's mood differed so drastically from the previous day. It was an incredible turnaround. Then another thought entered his head. Was this sudden improvement just a ploy to make him think she was feeling better, to stop him pestering her with awkward questions.

'No!' he said out loud. 'No!' He berated himself for being so negative. His wife had shown an encouraging disposition this morning, something that, for weeks, he prayed would happen. He must take heart from that. It was only slight progress, a beginning; but once more he dared to hope that their lives could find some measure of normality again.

As Mel walked back through the sitting room towards the kitchen, she stopped by the Indian coffee table. The horrific sight of Scrivens' mutilated body flashed through her brain. There he was – twisted, lying at her feet in a pool of his own warm blood. Shockwaves racked through her body as the vivid image of his corpse abused her senses. *Keep moving*, she told herself. *Keep moving*.

On unsteady legs, Mel continued on to the kitchen. She sunk into the chair, placed her hands on the table and dropped forwards, letting her head bang on the wooden surface. The action was repeated. She felt no pain as her thoughts scrambled. She could now see Ballack's bulbous eyes, staring, inches from her face, feel the crushing weight of his body on her chest as he pounded into her – the stale smell of alcohol mixed with his acrid sweat. She had no control over these invasive memories. At that moment she hated herself.

The thought of having Ballack's child, his blood, his DNA, his odious characteristics inside her, changing her body's metabolism with each ensuing day, made her feel sick to the stomach. She had wanted a baby so much. Her husband's baby. To have part of Nick inside her, a man she loved deeply, was her dream. The obnoxious reality of her present condition had become her worst nightmare.

With a sudden rush of adrenalin, she pushed herself upright, realising she had to be strong. She was pregnant. There were decisions to be made. Suddenly, the future was clearer. The fog inside her head was beginning to lift. She looked out of the kitchen window. The sun was shining. She was aware that a smile had made its way across her lips for the first time in weeks.

Then her attention focused on the cupboard below the sink. She couldn't make those decisions on her own. She needed some help. And what lay behind that cupboard door could provide it.

CHAPTER 61

The weather had made an unexpected turn. A cerulean blue sky provided a breathtaking, infinite canopy over South East England. Nick's dense mane of hair was plastered to his head, his shirt clung to his body as he laboured beneath the surprisingly hot spring sunshine. By one thirty he had cleared the tired and the dead shrubs, weeds, crisp packets and fizzy drink containers from the two brick-enclosed, raised flower beds that were designed to give the entrance to the Ashtead Job Centre some quota of appeal. Nick's van was stocked with an array of colourful perennials that would lighten the mood of the building's employees and, hopefully, some of those out of work.

But the planting would have to wait. Nick wanted to check on Mel to see if this morning's progress had been maintained. He climbed into his vehicle, hot, sticky and dirty, and drove the short distance back to his home. His mind was searching, grasping for ways he could help Mel and to build on her more upbeat mood.

Maybe he could arrange some counselling sessions for his wife to help with her depression, he thought. But then again they would have to reveal too much detail to the analyst – that was a no-no. Outside assistance was impossible. They needed to get away from their present environment – from where it all went wrong – the vivid memories, the nightmares. A holiday. That was what Nick's mind settled on as he put his key in the front door.

As he entered the house, the first thing he noticed was the sound of the radio coming from the kitchen. It was tuned to a station that was playing pop songs – the volume filled the room. Nick frowned, then smiled. This was definitely an improvement from the silence that had ruled the house over recent weeks. He moved into the kitchen, still smiling, but was surprised to see it empty.

Then he noticed the bottle of gin on the table. This time it was empty. His heart sank. If this was going to become a regular outlet, her chances of recovery would be considerably slimmer. He was aware she needed help to silence her demons but disappearing into drink was not the answer.

'Mel, I'm home,' he shouted above the music as he turned, exited the kitchen and headed for the stairs. 'Where are you, darling?' he called again. As he neared the stairs he almost tripped over something on the floor. It was a high-heeled shoe. He picked it up, frowning. This was unlike Mel, she was normally so tidy around the house. It had to be the booze. Maybe she had gone to bed to sleep it off. This was another problem they were going to have to face, he thought, as he started to climb the steps.

He looked upwards and was about to call her name again. There she was, dressed in her silk Catherine Malandrino dress. The other high-heeled shoe was still on her foot, which dangled two feet above his head. Mel looked down at him with bulging eyes. Her bloated face and protruding tongue were a mixture of blue and purple. Around her neck and secured to the banister above her head was the belt from her dressing gown.

Nick's legs gave way as he slumped backwards and slid down the few steps he had just climbed. The sudden and drastic loss of oxygen to the brain caused his body to lose all muscle control and coordination as he went into shock. From his prone position at the foot of the stairs, he looked sideways. He felt drunk. His eyes were unable to focus clearly on anything, as if he were underwater. Time ceased to exist as he failed to recognise his formless surroundings.

Visions of Mel began to seep into his confused state; the four years of happy marriage; the first time he saw her; the imagined sight of her in that dress, beautiful, majestic. He tried to get up but his brain, still fused, was sending out muddled, incomplete messages to his nervous system. He looked up once more. The sight that met his eyes caused a long agonised moan to squeeze from his deflated lungs. 'No!' was the only word that managed to escape from his mouth as he lay on the stairs beneath the crudely suspended body of his wife. 'No, Mel. Not this,' he pleaded, as his strength gradually returned. He pulled himself to his feet, reached up and touched Mel's bare foot. It was icy cold.

Then, buoyed by a sudden sense of urgency, thinking he may still be able to save her, he climbed to the top of the landing, put his hands under her armpits and, using every ounce of his power, he managed to pull his wife up and back over the banister. He untied the belt, carried her into their bedroom and laid her on the bed.

After minutes of trying to resuscitate her he realised it was a hopeless task. She had gone. He sat up, exhausted, heartbroken. Leaning forward onto his fists, his eyes closed, his head spinning; he felt faint. Overwhelming pain coursed through his entire being.

Just as he thought he was going to pass out, his lungs filled to capacity and held the large volume of air within. He threw his head back: the word "no" escaped from his chest once more. But this time it exploded as a roar that shook the windows and walls of his bedroom.

The veins in his neck and forehead bulged to the point of bursting as a mixture of rage and frustration was released from every nerve end in his body, rising up like molten lava and pouring from his open mouth. It lasted until his lungs were powerless to continue.

Spent, his head and shoulders slumped forward as he broke down. He cried like he had never cried before. Huge sobs convulsed through his unresisting body. His brain was now incapable of thought. He looked to the ceiling, closed his eyes once more and fell backwards next to Mel's lifeless body. He lay next to his darling wife, holding her soft, cold hand, devastated, unable to move. Eventually, he turned to look at her face. Even now she was still beautiful. He raised himself up, leant towards Mel and kissed her gently on the cheek.

As he did so, he noticed two white envelopes on the pillow next to where Mel's head lay. He picked them up. One was marked 'To be opened first'. The other was simply marked 'Nick'. His trembling hand picked up the first envelope, pulled the note out from inside and started to read:

My darling Nick,
I carried out two pregnancy tests yesterday and another this morning. They were all positive. Since we last made love I have had a period. I am therefore carrying Nathan Ballack's child. Because of my beliefs I can't go through with an abortion but I can't give birth to a victim of rape either. I am in an impossible situation. I cannot see any other way out. Please try to understand. Too much has happened to me. My life is worthless. I know you will find someone to give you the family you deserve. But you must destroy this first letter before you call the police for obvious reasons. I have hidden the pregnancy tests under the bonfire remains. I've written another letter so the police will not know the truth of what occurred in this house.
Whatever happens don't make it easy for them.
I love you,
Mel.

Tears rolled from his eyes, falling onto the note as he read the contents once again. He then opened the other letter:

My darling Nick,
I know how much you have wanted children and I have failed you. I hope you find someone who can fulfil that dream. Please forgive me.
I love you,
Mel.

Nick felt as though his brain was shrinking inside his skull. He could not make sense of anything that was now confronting him. He looked down once more at the body of his wife. She looked so small, so fragile lying there next to him.

He knew Mel had been deeply depressed these past weeks – but to kill herself? And how could she be so disturbed as to take her own life yet be so clinical and together to think of leaving two suicide notes?

'Pregnant!' Nick whispered. The cruel irony was a dagger thrust deep in his heart. He could only guess at the despair and confusion within her when she discovered her condition. Could he have persuaded her to get rid of Ballack's child? Tragically, he had never had the chance. Could they have brought up a child conceived in such distressing circumstances? If only she could have discussed it with him.

But it was too late. She had made those decisions for him. Were her actions brave and noble or cowardly and selfish? All Nick knew for sure was that the woman he loved had deserted him forever.

Any guilt that had remained concerning the death and disposal of Nathan Ballack was quickly diluted. He hated him. He had taken everything away that was good in his life – his peace of mind, his morals and now Mel, his beautiful wife.

Nick made his way downstairs to the telephone and picked up the receiver. He was tempted to end the whole charade and confess all to the police as he dialled 999. He held the envelope containing the first note in his hand as he told the operator of his wife's suicide.

Then it hit him as sure as someone had kicked him in the stomach. He realised that if he confessed it would mean that Ballack and Scrivens had won. Mel would not have wanted that. It was not going to happen.

He decided there and then to honour Mel's wishes. If the police were clever enough to discover his secret then so be it. But he was certainly not going to make it easy for them.

After he put the phone down, he walked into the bathroom, tore the first envelope and its contents into small pieces and flushed them down the toilet.

However much evidence he destroyed, the strangled body of his lovely wife, hanging limp from the stair rail, would be a sight engraved across his soul for the rest of his years.

CHAPTER 62

When the call came through to Ashford Police Station of the suspected suicide, two uniformed officers were assigned immediately to the location of the incident. One of them was PC Ben Woodhurst. Ben immediately recognised the dead woman's name. He remembered that Nick and Mel Summers had been linked socially with Jo and Ballack just before the detective's disappearance. He picked up the phone and rang Jo Major.

It was just after three o'clock when Jo took the internal telephone call from Ben informing her of the death of Mel Summers. Her initial reaction was one of complete shock. She had liked Mel; they were at the beginning of what she had hoped would be a lasting friendship.

But she was deeply upset for Nick. What must he be going through at this moment? Then her detective's brain kicked in. This confirmed her suspicions that all was not sweetness and light with the Summers.' Mel would need a powerful reason to take her own life, surely?

She began to imagine the dreadful sight that must have confronted Nick on his arrival home. As she did so, transient flashbacks of finding her own mother in her bath interweaved with visions of Mel's cold, lifeless body hanging from the stairs. Jo screwed her eyelids together as tightly as she could and then blinked them open, attempting to oust the unsettling images.

The memories of her mother's death were still too raw. Mel's suicide, if it was suicide, was going to tear her slowly healing wound wide open again. Her involvement in this was not going to be easy.

She tried to focus on the facts as she knew them. Not for one moment did she suspect that Nick had anything to do with his wife's death. But she was convinced something had happened to upset this couple – something drastic that had changed their lives.

Jo had to tell her boss of this latest development. It may have nothing to do with Ballack but the proximity of these events both in time and distance aroused her suspicion. She rose from her desk, headed straight for Jack Jolley's office and knocked loudly on the door.

'Come in,' Jo heard Jack call. She entered the room and strode directly up to his desk. Jack looked up from a pile of papers spread out in front of him and into the face of his detective constable. Her mouth was slightly open, her eyes wide and fixed. Jack sensed this was not a social call. 'Coffee?' he asked, a hopeful look on his face.

'Guv, Nick Summers has just called the police. He arrived home to find his wife dead. She's hanged herself from the banisters.'

'Oh my good God!' Jack said, shaking his head. His eyes narrowed, then slowly panned down to his desk. He picked up his gold pen, leant back in his chair and began tapping the underside of his chin. After a few seconds he let out a low, contemplative sigh. He looked back up at Jo. 'What do you think?' he asked her.

'It doesn't make sense, guv. When I first met them a few months back they seemed the perfect couple. Though recently, I sensed that there was a bit of tension between them. Mel appeared to be under some sort of pressure I think. But I didn't see this coming. Not suicide.'

'Well, the pathologist's report will tell us if there's any foul play involved,' said Jack, expanding his white eyebrows.

'I don't know. I find it hard to imagine Nick Summers murdering his wife. But there's more to this than meets the eye here, I'm sure, guv. Don't ask me what, but there are too many strange things going on in a quiet little town like Bourne.'

'There's such a thing as coincidence, Jo,' said Jack.

'Coincidence! If my memory of police-worthy incidents in Bourne over the past five years serves me correctly, I think we've had a cat stuck up a tree, a couple of flashers in the park, a few noisy late night parties and a stolen car – which wasn't stolen at all. The lady owner had just forgotten she'd parked the bloody thing in Tesco's car park,' was Jo's stout reply.

Jack smiled at Jo's punchy retort. 'Okay, point made. Look, I'm going to assign DS Sam Geddy to lead the investigation on this, Jo,' he said, picking up the phone. 'I have to have an unbiased view to protect the integrity of this inquiry. I assume we've got uniform on their way over there?'

'Yes, guv. But...' Jo halted her reply as Jack spoke on the phone. He arranged for Detective Sergeant Geddy to attend the scene of the crime as head of the investigation. He placed the phone back on its base.

Jo went to speak but Jack got there first. 'That doesn't mean to say you can't get over to the house and keep your eyes and ears open, does it?' he said, anticipating Jo's wish to still have some involvement with the case. 'Perhaps you can use your knowledge of the couple to spot something that Sam can't see. But don't get in his way. Do you understand?'

'Yes, guv. Thanks,' replied Jo, relieved.

'You know Nick Summers quite well, don't you?' Jack asked.

Jo responded with an uncertain nod of her head.

'Right. Just watch and listen,' he said to the young detective.

As Jo was about to leave, Jack spoke again, 'Do you think this has anything to do with Ballack's disappearance then?

Jo's face looked pained. 'I don't think so, guv. I can't put my finger on it, but something's not right somewhere.'

CHAPTER 63

Jo waited half an hour at her desk. She didn't want to arrive at the Summers' house before DS Sam Geddy. It was his show and it would not have been right to be on site before him. But she was pleased Sam had been chosen to run the investigation. He was a friendly, fairly laid-back character. She was pretty sure that he would not have a problem with her presence at his crime scene. She wanted in on this but she still had to tread carefully.

When she arrived at Nick Summers' house, a handful of emergency service vehicles were already parked outside. She pulled in behind the ambulance and turned off the ignition. The vehicle's rear doors were wide open. She could see through her front windscreen that there was no one inside.

She sat in her car for a while in contemplative mood, watching the rain hit the bonnet, until she was unable to see clearly through the glass in front of her. She turned to look out of the side window. Every light in the Summers' house was on, making the afternoon dusk appear darker.

Either side, neighbours peered through curtains at the worrying presence of the police and ambulance vehicles in their quiet road. Directly opposite, one white-haired old lady wrapped in a bright red tartan shawl, arms folded, stood under the shelter of her front porch. They would all have plenty to gossip about tomorrow, Jo thought.

Realising the rain was not going to ease, she got out of her car and hurried up to the Summers' front door. She rang the bell and waited. The door was opened by PC Ben Woodhurst.

'Ah! Hello, Jo,' whispered Ben, standing aside to let her enter the hallway. 'DS Geddy's taking a statement from Mr Summers now. It appears he's been gardening down at the Job Centre all morning. Then he comes home to find Mrs Summers hanging from the banister. The doctor's upstairs examining the body now,' he continued.

'How is Mr Summers?' asked Jo in hushed tones.

'Wrecked, I'd say. If he had anything to do with her death, he's a bloody good actor. And I've seen the body. It's not a pretty sight. Her face...'

'Yeah, all right, Ben,' Jo interrupted as she gave the police constable a look. He understood.

Jo walked into the sitting room to see the detective, who was sitting in an armchair, close his notebook. Sitting opposite him on the sofa was the hunched figure of Nick Summers. But this wasn't the man she knew. He appeared smaller than when they had last met. He was wearing what appeared to be damp clothes that clung to his shivering body. It was a pathetic sight that would have moved her to tears had she not been on official business.

Sam Geddy stood up and walked over to her. 'Hello, Jo. I understand you were friends with the Summers,' he said quietly.

'Sort of,' Jo replied.

'This must have come as a shock, then?' he said. Jo realised this was a probing question and not words of comfort.

'Yes, it was. A total shock.'

'Well, I've finished interviewing Mr Summers for now. I've got a few other things to do before I'm finished here. We'll talk later, back at the station,' Sam said, as he headed towards the kitchen.

Jo's attention was now focused on Nick. As she approached him, he raised his head to look up at her. It was a face drained of all expression and colour apart from the red surrounds of his weary eyes. 'Jo,' he said quietly.

Jo sat down next to him and held his cold, unresponsive hand in hers. Nick went to speak but stopped as he broke down in tears. 'Okay, Nick,' Jo said, lost for any meaningful words to comfort the distraught figure beside her. She took a tissue from her handbag and pressed it into Nick's quivering hand. 'The first thing I want you to do is get out of those wet clothes and have a hot shower. I'll be here when you come back down,' Jo said. She helped him to his feet. 'Go with him,' she told the police constable nearby.

The police officer stepped forward and took Nick's arm. Jo followed their slow progress up the stairs; she shook her head, bewildered.

Half an hour later she watched as the blanket covered body of Mel Summers was carried out of the house. She walked behind the two ambulance men as far as the front door, then looked on in disbelief as they carried the corpse of her friend carefully down the wet path to their waiting vehicle. She breathed the cold evening air deep into her lungs and exhaled forcefully, producing a white trail of vapour.

Her move to the door was not just to follow the stretcher that contained the young and vivacious Mel but to avoid making eye contact with the two police officers in the room. She felt that any show of emotion, witnessed by her colleagues, would weaken her credibility as a police officer. Once more, she questioned whether she was cut out for this type of career.

Shortly afterwards, she was sitting next to a slightly stronger looking Nick Summers. The shower and change into warm, dry clothes had gone some way to improving his outward appearance.

Jo listened carefully to Nick's short, heart-rending story. This man, who was normally so confident was, at that moment, a little lost boy. It was heartbeaking to witness. Now was not the time to delve further into his relationship with his deceased wife. As far as Jo was concerned it appeared to be an obvious case of suicide, but they would have to wait for the post-mortem report for confirmation.

If there were no signs of a struggle in the form of suspicious bruising or restraint marks and no evidence of Mel being drugged, then it was an open and shut case. The addition of the suicide note, once the writing had been proved to be that of the deceased, would be enough to satisfy the coroner.

But there were still unanswered questions, nagging worries that made Jo feel uncomfortable. Not being able to have children could certainly send a woman into a deep depression, but was it enough, on its own, to impel her to take her own life? She had her doubts.

When Jo climbed into her car to drive home, her professional mask fell from her face with a crash. She turned on the ignition, then turned it off again. She hadn't realised how on edge she had been in the Summers' house. The muscles beneath the rear of her skull felt pinched, causing a tension headache.

She was a young policewoman not yet hardened to these kind of situations. And this was no ordinary incident – this was a friend – a beautiful young woman who had taken her own life. Here was a charming young man robbed of his future, destroyed by the loss of the woman he loved.

The pain she had seen on Nick's face was unbearable to witness. The hopelessness that bled from his eyes was infectious. In the house she had stayed strong for him, but now her tears came. They came for Nick and Mel, and her own mother.

CHAPTER 64

Jo stared at her office computer screen as if it were a sounding board in the vain hope that her reflected thoughts would reveal some answers to the many questions gnawing away in her head. Her eyes fell to the bottom of the display. It told her it was ten a.m., Wednesday 6th January – two days after Mel's suicide. They were two of the most unsettled days of her life. Her concentration, as far as office work was concerned, rose and fell at will. Her brain was like a tumble dryer throwing assorted theories and graphic images round and around in mind-numbing circles.

Her moods, uncontrollable – causing her mind to wander off to places she would rather not visit. One of the distractions was Nick Summers. The fact that he was living on his own in the same house in which his wife had taken her life was of concern to her. It was not a healthy state of affairs. She'd had a similar experience recently and knew what it was like to be alone with those memories.

But she had lost her mother, an ailing old lady in the autumn of her years. Mel had been not much more than a girl with her whole life in front of her. The thought crossed her mind that if Nick could not see a future for himself now, he may decide to take the same route as Mel.

The phone on her desk rang. It was Bill Montgomery the pathologist. She had known Bill for over ten years. He was in his late thirties with shoulder-length honey-blonde hair and still happily single. They were good friends. When she found out that he had been assigned the job of carrying out the post-mortem on Mel Summers, she had rung him to discuss a few details of the case. Now he was returning her call.

'Bill Montgomery at your service, Miss Major. How's life in the fast lane?' was his opening line.

'Hi, Bill. Oh! You know – fast. Arses and elbows come to mind,' Jo replied.

'Arses and elbows? Weren't they a seventies punk band?' said Bill.

Jo giggled. 'Your humour doesn't get any better.'

'Listen. Mel Summers. I've finished the autopsy and you'll be pleased to hear there are no suspicious circumstances surrounding her death. No signs of a struggle and no drugs had been administered. She had consumed the best part of half a bottle of gin, but that's it. I'm happy and confident to give a verdict of suicide.'

'I thought as much. But I'm relieved to hear it from the horse's mouth,' said Jo.

'The horse's mouth has got something else for you. This has no bearing on the validity of my verdict of suicide, but there's something, unofficially or officially, you might want to know. Having had our discussion about the circumstances of this death and how you were friends with both of them, I'm prepared to keep this out of my report if you think it will help the husband.'

'God! Bill, this is killing me. What is it?' Jo said, keeping her voice low. Her colleague Mark Smallwood never listened to her phone calls and was probably far enough away not to hear anyway. But creepy 'Merrill' Lynch, who was one desk closer, always seemed to be trying to ear-wig on her conversations.

'She was pregnant,' said Bill.

Jo was stunned. *No, it can't be true,* she said to herself. 'How many weeks?' she asked Bill.

'About six,' came the reply.

'So she must have known?'

'Probably,' Bill said.

'Then why?'

'You're the detective, Jo. Look, I need to know whether you're going to reveal this to anyone. If so, I'll have to put it in my report. But what with the contents of the suicide note and all, I thought you might want to save the husband more pain. If he knows that she was pregnant, well, what's that going to do to the poor bugger? He'll have to live the rest of his life never knowing the real reason that she killed herself. Another possible scenario, of course, is that maybe she didn't know she was pregnant, and that would be even more tragic. Either way, it could devastate the husband.'

'Thanks, Bill, I really appreciate this. And no, I'm not going to tell anyone about it. I think that would tear Nick apart. If you're convinced that it was suicide, then this piece of information can remain a secret between you and me. I can't see who would gain from knowing that Mel was pregnant.'

'Still, it's a funny one. Unless...' said Bill.

'Unless what?'

'Unless it wasn't her husband's baby.'

Jo took a few seconds to digest Bill's words. 'No way! She wasn't that type of girl. Those two may have had some sort of ongoing problem but they were inseparable.'

'Just a thought,' replied Bill. 'Look, I've got to fly. So this thing is just between us, yeah?'

'Yes, of course. Thanks again for you-know-what, and take care,' said Jo.

'Bye, *mon petite* detective,' said Bill in a heavy French accent.

'It's feminine – it's ma,' corrected Jo.

'Oh, sorry. Bye, ma,' Bill said as he put his phone down.

'Bye, you bloody fool,' Jo said to a dead phone line. She smiled at Bill's last comment. Considering the stomach-churning procedures that he had to carry out, he was a breath of fresh air. Maybe the only way he could do that kind of job was to have a crazy sense of humour.

Then it hit her again. Pregnant. God! *This changes everything,* thought Jo.

CHAPTER 65

After Bill's phone call, Jo went straight into Jack Jolley's office. 'Guv, the pathologist has carried out the post-mortem. He confirmed that Mel Summers died by means of strangulation. There were no suspicious circumstances. The coroner's verdict will be suicide.'

'Good. We can do without a local murder investigation right now. But you still think this is, in some way, tied up with the Ballack case,' said Jack.

'I'm not sure, guv. Maybe this tragedy is just a coincidence, as you suggested. Perhaps I'm seeing something that isn't there.

'Grasping at straws, possibly?' Jack said, his eyebrows forming twin arches. Jo displayed a pained face in response. 'Well, there's nothing wrong with that. Sometimes we surprise ourselves with what we find,' he added.

She knew that she should inform her boss of Mel's pregnancy but something was stopping her. Only she and Bill Montgomery knew of this turn of events, and she was confident the trust between them would not be abused. For

Nick to lose his wife to suicide because she failed to give him a child was pain enough. If he knew she was pregnant, well, that would surely destroy him. But that, if she was honest with herself, was not the only reason to withhold the information.

Since her mother's death, the feeling of solitude had triggered a change in Jo. A deeper sense of ambition began to edge its way into her thinking. She needed financial security, and if it wasn't going to be achieved through marriage, it had to be via her job. Something in her mind told her that if she could solve all these puzzles on her own it would give her, the new girl on the block, a great deal of kudos with Jack Jolley and her colleagues. With Ballack out of the picture there was a need for someone to run the team. Maybe it was too early in her career to expect to get that position, but there was no harm in trying.

'Look, Jo,' said Jack, popping her thought bubble, 'we've got a lot on our plate here at the moment, and with being one man down on your team it's not going to get any easier for a while. So I want you to concentrate all your efforts on the team's pending cases whilst still trying to get a lead on the whereabouts of Ballack. DS Geddy will tie up the Summers' inquiry in the next few days. I've seen his report and there's nothing to suggest otherwise.'

'Okay, guv,' said Jo, as she left Jack's office. Back at her desk, she played the conversation with her boss over in her head. She had been dishonest, or at least held back information from him. Suddenly, her mind was a battlefield of conflicting emotions. Part of her wanted to show the men around her that she was as good a detective as them – if not better. But she was capable of deceitful tactics. Hardly the actions of a team player.

This was the first time in her career she had cause to doubt her integrity. *But, surely, if I solve these cases, the end product would justify the means, wouldn't it?* She asked herself.

Until now she had done everything by the book. When she had first joined the drug squad within the SCD unit as a fresh-faced novice, she had visions of at least making every school and college in the area safe from drug dealers and users. It was never going to happen. They were far too devious, much too slippery.

Jack once told her that the big picture was huge, ineradicable. They could win the occasional battle, but the war was unconquerable. This situation was different. The mysterious disappearance of Nathan Ballack was the battle that now challenged her every skill as a detective.

Could she conquer this one? She was sure that she could.

CHAPTER 66

Mel Summers' funeral had been held in the late afternoon at the nineteenth-century Catholic Church in Bourne. The interior of the church, with its high vaulted ceiling and Caen stone walls, was not a lot warmer than the temperature outside. Central heating, it appeared, had not found its way into this beautiful, old structure. Despite the freezing weather conditions the church had been packed to its arch-braced rafters.

The suicide of Mel Summers had spread throughout the local community in a matter of days, putting the inhabitants of the small village into a state of shock. Large numbers of mourners, ranging from the sympathetic to the morbidly curious, had emerged from the warmth of their homes to attend the church service.

Jo Major attended the funeral and had been one of the few to be asked back to Nick's house after the church service. She was surprised by the invitation.

As she entered the church, she nodded to the vicar and took her seat behind and to the side of Mel's parents. They had flown over from Spain two days earlier. She wondered how Nick had managed to explain to them how his wife – their precious daughter – had come to take her own life.

Whatever the reason he gave them, surely they would have doubts as to his culpability in the death of their daughter.

She was soon to regret sitting in such close proximity to them. Mel's mother was inconsolable throughout the entire proceedings, sobbing audibly into a handkerchief. More than once she saw her reach her arm up towards the nearby coffin that contained the body of her only child. Jo expected her, any minute, to rush forwards and throw herself across the pine casket.

Mel's father was in his early sixties. Jo guessed that under normal circumstances he would have been a good-looking man. But the person she saw appeared stunned. His body, rigid in his seat, looked like a waxwork dummy. The face, lightly tanned, looked drawn; his vacuous eyes were fixed on a point above and beyond the coffin. She realised he was trying desperately to hold himself together for the sake of his wife.

Eventually, the tension became infectious. The shared pain Jo witnessed between the two of them finally got to her and she wept silently behind them.

After the ceremony, on his way out of the church, Nick had not recognised half of the faces in the congregation whose heads sat deep amongst a collection of multi-coloured scarves and heavy overcoats. He had the feeling that they had all turned up to witness a public execution – his.

Back at the house, Nick's mother had prepared a cold buffet for the guests at the wake. 'I hope we've got enough food for everyone,' she said, as she arranged plates of sandwiches on the kitchen table. 'How many are coming back?' she added.

'Stop fussing, Mum. It doesn't matter,' Nick said dismissively. 'If I had my way, we wouldn't have any of this – just say my thank yous and goodbyes at the church.' He picked up a bottle of wine from the kitchen worktop and filled a large glass. 'Mel's taken her own life. What's there to talk about? What's to celebrate?'

Nick's mother looked forlornly at her husband, who widened his eyes and said nothing, then back at her son. She too was stuck for words.

The doorbell rang. The first guest had arrived.

The invitations to the wake, back at Nick's house, had been limited to relatives, a few close friends and Jo Major. Despite being a police officer and a potential threat, he was grateful that she had been such a comfort to him on the day of Mel's death. She had called, subsequently, and appeared to be concerned as to his frame of mind.

As the guests poured in, he stood at the door with a polite smile and a handshake. It was an uncomfortable process listening to the offers of condolences from each sympathiser. He didn't want a ceremony. He certainly didn't want a fuss.

If Mel had died from an illness or an accident, it would have been different. But she hadn't. She had hanged herself in their home. He was certain that a fair percentage of the mourners in the church and back at his house would be wondering whether he was to blame in some way.

How self-indulgent, how uncaring must a man be not to notice that his wife is on the edge of taking her own life? The thought bit deep. But if he had been in their shoes, that is exactly what he would have been thinking.

But none of them knew. None of them could be told.

CHAPTER 67

Jo was talking to Nick's mother and father in the sitting room. She could see that they both looked utterly bewildered by this unforeseeable tragedy. That their only child could be involved in such a scandal was deeply shocking to them.

'And what do you do for a living,' said Nick's mother in a hushed, courteous manner.

Here we go, thought Jo. 'I'm a police officer,' she replied. As soon as the words left her mouth, she noticed an immediate change in them. They both looked visibly surprised as their demeanour towards her suddenly shifted. It was as if they thought she was spying on their son. Maybe she was; she was still not sure what to make of the tragedy.

She glanced across the room at Nick, who was speaking to a plump, middle-aged woman holding a plate stacked with sandwiches. The detective in her wanted to get him on his own, ask him questions about the events of the past few months – questions that would be both intrusive and painful to a man who had suffered more than enough misery already.

But now was not the right time. Maybe she would never find the appropriate time.

Eventually, Nick got around to speaking to her as he poured her a glass of wine in the kitchen. 'I can't believe how many people were at the church,' said Nick.

'You live in a small village, Nick. Something like this is big news, I'm afraid. Everyone wants to pay their respects,' said Jo, trying to play down the curiosity aspect of the proceedings.

'I've never seen half of the faces there before,' said Nick, shaking his head.

'And I doubt you'll ever see them again. At least they helped to warm up a freezing cold church,' said Jo, trying to lighten the mood, still feeling chilly. But the rest of the conversation was polite and stilted. She could see that Nick wanted to be anywhere else but there.

As he moved on, she watched him walking dutifully around his house, thanking the guests for attending the church service, smiling at their awkward attempts to cheer him up.

Taking the hint and hoping others would follow suit, Jo decided to leave after an hour. She performed her round of goodbyes, kissed an uncomfortable looking Nick on the cheek and departed.

As soon as she entered her flat, she took off her black mourning clothes and changed into tracksuit bottoms and sweatshirt. She hoped the change of outfit would lighten her mood. She headed straight for the kitchen. A chilled bottle of chardonnay was released from the fridge. Over the next two hours it was consumed to the melancholic accompaniment of Dido.

When she retired for the evening, her brain was dominated by the face of Nick Summers. The face was empty, as though it had been drawn in pencil on see-through plastic. It appeared to be a window that led to nowhere. But she suspected that this grieving man had closed the curtains on that window. What were they hiding? What couldn't she see?

CHAPTER 68

Three weeks after the funeral, there had still been no new leads on Ballack's disappearance. Jo was sitting at her desk immersed, almost to the point of drowning, in oceans of administrative work. She was halfway through typing a report when her office phone rang. Jo picked up the receiver, cradled it between head and shoulder and continued to type. 'Hello, Jo Major,' she said.

'Hi, Jo. It's Ben Woodhurst.'

The last time she'd seen or spoke to the police constable was at the Summers' house on the day of Mel's suicide. 'Hi, Ben. How are you?'

'Fine. But listen to this. The station got a call from some bloke earlier today who works for the Kent Wildlife Trust. He's been down to Dunley Marsh this morning. Do you know it?' asked Ben.

'Yeah, I know Dunley Marsh. And?' Jo said a little impatiently.

'Apparently, they've been thinking of marking off a large piece of land there for a bird sanctuary or something. God knows why, the place stinks. Every time I've had to drive out that way I close the car windows,' said Ben.

'This better be good, Ben, I'm up to my eyeballs in paperwork at the moment,' said Jo, wishing she had never answered the phone.

'So, he's checking out where the boundaries should go and seeing what parts of the land are solid enough to erect one of those lookout places on.'

'Well, if he was successful, we can all sleep well in our beds tonight,' said Jo.

'He edges around a row of bushes and finds himself standing over a hole that's probably been dug by a badger or a fox or something. And in the middle of the hole, sticking up from the mud, is a human hand.'

Jo stopped typing immediately and grabbed the telephone. Ben had finally got her attention. 'Go on,' she said.

'I'm calling you from the crime scene, and believe me, if you thought that this place stunk before, you should be down here now. We've found two bodies,' continued Ben.

'Two?' said Jo.

'Buried virtually on top of each other. The crime scene manager and her team are down here right now. I watched them pull the corpses out of the makeshift grave. It wasn't a pretty sight. But I thought you'd like to know that one of the bodies, as far as I could make out, was wearing a black, leather, knee-length coat.'

'I'll be straight down,' said Jo.

'Bring your wellies, you're gonna need 'em,' replied Ben.

'Okay. Bye,' Jo said as she put the phone back on its base.

She rushed in to Jack Jolley's office to tell him of the latest development.

'Mm! Two bodies. That doesn't happen every day,' said Jack on hearing the news.

'I'm off down there now, guv,' said Jo.

'Good,' said Jack, as Jo got up to leave. 'Take a warm coat – I know that place. It's cold, damp and horrible,' he added.

'Will do,' Jo replied.

Jo returned to her desk and briefed Mark and Colin on the latest piece of news. Their faces dropped at the probability that one of the bodies in the Dunley Marsh grave was that of their team leader. Jo had no time to discuss the matter further. She retrieved her coat and left the office with her colleagues still looking stunned.

On the way to her car, Jo was not sure whether she wanted one of the dead bodies to be that of her old boss. Her stomach was in knots. Part of her was excited by the find and the other part was fearful that Nathan Ballack had been callously murdered.

CHAPTER 69

Darkness had descended by the time Jo arrived at Dunley Marsh but it was not difficult to find the exact location. The entrance to the place had been lit up like a funfair and was crawling with what appeared to be half of the Ashford police force and ambulance service.

Jack and Ben Woodhurst were not wrong. The place was remote, damp and unwelcoming. When Jo got out of her car, the famous Dunley Marsh odour draped itself over her like a heavy, mildew-soaked cloak. Although March had just made its appearance on the calendar, the early evening air was still uncomfortably cold.

She pulled on a pair of wellingtons, which she always kept in the boot of her car, and fastened the buttons of her coat up to her neck. She wished she had worn a scarf that morning.

Ben was waiting for her at the entrance to the narrow, winding path that led to the burial site. 'Hi, Jo. Welcome to the house of fun.'

'Hello,' Jo replied. Ben was in his early twenties and stood six feet tall. His short-cropped black hair sat neatly above a face in which the highlights were a set of sharp blue eyes and a cheeky grin. It was difficult not to like Ben, Jo thought. She had always wanted a brother and he would have fitted the bill perfectly – good sense of humour, nice looking and, above all, thoughtful.

'Follow me,' was all he said as he trudged off along the slimy, uneven path back into the darkness. Jo followed, plodding through the puddles and ankle-high mud. Their slippery, windy way was lit only by a small torch that Ben held out in front of them. Menacing shapes and shadows flickered and danced in and out of the gloom, disorientating Jo as she walked closely behind the dusky figure in front of her.

Spindly, finger-like twigs dangled in the mist above her head. Occasionally, the soggy tips would brush through her hair, making her shrink down as the two of them crept towards their destination.

This place was not for the faint-hearted. But it was a great spot if you wanted to bury a body. Who would want to come here for a day out? The chances of that wildlife fella stumbling across the grave must have been a million-to-one, Jo thought.

After they had been trudging through muck and grime for what seemed like miles, Jo noticed an illuminated area ahead. Finally, they reached the edge of the crime scene. Ben stopped. 'I've seen enough up there already. It's all yours,' he said as he waved her forwards.

Jo approached the pit that had been cordoned off by the forensic team. The area was lit up by four powerful spotlights mounted on metal stands. She showed her warrant card to the attending police officer and ducked under the tape.

The stench permeating the air was gut-wrenching. She took a handkerchief from her coat pocket, which she had sprayed with her perfume before she left the office, and held it over her mouth and nose.

Two mud-coated bodies had been laid on stretchers beside each other near the perimeter of the grave. The putrefaction that had occurred within the corpses had made it near impossible to identify them. One was certainly big enough to be Ballack. And there was the black, three-quarter length leather coat.

She caught the eye of one of the forensic team who was depositing mud samples into a small plastic bag with a large pair of tweezers. She asked her, by way of mouthing words and pointing, whether she could approach the bodies. The request got a nod of approval from the white-suited female.

When she reached the largest body, she bent down and looked into the grey, decomposing face. But the whole head was covered in too much mud for Jo to make out any distinguishing features. Was she looking at the face of her old boss? She could not be sure. An involuntary shiver tripped through her body.

Just as she was about to stand up, a small glint of light caught her eye. Amongst the grime, settled in a crease of the leather coat, something glistened in the reflection from the beam of one of the spotlights.

Jo leant forwards poked her fingers in the crease and plucked the small object from its grimy home. She pulled out a tissue from her pocket, wiped a lump of mud off and cleaned the rest with the tissue.

It was a wedding ring with a small diamond set in the top.

She had seen this ring before. Instinctively, although she was not absolutely sure why, she looked around to see whether anyone was watching her. Her subconscious mind was now ruling her actions. This could be her chance to solve these murders entirely on her own. Recognition. Promotion maybe? Luckily, the forensic scientist next to her had her back towards Jo and everyone else on the scene appeared to be busy doing their own jobs.

Using only one hand, she wrapped the ring in the tissue paper and casually put it back in her pocket. Then she stood up and returned to Ben, who was involved in a deep, painful-looking conversation on his mobile phone. By his whispered tones Jo guessed it to be a discontented girlfriend on the line.

When he saw Jo draw up alongside him, he raised his eyebrows at her. 'Look, I've gotta go. Speak to you later. Bye,' Ben said hurriedly down his phone. He slid the pencil-thin wonder of technology into his trouser pocket. 'See anyone you recognise,' Ben said flippantly.

No one I'll be inviting to my birthday party, that's for sure,' Jo replied.

'Do you think it might be Ballack?'

'Might be. We'll have to wait for the DNA analysis and dental records from forensics. Anyway, I've seen enough, thanks. Get me out of here,' said Jo.

On the journey home in her car, Jo could still taste the pungent, suffocating smell of the crime location. But far worse than that were the faces of the rotting cadavers. They were high-definition, full-colour images that were present in the car with her every time she blinked.

When she stopped at the first red traffic light, she reached into her pocket and pulled out the piece of tissue paper. She unwrapped the ring and stared at the small piece of gold. Her head started buzzing with all sorts of theories.

As a detective, she had learned not to trust coincidences. A wedding band with an oval-cut diamond inset. She was convinced she'd seen this ring before – in fact, she had held it in her hand. *Surely, this could only belong to one person*, she thought. Nick Summers.

In a few days, the lab results on the Dunley Marsh two would be known. But she thought she already knew the outcome. The dead bodies she had stood over earlier that afternoon would surely be those of Scrivens and Ballack.

Jo arrived home shortly after seven p.m. It had been a hectic and tiring day but the blood was pulsing through her veins. Today's breakthough had provided long-awaited clues to this investigation. Immediately, she took the ring into the bathroom and scrubbed it clean with a nail brush under the running tap.

She needed to think. It was too late tonight to act on her discovery. Tomorrow she would have to put everything down on paper in chronological order – every incident, every suspicion, every conversation that she could recall during the past three months.

Later that night she sat wearily on the side of her bed, holding the gold band in the palm of her hand. Each time she looked at it, all she saw was the strip of white skin on Nick Summers' wedding finger.

Trophies were usually awarded to the victor after the contest, she thought. In this case, the trophy had presented itself to her prematurely. She dropped the ring in a small zipped compartment in her handbag and placed it on her bedside table. She would carry that with her until it was needed. It was this prize that would win her the contest.

CHAPTER 70

The headline screamed out at him from the front page of the *Daily Mail*: TWO BODIES FOUND IN ONE GRAVE IN KENT MARSHLAND. Nick sat at the breakfast table, paralysed. The impact on his body as he read the shocking news caused his neck and shoulder muscles to lock onto his spine. His head suddenly felt half its weight.

'No. How can that be possible? The spot was so remote. So inhospitable,' he said, as he studied the report. He shook his head in disbelief. 'Kent Wildlife Project – what were the chances? The place is immense. Millions-to-one, it had to be.' When he finished the article, he raised his head to the ceiling. 'So this is it,' he added.

Relief jostled with fear; his heartbeat increased as he got up from the table. He couldn't think straight. *Well, at least Ballack and Scrivens can have a proper burial now*, was all his muddled brain could think of at that moment.

All of a sudden his world seemed a much smaller place. Was the net closing in? Would this discovery lead the police to him? The probability of finding those bodies in that remote hellhole were extremely slim. But they were found. Would they find his wedding ring?

Since Mel's death he had been living in a false world, hoping that one day he could put these harrowing events far enough back in his mind to be able to live with himself. Maybe even start a new life. He had found it impossible. The grim truth of the past months was too much to bear. He had gone to a place no man should ever go. Now he was on his own. That was the worst part.

CHAPTER 71

Two days later, the pathologist's report, along with the forensic evidence, was faxed through to the station. The results confirmed what Jo already knew – the bodies were those of Scrivens and Ballack.

Scrivens had been dead for approximately three months. He'd died from a severe blow to the left side of the head that crushed his skull, driving large fragments of bone into his brain. Jo noted that he had sustained other, particularly nasty, injuries. Whoever had killed him had not done it cleanly.

Ballack had died three to four weeks later but, interestingly, had then been buried in the same grave as Scrivens. The lab report was not totally conclusive. It stated that there had been a significant compression of the hyoid bone and corresponding bruising around the neck, suggesting attempted strangulation. Further investigation revealed that the detective had sustained a myocardial infarction. *So he had a heart attack as well*, thought Jo. The report concluded that the likely cause of death was from the heart attack.

Jo studied the report once more. So, he was being throttled and then had a cardiac arrest. The information was fed into her brain and logged. But what mattered now to her was that they had finally discovered Ballack's corpse and he had been murdered. She knew Nick Summers had to have buried the bodies, but she couldn't believe he was a cold-blooded killer. What would be his motive?

A full-scale investigation swung immediately into operation, led by DS Jack Jolley. The morning after the discovery of the two bodies, a team of ten officers were gathered together in the briefing room.

'Some of you in this room may still not be aware, though I doubt it now, that Detective Sergeant Nathan Ballack was a user and dealer in class A narcotics,' said Jack. Low mumbling filled the room but only two jaws dropped. News, such as yesterday's gruesome find, scuttled across the police grapevine in the blink of an eye.

'His murder and that of his supplier, Tony Scrivens, was almost certainly drug-related. I want every nark, pusher and dealer pulled and interviewed in connection with this double murder. Any associates they may have had. Dodgy pastimes, websites visited. A house-to-house with the local residents around Dunley Marsh, the same with Ballack's neighbours, and I want a thorough search of his home carried out,' instructed Jack.

He continued, 'This is one of our own and he was dirty. It doesn't look good on this station. The press will be crawling all over us on this one, so I want it cleared up as soon as.'

Jo and Mark Smallwood were assigned to carry out the house-to-house investigations.

Jo knew she had a headstart on her colleagues and decided where her focus would lie. To that end, she suggested that Mark cover an area that took in Ballack's immediate vicinity whilst her half of the area would include Nick Summers' surrounding roads. *Most neighbours are inherently nosey,* thought Jo, *someone must know or suspect something.*

That afternoon she spent two hours knocking on doors the length and breadth of Bray Road, but her efforts, so far, had been in vain. Then she came to the house where she had seen the white-haired old lady standing beneath her porch on the day of Mel's suicide. She rang the bell on the olive-green door. After a short wait she rang again. Just as she was about to leave, the door was opened, still attached to the safety chain. Jo recognised the white hair and the red tartan shawl through the small gap.

She pulled out her warrant card. 'Good afternoon, madam. Detective Constable Jo Major. I wonder whether I can ask you a few questions? I won't take up much of your time.'

'I know who you are. I saw you over at Mrs Summers' house,' replied the old lady as she closed the door, took off the chain and reopened it to the width of her shoulders. 'I won't say a bad word about that couple. She was always helpful to me, a lovely lady. And Mr Summers always smiled and waved when he saw me. It's such a tragedy. Poor woman.'

'May I ask your name? It's just for my own record,' asked Jo.

'Mrs Godsell,' replied the old lady proudly. 'Suicide, was it?'

'Yes, I'm afraid it was,' said Jo, writing down her name on a small notepad. 'I wondered whether you may have noticed anything unusual across the road these past few months, or whether Mrs Summers may have talked to you about anything of particular interest?'

'Is Mr Summers in any trouble then?' asked Mrs Godsell.

'No, no, it's just a routine enquiry. It would help our records if we had some idea of why this may have happened.'

'Well, there was a man,' she replied awkwardly.

Jo waited for her to continue, and when Mrs Godsell was not forthcoming she asked, 'could you be more specific?'

'I just happened to be looking out of the window and I saw a man walk up to Mrs Summers' door. What worried me was that he came from round the back of the house, which is very unusual. And it had just got dark, so I wondered what he was doing round here. But when she opened her door, she seemed to know him,' Mrs Godsell said, surprised. 'They stood talking under the porch light for a bit, then he went inside.'

'What was he wearing, this man?' asked Jo.

'Ooh. Erm, let me think. It was a black coat, I think. Yes, that was it. He had on a black shiny coat with the collar pulled up,' said Mrs Godsell, pulling up an imaginary collar.

Jo looked closely at the old lady. Her eyes narrowed. 'Can you remember when this was?'

'Oh yes, that's easy. It was my grandson's birthday. I'd just got off the phone wishing him a happy birthday. I may be old but I have a good memory for birthdays. It was the fourteenth of December,' said Mrs Godsell confidently.

Jo's eyes opened wide. It was the day Ballack had gone missing.

'I was a bit worried for a while, but when I saw Mr Summers come home a short while after that other fellow went in their house I realised it must be okay,' Mrs Godsell said.

Jo looked away as her brain tried to assimilate all this new information. Involuntarily, she shook her head.

'Oh! I hope I haven't got anyone into trouble, have I?' said Mrs Godsell.

'No, of course not. But you have been very helpful. And thanks for your time,' said Jo, getting up to leave.

'Would you like a cup of tea?' the old lady asked.

Jo's head was spinning. All she wanted to do was get home, assemble all these facts and try to construct a plausible story for what happened on the afternoon of 14th December.

'No thanks, Mrs Godsell. I have to fly, I'm afraid. But thank you for the offer. Maybe when I have more time I'll pop in and take you up on that cuppa. You've been a great help, thanks. Bye-bye,' said Jo as she opened the front door of the house and departed.

On her way to her car, she realised that she had to do one more thing before she headed home. She walked round to the path that ran along the rear of the Summers' house. From there she noticed that the upper windows were clearly visible to any passer-by.

Then she retraced the route that Nathan had to have taken from his house that afternoon. Cathy had told Jo that Nathan said he was going to the pub. But this was not the route to the pub at all and she already knew he had not been in that night. Furthermore, Mrs Godsell said that it had just got dark when she saw him. So Nathan must have decided to head straight for Mel Summers' house immediately after he assaulted his wife Cathy.

When she got back to her car, vital pieces of the puzzle were beginning to fall into place. On the drive home Jo's mood was one of excitement. Mrs Godsell's information had shone a much-needed light on the investigation. By the time she reached her flat, she had already started to piece together some of the events of that day.

From the rear path Nathan could easily have seen Mel through one of those upstairs windows. He had been drinking, his wife said, so goodness only knows what was on his mind. He must have seen that Nick's van was not outside the house and chanced his luck.

'God! Did he rape Mel?' she said out loud as she sat in her kitchen, trying to imagine the scene. Jo hunched over the kitchen table. This meant that Mel could have been pregnant with Nathan Ballack's child. She would have been devastated.

Mel's brain quickly moved through the gears and was now working at full speed.

Then what happened when Nick arrived home? Had Nick attacked Nathan or had he escaped retribution from Nick only to be captured later and killed by a hired enforcer of some drug dealer? But then, there was the ring. Merrill had already delved into Ballack's financial affairs – his overdraft and credit card debt totalled more than twenty-five thousand pounds. He surely must have been in heavy debt to his supplier as well.

Her mind went back to the broken window in Nick's kitchen and the tense atmosphere that was present between them. And on the night of their drink together Scrivens had turned up at the pub.

Had he chosen to break into Nick and Mel's house before they got home that evening? If so, how had he ended up dead?

The more she tried to unravel the web of clues, the more confused she became. The whole series of incidents seemed incredible to her.

By the end of the evening Jo was fairly certain of two things: the ill-fated Summers had suffered not one but two separate and terrible incursions. Even if they had not been responsible for the deaths of Scrivens and Ballack, they had still decided not call the police. Why?

She was getting close, she could see the finishing line. But how was she going to handle this information? She was playing host to two powerful emotions – an adrenalin-fuelled urge to unravel this complicated series of events as a copper, and an ill-fitting desire to protect Nick Summers as a human being. She was torn.

CHAPTER 72

The following afternoon, Jack Jolley called Jo into his office. As he looked up from a report he was studying on his desk, her eyes moved their focus from his rich crown of white hair to his face. She thought he looked vexed. He nodded to the seat opposite him. She sat.

'Jo, it's still early days, but the team have uncovered nothing as yet to give us even a sniff of a lead concerning Ballack's murder.'

Jo said nothing.

'The fact that the dealer and supplier were discovered together convinces me, and most of the investigating officers, that this was a drug-related double murder. Why else would they both be buried in the same grave? It's the kind of message these people like to give out – "fuck with us and suffer the consequences". These bastards don't do compromise.'

Jack stood and began moving around his office. 'We have not yet found any witnesses to the events carried out at Dunley Marsh and no clues, so far, have been discovered at the scene. I'm told, due to the heavy rain over the last few weeks the only footprints they could find were those of the Kent Wildlife employee.'

Jack returned to his desk. Still standing, he looked at Jo. 'The press, as you know, have already reported that two bodies have been found in the same grave but the identities were not yet known. I've held back on releasing their names to the media.'

'Why, guv?' said Jo.

'Because once that information is released, the press will have a field day. There will be a great deal of intrusive and potentially awkward questions asked of all of us. This would generate an unwelcome amount of adverse publicity for the station and the police force in general. It only takes one bent copper to undermine the integrity of the whole shebang. The media will lap this up. To that end I want the investigation to be concluded as soon as possible and with the least amount of fuss,' Jack said, with an intensity Jo had rarely seen from her boss.

Jo was aware that Jack was due to retire in a year or so's time. She gathered from the way he was handling this that he didn't want his name to be remembered purely for a scandal at his police station. She knew he had to be sure of his facts and convince the press of his team's findings when he issued his official statement to them. If the sharp-eyed hacks thought there was any doubt surrounding these killings, they would inflate this story out of all proportion and string it along for weeks.

Her boss returned to his seat. 'If, after another day or two of intensive investigations, nothing new has turned up, I will release the names of the deceased and inform the press that these were drug-related murders and we will do everything in our power to bring the perpetrators of these crimes to justice. But, I have to say, in my experience these drug network slayings are usually carried out by faceless professionals. They are rarely caught.'

But Jo hoped that she could pre-empt Jack's statement to the press by giving him the solved case on a plate. She wasn't sure how to handle the matter with the ring but maybe she wouldn't need it. There must surely be traces of Nick's DNA on the bodies and more evidence at his house. With the information she received from Mrs Godsell, she was almost there. It was simply a matter of careful timing.

Jo knew what she had to do. Back at her desk she looked at her watch. It read 1.35. She knew Nick would probably be at work. She rang his mobile number.

The phone rang five times before it was answered. But there was only silence from the other end of the line. 'Hi, Nick? It's Jo Major.'

More silence.

'Hello?'

'Hello, Jo,' came Nick's flat reply.

'Nick, are you at home later this afternoon? About five?' she said, assertively.

There was a pause before he answered. 'Yes. I think I could be back by then.'

This wasn't the Nick Summers that she knew. Hardly surprising, she thought. She was sure that he must have read in the paper of the findings at Dunley Marsh.

'Okay. See you then,' she added. She waited for a reply. None came. She put the phone down. Jo knew she should interview him at the station but then he would be far more defensive within that environment. She wanted to confront him in a less pressurised situation and then present him with the ring.

There was still a small amount of uncertainty in her mind. Nick was a friend. A definite plan had not formed in her head of what to say to him, but the hope was that she could get him to open up to her.

If she was right, Nick Summers, in some way, was responsible for the death of two men. Suddenly, she felt very nervous.

CHAPTER 73

Nick had been anticipating Jo's phone call ever since he had read the article in the daily paper. It had been an incredible stroke of bad luck, he thought, for that bird sanctuary man to have stumbled across the burial site. At first the news came as a shock. But after a while he realised the find had brought a sense of relief. Now he was just going through the motions at work – existing, waiting for the knock on his door to tell him he'd been found out.

In his head he had become two separate people, neither of which he could relate to. One was a mixture of anger, desolation and loneliness, the other was remorseful and confused. Both personalities haunted by the constant nightmares and consequences of his ill-judged actions.

The month of March, for Nick, was usually the best time of the year to be working in tandem with nature. But his excitement at seeing young, vibrant life emerging from a barren environment had been stolen from him this year. It was as if his soul had withdrawn from his body and was watching himself, evaluating his every move. He could see himself shrinking, disappearing.

Nick pulled up outside his house at three thirty. He closed the front door behind him and looked at his wristwatch. He was expecting Jo at five o'clock. He didn't know what she wanted to talk to him about but he was anticipating bad news. He was nervous but he was also tired of trying to quieten a guilt-ridden conscience, of living a lie. He was tired of his life.

CHAPTER 74

Throughout the afternoon, Jo found it impossible to concentrate on her work. Her mind was parked deep in the Summers' case and, for a reason she didn't want to evaluate, her stomach was in knots. She checked her watch every fifteen minutes waiting for it to tell her it was four forty-five. That was when she would leave the office and drive to Nick's house. But, as usual in these situations, the time dragged.

'Are you all right, Jo?' her colleague Mark asked. 'You've not said a bloody word all day. Come on. What is it? You've finally got a boyfriend but you've just found out he's gay. Or worse – he's a Morris dancer? I know, you've had it off on the lottery and you're not sure how much to give me?'

The last thing Jo wanted was to appear anything other than her everyday self. She didn't want to alert anyone to what she was doing until she had the case tied up. 'Me? Pfft! Chance'd be a fine thing. No, just a bit tired, that's all,' she replied, matter-of-factly. She rose from her desk and exaggerated a stretch. 'Coffee, anyone?'

Two yesses.

Jo stood in the narrow kitchen preparing the drinks, her mind skipping from one subject to the next. She was pleased that her boss was not there to threaten her in the confines of the small room this time. He had abused his position in the most awful way and if she was right, that selfish, twisted bastard had raped and impregnated Mel. That, surely, was more reason for her to take own life than the one she put forward in her suicide note. As her jaw tightened, she thought there would be few, if any, shedding tears over this man's demise. As far as she was concerned, Detective Sergeant Nathan Ballack was where he belonged.

To solve the mystery by herself would be a big feather in her cap and do no harm to her prospects of promotion. Then the thought suddenly hit her that Jack Jolley may not welcome her barging into a case that he was eager to close. He had already mentioned that he was happy to treat it as a drug-related double murder. As she poured the hot water into the three cups, she decided she would just have to take that chance. This was an opportunity she couldn't miss.

Her focus then went back to Nick. The memory of her recent dream flashed through her mind – his handsome face, powerful hands, fit naked body, the relaxed joy of utter fulfilment. Bringing him to justice was filled with conflicting emotions. But, just as rapidly, her thoughts darkened. She began to imagine the sight that confronted him when he arrived home on that fateful day – the bloated face of Mel; her ragdoll body hanging from the banisters in their home; her twisted neck; marble-like eyes, wide, staring, blinded forever. She now asked herself the question. If Nick thought she was coming to arrest him, well... was that how she was going to find *him*? A shiver swept across her shoulders and down her arms as she picked up the hot beverages.

Very soon, she was going to be instrumental in his incarceration amongst cold-blooded murderers and all manner of unsavoury, unethical low-lives. Prison was going to be hell for him, but he could at least still have a life after his release. She prayed her phone call hadn't spooked him and that she would find him alive and well on her arrival at his house.

She took the coffees out to Mark and Colin, sat down at her desk and tried to direct all her attention onto her daily duties. But the question kept entering her brain – why had she kept the discovery of his wedding ring at the grave site to herself? Was it due to raw selfish ambition or because she was attracted to the handsome landscape gardener? Maybe it was a bit of both.

Neither motive, she decided, filled her with a sense of pride. What was she searching for? Was it happiness or success? Was she the beautiful but tender and vulnerable flowering clematis or the tough, rampant ivy, climbing over everything in its path?

At four thirty Jo got up from her desk and went to the ladies restroom. She moved to the hand basin and looked at herself in the small wood-framed mirror. Her face reflected her mood. She felt the same as the day she went for her first job interview. But within that feeling of apprehension there was also an element of excitement that she was about to move in for the kill. This was the first time she had sat on the edge of such a significant result – and it would all be hers. She just wished it didn't have to involve someone she knew and to whom she felt attracted?

She checked her watch again. Twenty-five to. Time to clear up and head off, she thought as she left the room.

As she returned to her position, Mark was on the phone. When he saw her approaching, he shot her a weird look. One that she had never seen on his face before. His eyebrows arched wildly upwards, pulling his eyes open wide, his mouth fixed, gaping. It was a mixture of shock, confusion and excitement. Jo stood by her desk. She suddenly felt uneasy.

Mark Smallwood finished his conversation, put the phone down and stared at Jo. He went to speak but simply shook his head.

'Well?' said Jo, turning her palms towards the polystyrene tiles on the ceiling.

Mark was struggling to speak.

'For Christ's sake, Mark!'

On hearing Jo's words, Merrill stopped working and looked up from his PC. It was a rare moment.

'That was Jack Jolley. You're never gonna believe this,' he began, still looking stunned. 'Nick Summers, your Nick Summers, Jo, has just walked into the station and confessed to the murders of Nathan Ballack and that little scrote Scrivens.'

It was now that Jo's mouth took its turn to drop open. She hadn't seen that coming at all. She sat down behind her computer screen, linked her fingers and put her hands on her head. Slowly, she sank back in her chair. While she was taking in the unexpected news, Mark spoke again.

'I've been asked to go down and take his statement,' he said, looking at Jo. She met his look and opened her mouth to speak. 'Before you say it, Jack thinks you're too close to this, Jo. But he's happy for you to sit in,' he said. He looked at

Merrill, who reflected the mood of the room. 'Wow! That's come from out of the blue,' Mark added. He turned back to Jo. 'You were quite friendly with him and his wife, weren't you?' he asked.

Jo nodded, looking at the blank screen in front of her.

Mark rose from his desk. 'Right! Ready?' he asked Jo.

'Give me a minute. I need the loo again,' she said, scooping up her handbag and scurrying from the office.

When she returned, she put her bag on her desk and turned to DC Mark Smallwood. She sucked air into her lungs and quickly got rid of it. 'Okay. Let's do this,' she said.

CHAPTER 75

The custody sergeant acknowledged the two officers as they entered the interview room and informed them that the detainee had declined the offer of a solicitor. Nick was sitting behind the small wood-veneered table, his hands resting on the worn surface. He looked up at them as they approached. The last of the dwindling sun's rays speared through the room's single-panelled window hitting the grey-painted far wall and highlighting one side of Nick's face. Jo looked into his eyes. They appeared tired, defeated; his once proud stature now concave, acquiescent to its fate.

'Hi, Jo,' said Nick, in a whisper. Jo nodded as she took a seat next to Mark.

During the next thirty minutes Nick poured out his incredible story to the two stupefied detectives. It was one that elicited many contradictory emotions from the two officers. It was certainly a tale that no one could invent. When his statement had been taken and the tape recorder turned off, Mark and Jo stood up from the table. The custody officer went to open the door and Mark followed him. Jo leant forward and went to shake Nick's hand. 'It was the right thing to do, Nick. Try to stay strong, and good luck.'

As their hands met, he felt an object pressed into his palm. The sullen expression on his face changed as he saw the ring. His hand closed around the precious piece of jewellery as he looked up into her eyes. 'I have no need of this now,' she said, in a barely audible whisper. She turned and left the room.

That evening, as Jo drove back towards her new flat, her emotions were tearing themselves into strips. On her return to work she had said nothing to her colleagues of the last twenty-four hours. Was she really cut out to be a police officer? She had been dishonest by withholding important information that was almost certainly encouraged by her feelings for Nick. But she had also been driven by personal glory. Now, she was left with nothing.

Clouds of confusion swirled in her head. She questioned at length whether or not she should remain in the force. Then it dawned on her. The yearning to be successful in her career – the recognition, the trust, the affection – and the yearning to be loved, were one and the same emotion.

When Jo arrived back at her apartment it was in near darkness. She went to switch the lights on, then changed her mind. She stepped out of her shoes and, with only the reflection from the streetlamps to guide her, moved slowly through the sitting room to the picture window. She stood, a solitary soul looking out over the undulating tiled roofs of the village and across the moon-decked, shadowy Kent countryside. The tears came. She had made many mistakes.

So had Nick. But he had been fighting for his survival. She realised that giving himself up would undoubtedly go in his favour. And the circumstances of the crimes may afford some degree of leniency in his sentence. She hoped so for both their sakes.

CHAPTER 76

In the months leading up to the trial, the media hacks and the main television networks had clambered all over the story, covering it from every angle possible. The case had generated enormous interest throughout the country. The public gallery of Canterbury Crown Court was packed to the rafters with journalists, family and friends and captivated spectators. More had gathered on the steps outside the building.

Whatever personal feelings were held for their colleague before this incident, Jo and the entire police investigative team all regarded DS Ballack's behaviour as reprehensible and a disgrace to the force. They felt that the adverse publicity reflected badly on the whole station and not one of them was sorry he was dead. The team's sympathies now lay firmly on the side of Nick Summers – their reports and testimonies reflected that fact, no better highlighted than by Jo Major's character reference of the defendant in court that concluded her evidence.

'I would like it recorded that the Nick Summers I know is an honest, hard-working man who loved his wife. On each occasion that I met him, he was charming, helpful and always sympathetic to others.' It was a heartfelt endorsement from the police officer delivered whilst looking directly at Nick. A few of the jury members were visibly moved by her declaration.

When the judge began his summing up of the case no one in that courtroom was aware that his own house, just six months earlier, had been broken into during the night. The judge, on hearing a noise downstairs scared the intruder off before he had time to steal anything from the property. But he didn't report the break-in. The reason for this was out of pure embarrassment. He had forgotten to lock the back door that evening before retiring, affording the thief an easy entry. Although he had taken steps to tighten the security around his home, the incident had left his wife feeling vulnerable whenever she was alone in the house. It had left *him* with a smouldering anger directed at himself and the intruder.

As the judge spoke to the jury, certain sections of his address left few of the spectators in any doubt as to his feelings about the case.

'Indeed, if it wasn't for the imprecise law of reasonable force there would have been no need, no temptation, to bury the body of the thief. The defendant has also stated that he was persuaded to carry out this deed, after he turned to Detective Sergeant Ballack for guidance, who, in turn, recognised the intruder as his own drug supplier. The police evidence has confirmed this. The phone records show that the defendant rang DS Ballack late that night and his wife has testified that she heard him leave the house to return approximately forty five minutes later.'

The tension in the courtroom now was palpable as row upon row of fixated eyes arrowed down from the public gallery, swinging back and forth from the solitary figure of Nick Summers to the intermediate faces of the jury and across to the judge.

After informing the jury of the more technical facts concerning the case, he continued. 'In the act of protecting his home and family, Mr Summers killed Tony Scrivens, a habitual thief and convicted drug dealer. This, I am convinced, was an accident. An act of self-defence, albeit an imprudent one. No person of right mind intends to kill another human being in circumstances such as these. Moreover, no one can foresee how they would react in such a highly-charged, terrifying and unexpected situation that Mr Summers found himself.'

The judge's summing up eventually moved on to the death of Nathan Ballack.

'Ballack's pregnant wife, in her statement, admitted that he had left their home in a fit of temper. Earlier that afternoon she had stumbled across his store of cocaine. Mrs Ballack goes on to say that on his return home, and worse for wear with alcohol, a heated row ensued after which he struck her across the face and stormed out. 'Detective Constable Major's witness, Mrs Godsell, a nearby neighbour, states that she observed a figure resembling that of DS Ballack entering the Summers' house. This sighting was minutes after he had left his own home. Mrs Godsell then saw Mr Summers return to his home shortly afterwards. According to the defendant's testimony, Mr Summers is then witness, in his own home, to the horrific sight of Detective Sergeant Ballack in the act of raping Mrs Summers. What husband would not want to kill the man caught attacking his wife in this way, and in his own house? But he doesn't kill him. In his anger he puts his hands around his throat but desists from the final act of murder. The pathologist's report states that DS Ballack died of a myocardial infarction. A heart attack. His medical report indicates that Ballack was suffering from cardiomyopathy, a form of heart disease due, most likely, to him being overweight added to his intake of alcohol and long-term use of barbiturates. The assault by Mr Summers may well have been a contributory factor in bringing about Ballack's heart attack but that can't be proved. No other motive has been found, apart from the one I have just read out, for the attack on DS Ballack by the defendant. I have no valid reason to disbelieve the defendant on this point.'

After the judge had told the jury that Nicholas Summers' crimes had not been discovered by the police, but that he had listened to his conscience and walked into a police station to confess all, he delivered his last words. 'I am fully entitled to form a view about anything to do with the facts of this case. I am fully entitled to let you know what my view is. But please bear in mind that your task is to decide the facts. It is not my task. You have to reach a decision on the evidence you have heard.'

After the judge had given the jury the verdict options open to them, they retired to discuss their decision.

Five hours passed before the twelve members of the jury returned to the courtroom. The judge addressed the foreman. As the slim, middle-aged man rose tentatively to announce the result of their deliberations, the only sound to be heard was the occasional creak of a wooden seat as the crowd leant forward in anticipation. Nick Summers stood, hands clasped tightly, looking straight ahead, his mind in a suffocating bubble of fear and uncertainty. Jo Major held her breath.

The foreman read from the piece of white paper clasped in his unsteady hand:

'In the case of Tony Edward Scrivens, we find the defendant guilty of involuntary manslaughter.'

There was an audible gasp from the public gallery.

'In the case of Nathan Ballack, we find the defendant guilty of assault. We also find the defendant guilty of the prevention of the lawful and decent burial of both bodies.'

All eyes turned towards the man in the dock. Nick Summers took a few seconds to digest the verdicts issued by this complete stranger. He then inhaled deeply and slowly breathed out as the muscles throughout his body began to unwind, returning much needed blood to his brain. Excited news reporters scribbled madly on their notepads, some jumped from their seats and headed for the exit as a rumble of whispered voices filled the room.

After the judge deferred sentencing for psychiatric reports, Jo took one last look at Nick, rose from her seat and left the courtroom.

CHAPTER 77

Jo Major sat at her desk typing out a report on a fifteen-year-old heroin user and dealer. It had been four long days since the trial and she was still waiting for news of Nick Summers' sentence to come through. She picked up the bottle of water in front of her, went to take a drink and realised it was almost empty. As she stood to go to the kitchen for a refill, Merrill looked up from his computer. 'Google... five years!' he announced triumphantly, pointing at his screen.

'What?' said Mark.

'Nick Summers. Five years.' Merrill repeated.

Jo immediately sat down again. The words hung in the air. Five years. The sentence filtered through her system as she absorbed the news. With good behavior out in three, maybe less, she thought. She threw her head backwards. 'Oh! Thank God,' she said to the ceiling, her eyes screwed tight.

'I reckon that's a result,' said Mark.

'It may be a result for you,' Merrill piped up, 'five years in the slammer? Rather him than me.'

Mark looked across at Jo. He recognized the look on her face. He turned back to Merrill. 'Rather you than him, if you don't shut up.'

During the days that followed, the media lauded the relatively lenient sentence, claiming it as a major breakthrough towards householders being able to protect their property and loved ones without fear of prosecution. Two of the red tops were even pushing for the law of reasonable force to be scrapped entirely.

As the days passed, Nick Summers, little by little, was beginning to be held up as the people's champion. Jo had read all the reports, watched all the television programmes covering the story. It seemed to her that most of the country was in support of the handsome landscape gardener.

The spartan room had the faint smell of stale cigarettes and cheap perfume. Jo Major sat on the metal-framed chair, waiting. She looked at her watch. It was 3.07 p.m. All the other inmates had arrived at their tables at three on the dot and were already sitting down talking in hushed tones to their friends and family members. She now thought she had made a mistake coming to visit Nick. She got up to leave just as he appeared at the door. Instantly, she sat down again and watched him walk slowly towards the table. She thought he wore a look of uncertainty on his unshaven face. A few of the other people in the room looked over; some whispered and pointed at the man who had been plastered all over their TV screens for the past weeks.

'Hi, Nick,' said Jo, 'how you doing?' It was a stupid question and she immediately regretted it. She felt nervous.

'Yeah! Okay, thanks,' said Nick, guardedly. The conversation continued on a polite level for a few minutes, then fell into an awkward silence. Eventually, Nick spoke again. 'There's a question I've been wanting to ask you.'

Jo shifted in her seat, unfolded her arms and put her hands on the table. She said nothing.

'Why did you keep the ring? Why didn't you hand it in?' he asked.

She wasn't expecting the question. She decided, immediately, that she had to answer it honestly. 'I think, for two reasons. The ring represented something I had never had in my life. Firstly, it was the catalyst to solving this crime on my own – a chance to be noticed in my job. To be accepted by men, even respected.'

Nick nodded once in a deliberate motion. 'What was the other reason?'

'I had part of you in my possession – an intimate part of you that, if not revealed, could protect you. And a big part of me wanted to protect you, Nick. I have had time to reflect on my motivations now and I realise that my needs within both of those reasons were probably one and the same.'

Nick said nothing at first. He stared at Jo. She felt as if he was trying to see inside her head. Jo went to speak but Nick beat her to it. 'Ever since I was a kid, I've not been a lover of the police. I haven't had much trust or respect for them. But you, by keeping my wedding ring a secret, a damning piece of evidence, whatever your reason was, enabled me to hand myself in, to have a bit of long-forgotten pride in myself – to be in charge of my own destiny. That has meant a great deal to me and almost certainly shortened my prison term.'

Jo held Nick's look. 'Nick, it would mean a great deal to *me* if, in time, you could grow to love just one member of the police,' she said, with a wavering smile.

Nick's head dropped gradually down towards the floor. He sat motionless. Jo then saw his chest fill with air as he leant forward in his seat. Slowly, he moved his hands across the surface of the table until the tips of their fingers touched. He then raised his head to look at Jo. They stayed like that for minutes. She watched his eyes narrow, searching for something.

She saw pain behind those soft blue eyes. She saw doubt. But she saw hope.